MY
NAME
IS
NOT
ISLA

Eliza Freed

ALSO BY ELIZA FREED

MY
NAME
IS
NOT
ISLA

Eliza Freed

Brunswick House
New York

For all those who've been silenced.
The time is now.

Evil creeps in the same way a person dies in their sleep.
Peacefully and comfortably.
Until one moment you realize, your entire world is dark.

Isla, my love,

I'm dying inside. I can't get through to you. You've stopped listening, or is it that you refuse to believe me? You showed up at the bar last night and sat next to me without an ounce of love in your eyes. Just floated in as if you weren't there for me. Your phone, the bartender, and the fans who stopped by to annoy you and finally made you leave—they all seemed more important than me.

When I said your name, I saw it. The rejection in your eyes. The dead stare. The end is coming if we don't change something. I wanted to shake you and scream, "It's me. Ian. The one person who really knows you."

The only person who truly loves you. The others are using you. All they care about is the money. You're exhausted. You need a break. I get it, but it's me. It's always been me.

I'll never let you go. You are my whole life, and we belong together. You know it as well as I do. You're the only thing that matters in this world to me.

Love,

Ian

CHAPTER 1

Isla

THE AIR CONDITIONER KICKED ON again, and a ray of light beamed through the thick curtain where it billowed away from the window. I pulled the comforter up to my neck and rolled onto my stomach. It was June, and I was freezing. The great Cruz Allen always felt hot when he did too much cocaine, so the thermostat was turned down to a chilly sixty-one degrees. Wouldn't want him to sweat while he was snorting powder up his nose from the center of my glass-topped coffee table.

The stale light and the frigid air made me feel as if I were waking up in a morgue rather than my apartment overlooking the park. I guess that was what I got for picking the view and tiny balcony. I didn't want a grand terrace where I could entertain fifty people. I wanted to be as close to alone as possible, even if just for a few minutes of the day.

I looked from the window to Cruz, whose broad shoulders hid his head almost entirely because of the angle he was lying. He'd taken up most of the bed and left me with a sliver near the edge. Cruz believed he was welcome everywhere. He rolled over, and the wretched sound of him clearing his throat while he slept repulsed me. I was the only person in the world repelled by him.

I hadn't always felt this away about him, and I knew it wasn't

Cruz's fault. He was only born this way, and I—like the rest of the world—was drawn to him at first. He was an undeniable magnet, but with every word he spoke, my attraction to him faded a little more. I imagined his mother, pregnant and surrounded by her publicist and therapist and makeup artist, going over the possible names of a demigod soon to be born with the last name Allen. She'd have toasted herself when the name Cruz was decided, as if she'd cured cancer or discovered a gene associated with Parkinson's. She had, of course, given birth to an icon. He was the vision of first love for every teenage girl around the world.

Cruz reached out and draped his lanky arm across my back. "Sorry about the coke dick," he said, apologizing for his lack of ability the night before. Coke dick, whiskey dick, weed dick. How many inoperable dicks could one man possess?

I wanted to say, "This magical powder, which when inhaled makes you feel completely invincible, renders you the type of man who can't make his dick hard." Instead, I allowed some sound close to, "Mmmh," to break free. I wasn't here to tell Cruz what I thought.

I slipped from the covers and tiptoed into the bathroom. He was obviously awake, but I wanted him to think he was still sleeping. Cruz was easily fooled. Especially when it appeared someone was taking care of him.

I shook the snow globe on the counter and watched the tiny white particles fall over the little girl with her arms in the air and her mouth opened wide as if she were singing. It was the last gift my mother had given me before she died. "Lift your voice to the Lord," she'd said.

"Why the hell do you have a snow globe in your bathroom?" Cruz had asked the night before when I brought him home to my apartment for the first time and he saw it perched on the counter next to my toothbrush.

I laughed, and he forgot the question as he sipped the vodka and cranberry his trainer had suggested to reduce his calorie intake. I didn't tell him that the bathroom was the only room where no one could see the little girl singing in the snow. She wanted to be hidden.

I splashed water on my face and searched for a glimpse of my former self. My skin was pale from sleeping in and working late. The tour had robbed me of my circadian rhythm. I wouldn't dwell on the other parts of me it'd stolen. I clicked off the light and opened the door to find Cruz still in bed.

"Come back to bed. I'm ready for you," Cruz said without rolling over to face me. Effort was a foreign concept to him. He was the son of an Academy Award-winning actress and her director ex-husband. Cruz hadn't lifted a finger since the first time he'd moved his arm. "Isla," he yelled, obviously not realizing I was standing right there. The name sickened me like rotten milk poured down my throat. "Take off your top and come back here."

I'd heard enough. Probably six months ago when I first spoke to Cruz, I'd heard enough, but at my publicist's insistence, I kept listening. Ramona thought Cruz and I were perfect together. Hollywood's elite and Billboard's number one pop star. The sun shone bright upon us, and together, we made Ramona's job easy. The only thing bigger than Isla Monroe or Cruz Allen was the two of us as a couple.

"Isla!"

I rolled my eyes, more at my reality than at Cruz, and strode from the room and into the kitchen. I filled the teapot and lit the flame. It felt proper. People with real lives took time to drink a hot beverage in the morning. It was a ritual shared by millions. While the water heated, I walked back toward my bedroom window, opened the curtains, and let the light drench the room as I ignored Cruz's grumble of annoyance. The street was already full of cars stopped in traffic because of the red light two blocks away, and the sidewalk across it was occupied by dog walkers, joggers, and two men standing next to each other talking. I knew their messenger bags were filled with cameras and tripods and cell phones. They were the familiar shadow wherever I went and were usually joined by several more just like them.

I squared my jaw and straightened my back. "I'm done with this."

"Daylight?" Cruz asked as he faced the morning.

"No." I swirled my finger in a circle between us. "This."

"What the hell are you talking about?"

I didn't want to be cruel. Cruz was so delicate. The soft cloud he'd been raised upon utilized alcohol and every other drug to solve the problems money could not. He wasn't used to conflict, confrontation, or rejection. The world was a horrible place, though.

"This. Coke dick, hiding out, going out . . . you not showing up when you're supposed to. Caring more about what we look like than what we feel like." He'd be sorry he asked, because I'd woken with a vengeance. "The constant need for validation and the search for it in the pages of a magazine. All of it."

He sat up in bed and studied me. "You're fucking with me."

"I'm not. You can have anyone you want. They're literally waiting at your doorstep."

"Yeah, so they can get knocked up or sell a picture of my dick to the tabloids." My gaze dropped down to his coke dick before I could catch myself. "Besides, I want you. I *love* you, Isla." Cruz dropped the word "love" like a grain of sand on the beach. It meant nothing since there were a million more like it to follow.

"You don't even know my name." I tried not to let the words sound as lost as I felt. Cruz might not have known my name, but I didn't recognize myself these last few years.

"I know you, and the fact that you're just lost since the tour ended. You get this way when there's no work, you know?"

"How can you say that? This is the first time I've had a day off since I've known you."

"Because unlike everyone else in this business, you never complain. You act like it's a real job and there's some way of having a life outside it, but you're no different than the rest of us."

I hated when Cruz tried to make sense. I wished he'd just leave.

"Isn't it? A job?"

"No. Do you actually think your life is equivalent to that of a chef or a sales clerk at Bergdorf's? This *work*, as you call it, is your reason for existence, and when it slows, you feel like you've died. You seek out the next thing like a drug. Every movie, every song, every appearance is to maintain your relevance. *That's* the only way you're alive. No one understands it."

He sounded like the men in this industry who used to enchant me. In my early twenties, I'd sipped vodka and listened as they described our existence as floating above the mere mortals working beneath us. Ours was an inconceivable reality and a gift bestowed upon us from the Gods, but Cruz's heaven was quickly becoming my hell.

"Until they've lived it," he said and climbed out of bed. His coke dick, as I would forever call it in my head, hung between his legs. The lean muscles in his thighs continued up to his trim waist and lanky arms. Cruz was not in amazing shape. That would require him to work at it, and he didn't have to. He had a big dick, a larger ego, and talent. Cruz Allen was unstoppable. "Maybe you just need to take a break."

"I just suggested that."

"Not from me." He leaned down and kissed my cheek as if I hadn't just told him we were over.

My phone knocked with a text notification on the side table. The message read *Call Me,* and was from Ramona.

"Have Jared call Ramona, and they can put out a joint statement," I told Cruz.

He stopped walking to the bathroom and turned on his heels. His wide eyes bore into me. "You're serious about this?"

"Yes. I'm done."

He roughly ran his hand through his hair and across the back of his neck. "Jared's on his honeymoon. I promised I'd leave him alone for a few days."

I shook my head and tried to retain my resolve. "Of course. There's no rush. They can break us up whenever."

"Then go out with me tonight." His smile was criminal. He'd been convincing me of stuff for months, but today, that was ending.

"I'm calling Ramona." I took my phone back into the kitchen and dialed the only person who was always on my side, even when it made her job harder. I poured a cup of tea and warmed my fingers around the cup.

"Did you sleep in?" she asked without saying hello. We spoke so many times a day that greetings were unnecessary.

"I did. It's good to be home."

"A fourteen-month worldwide tour will make you miss your bed."

I still missed my bedroom at Mama's house in North Carolina, but that'd been torn down years ago. "About that . . . I want to take some time off."

"That's what I was calling to talk about. We've received several offers from Caribbean properties that are exclusive enough to house you and whomever you want to bring with you. Not sure of Cruz's schedule. Jared's out of town."

I inhaled and tried to take it all in. "Offers for what?"

"Accommodations, drinks, excursions, whatever you want, as long as we leak a picture of you on the property."

"I was actually thinking of a few months . . ."

"What?"

"A significant amount of time. Maybe go home for a while."

"No." Even through the phone, I could sense her shaking her head violently back and forth. "You are the hottest woman in the world right now. You can't go anywhere. Unless it's to elope with Cruz Allen on a beach."

"Ramona—"

"Not Vegas. Britney ruined that one already. Maybe the coast of Africa. Give me a few hours." I knew she was already on her laptop.

"You're not listening. Cruz and I are done."

"He's in your apartment right now." She was indignant.

"How do you know that?"

"I just read it online. What's going on?"

"Nothing." Cruz walked into the room, and the sunlight behind him framed his body. He poured himself a glass of milk and sat on the bar stool at my kitchen island without a piece of clothing on. "I've got to go."

Ramona hung up, and I wrapped my fingers back around my cup. The Bible on the counter caught my eye. The papers hung out of the pages at random intervals. The cream-colored sheets carried words written by a man I never really knew. His notes spoke of love and connection and pushed me further away with each one that was delivered. They should have been in a shoebox, or the trashcan, but the Bible would protect me.

"Do you want pancakes?" Cruz asked, and I let out a resigned sigh.

CHAPTER 2

Isla

WE PASSED DICK IN MY apartment lobby. His name wasn't really Dick, not even Richard, but since he never actually spoke to me except in grunts, I'd taken to calling him Dick in my head. He was overweight and sweaty and somehow hired by Victor Addario to head my security detail. As president of my record label, it was not uncommon for Victor to have some say in all aspects of my career, including the team that surrounded me, but Victor's interests went far beyond what was customary in this insane industry.

Dick's eyes fell from my head, down to my chest, and finally rested near my groin. He was foul. His expression was one of disdain, as if he resented having to watch me, which was ironic, since it was what I hated him for.

He lingered too long in dressing rooms under the guise of thorough execution of his duties.

"Just doing my job," he had said, running his oversized hands through the clothes in my suitcase before we'd left Atlanta. "Some creep could've been in here."

"Or is right now," I'd said and pissed him off.

He always had a reason for his intrusions where no other security felt the need to be. Dick stared at me instead of speaking as I made my way to the front door. The urge to be away from him practically slapped me on the back of the head.

My instincts consistently told me to flee from him, but he was literally being paid to make that impossible. He was gross and another one of my shadows. When I brought it up to Victor, he asked, "Has he touched you?" The threat of death depending on the answer.

"No," I'd begrudgingly admitted. We'd had this conversation in various forms several times. I wanted this ape gone from my life, and Victor always insisted he stay.

"You're being dramatic, Isla. Having a security team may not be comfortable, but it's necessary. Now more than ever." Victor's most potent power was convincing me I felt differently than I actually did.

"Good morning, Ms. Monroe," Alex said with a generous smile and stood straight next to the front desk in my lobby. He was Dick's partner and always kind.

"Morning, Alex."

Dick continued to sneer as I brushed by. The cold hatred surrounding him stopped me from moving. I wasn't imagining it. I took a second to listen. My feelings were real. I was going to hear them from there on out. Dick was the first of many things I wasn't afraid to leave without saying goodbye.

Outside, Cruz helped me into the waiting car. The traffic had thinned, and Cruz told the driver to stop on a side street near the restaurant. There were no cameramen in sight, but that was temporary. The two of us together couldn't avoid them; although, it often felt as if I were the only one trying. Cruz loved the spotlight in any form.

The hostess did a double take when Cruz flashed his Internet-ready smile at her, but the waitress didn't recognize us at all. I used to wait tables in North Carolina. If you were good at the job, you didn't have time to care who you were serving. This waitress was excellent.

I perused the menu while Cruz glanced back at the couple behind me. I could hear them whispering our identities and assumed they were trying to figure out how to take our picture. Whether we'd pose with them or if they'd have to take it covertly. This was why I ate most meals at home. Not because I loved to cook. I tuned them out, thankful that at least if they interrupted our breakfast, I wouldn't have to meet them while I was wearing the sequined body suit and thigh-high boots I had to wear on stage.

Pancakes, French toast, a bagel . . .

"Shit. I can't eat. I have to fit into a batman costume." Cruz leaned toward me and whispered, "They're going to think I'm anorexic or on drugs." At times, I thought he was both. "Fuck. They're already taking pictures."

I abandoned the menu and focused on my soon-to-be ex-boy-friend. "Eat. It's just food. Going into your body."

"Yeah, right. You don't even believe that."

"Should what you eat be a topic for anyone other than you and maybe your physician?" I was getting the pancakes.

"If Jared's doing his fucking job right, it should be."

"We really do see this whole thing differently."

"What?"

"Our impact on society. We should be helping to keep plastics out of the ocean and finding new channels of accessibility for proper mental health care around the world." His mouth fell open at my words. His brow furrowed in repulsion. "There are more important things going on than what Cruz Allen has for breakfast."

He leaned into me. "Lower your voice. No one wants to hear what Isla Monroe thinks of the environment."

I put my menu down and grabbed my bag off the back of the chair.

"Isla," he pleaded. "I'm sorry. Please don't go." The smile on his face was easy and casual, but I knew he was only concerned with how my departure would appear. He was right. I let out a soft sigh and pretended to dig for something in my purse before putting it back down.

The waitress walked up, still seemingly oblivious to our identities, and asked if we were ready to order.

"We'll have two orders of the pancakes with sausage on the side," Cruz said.

We sat in silence while we waited for our food. Cruz read something on his phone. For my own mental health, I didn't ask him what. I stared out the window until the photographers began to cluster on the sidewalk out front. A picture, a hashtag, a call . . . something, or someone, had clued them into our whereabouts.

Cruz noticed them, too. He leaned back in his seat, satisfied with his continued relevance.

I tilted my head. It was Cruz who'd tipped them off. One corner of his mouth tilted, confirming my suspicion. I rested my hands in my lap and roughly rubbed my thumb against the inside of my palm. As my eyes raked over Cruz, my discontent was replaced with disdain.

Our pancakes were delivered, and even though I hadn't had them in a year and the smell of the warm butter mixing with the syrup was divine, I was too repulsed by Cruz to eat.

He cut his pancakes and moved them around in the syrup. "I can't eat these," he said. "You take a bite and kiss me so I can taste them."

"No," I said and forced down a huge bite. He reduced me to a taunting child.

Cruz sneered. The restaurant manager stopped by, stuttered through an awkward conversation, asked whether Cruz was satisfied with his uneaten meal, and comped our bill. The total couldn't have been more than thirty dollars, but Cruz allowed him to do it. I left sixty-one dollars—all the money I had in my wallet—as a tip for the waitress.

We stood next to each other but a million thoughts apart as the black SUV stopped in front of the restaurant. He paused for a moment, took my hand, and pulled me closer. When Cruz wasn't talking, it was possible to believe that he was thinking and that maybe he saw the world differently than how he always professed it to be. Surely, he couldn't believe all the crap that came out of his mouth. For a second, I thought he understood. Not just my behavior at breakfast, but me. Truly me.

Then, in a moment of weakness, I smiled up at him in time to see his eyes dart to the side. I did the same and spotted a diner recording us with his phone.

I rested my forehead against him in defeat. Every move Cruz made was for the cameras. Being in public with Cruz was more difficult than being alone.

"You ready?" he asked.

"Definitely." I couldn't wait for this to be over.

He took my hand and walked in front of me as if he were protecting me from the swarm of attention he craved.

"Isla, what's next?"

"Are you eating for two, Isla?"

"When will you two get married?"

"Isla?"

"Isla! Over here!"

Cruz helped me into the back seat like a gentleman. Ours was a great American romance complete with all the romanticized fictional elements.

As soon as the door was closed, Cruz let go of my hand and pulled his phone from his pocket. I was certain he was reading several articles about himself. He was a tragedy, and not just a guy who played one on the big screen.

He turned off his phone and leaned back against the headrest in complete satisfaction. There must have been something wrong with me. People, millions of people, including myself when I was younger, dreamed of having the life I'd created. The one where Cruz and I rode around Manhattan in the back of cars with tinted windows because we shone too bright for regular people to see us.

It was getting to the point where I couldn't see myself.

When the driver stopped in front of my building, Cruz barely glanced up when he asked. "Dinner tonight?"

I had to trust the voice inside my head because I knew there were no others around me to believe. "No. Thank you." I leaned over and kissed the lost boy. "It's been a fun run, but I'm out. Take care of yourself."

I exited the car without looking back. As of today, there would only be forward motion.

I was barely in the door when my phone rang. It was Victor Addario's office.

"Hello," I said. Dread throbbed behind my ears.

"Good morning, Ms. Monroe. Mr. Addario would like to see you today if possible."

I was surprised he'd waited this long. Cruz and I started dating while I was on tour. Victor always wanted to see me when a new boyfriend emerged. It was his pattern of abuse. His triumph of power.

"Of course," I said. "What time will work for him?"

"He's cleared his entire afternoon."

The words sank in one by one. Victor was in worse shape than I'd thought. Cruz plus my resistance in signing my latest record contract must have left him . . . frustrated.

"I'll be there at two. Thank you."

"Thank you, Ms. Monroe. Have a wonderful day."

I might have, but I was going to see Victor Addario, and nothing would be nice about that. The last time I'd been summoned, he screamed at me about an interview Hugh Rakling did where he'd teased that he was in love with me after recording a duet together. The duet that *Victor* had arranged. He didn't want me. At least not publicly. I had to date other people, mingle with other stars, but it drove Victor mad when I did.

When Victor's tirade of words ended, he'd stared at me until my blood froze in my veins. He threw me on the table and ripped my panties off. The tearing of the fabric had only fed his dark needs. He rolled me on my stomach and tied my wrists together with his belt. I'd left him in my mind. He was alone in the horror.

I never let Victor have me. Not all of me. Each time he'd tightened the belt, I thought of how my life would be when it no longer included Victor Addario. He'd yanked me to the edge of the table, still mumbling about how I was *his,* and drove his fingers into my dry and paralyzed body until eventually demanding I sing as he fucked me.

He'd flipped me over and unbuttoned his pants. The sound of his zipper lowering rang through the room as a warning bell. I closed my eyes.

"Say it, little one." The gentle words fought through his taut jaw.

I'd stared at the ceiling as Victor lined his dick up against me.

"Say it!" he'd roared. Victor wanted to believe that I had the power. He was my *choice.* Victor was not a rapist. At least not in his head.

"Please," I'd said, and he tore into me.

My back slid across the desk until he yanked me toward him as he thrust into me again. He fixated on the lower half of my body. The sight of him entering me always excited him. He was on the verge of drool falling from his lips.

"Now sing." His voice was rough. It'd been too long for Victor Addario to have denied himself this release. "Sing, or I'll take you to your apartment and tie you up until you beg me to let you sing."

"The greatest gift," I sang, and Victor entered me again without regard for my pleasure or participation. If he could have reached me, he'd have slapped me. That was why it was his least favorite position, but I hadn't given him time to think. To properly plan how he'd take me back in every way.

He leaned over me and bit my nipple until I winced. "Sing," he whispered. The beast inside him had been slayed.

I sang as he came and rescued himself from the cage he'd been in since the last time I let him have me. Victor would hate himself when we were through. I'd hated him for years, but without him, I'd have none of this. He reminded me of that fact often. With and without our clothes on, he would tell me how I wouldn't exist without him. His reach was far. His influence in the industry was remarkable. No one told Victor Addario no, especially not the star he created.

I could barely walk when Victor had finished making his point. He owned me—that was the only thing he'd needed to say. The rest was for his pleasure. The only sick, twisted way the great Victor Addario could get off was to first force me to submit.

"I could share you with my friends," he'd told me when I was barely eighteen. It was the most terrifying statement a man had ever made to me. "But that wouldn't please me. Do you understand?" he'd asked and tightened his grip on my hair. "Know that whomever you're with, you're still mine."

His fist tightened until some of the strands of hair tore out, and I said, "I understand, Victor."

He'd taken advantage of a girl with a dream and would never comprehend there was a reason to apologize for it. I learned from Victor that the world took what you let them have. He was violent and unrelenting, obsessed and narcissistic. The only difference between Victor and Mama's boyfriends was he held the power to get me out of her house.

In the very beginning, I'd thought I was in love with him—at least to the extent I had any idea what love was—but that was bad for business. The teenage pop star dating her label's president had no legitimacy. I needed a guy like Cruz Allen to define my talent, and Victor needed my success to define his. The Rakling incident hadn't been the first time he'd taken what he wanted from me, and it hadn't been the last, either. It was the day I realized just how Victor had taken advantage of my naivety. The moment the seed of hate for him had been planted. Each tear of my panties or song I was forced to sing for him made my hate for him grow.

His only weaknesses were his complete inability to accept the word no and me. Victor Addario always got what he wanted, but with me, what he wanted was the one thing he wouldn't let himself have. At least until someone else threatened to take me away. Once he'd claimed me as his own, Victor could never completely let me go.

I wasn't sixteen anymore, and I wasn't afraid to end this life.

CHAPTER 3

Isla

I LEFT THE DARK GLASSES on even after entering the skyscraper that housed the executive offices of my record label. The scarf wrapped around my platinum blond hair did little to hide my identity. Sometimes I felt it was more of an attraction than a disguise.

"Ms. Monroe, right this way," the receptionist said before I'd even fully cleared the doorway. "He's waiting for you."

"Isla." His secretary greeted me warmly, kissing me on both cheeks. "Can I get you some tea?"

"No, thank you. How's that new puppy of yours?"

"Crazy!" She laughed. "I named him Cruz after that boyfriend of yours."

I laughed, even though nothing was funny about it. "Well, let's hope he's better behaved." It was scary how easy this came to me—the *being* of Isla Monroe.

She stifled her hysterics as she opened the door to Victor Addario's midtown office on the seventy-fifth floor.

Victor was staring out the floor-to-ceiling windows with his hands safely in the pockets of his suit pants. I steadied myself for the inevitable transfer of my power to him. He stole it from every person who entered the room. I was never an exception.

He glanced back over his shoulder with the corners of his mouth tilting up on the sides. Victor rarely smiled. His lure was born in confidence. His insistence that he was right. Just standing near him made you want to believe in him. The man in front of me had never had coke dick. That I was sure of.

The familiar feel of his hands touching my body flowed through me as he walked over and silently kissed my cheek.

"Isla." He stared into my eyes as if he could take the little bit he'd left behind for me to perform with, but he couldn't. I didn't belong to him.

"Victor."

"Thanks for coming by," he said and motioned to the chair in front of his desk.

"I was summonsed." I sat in my usual seat. Today, it felt like it should be in the corner facing the wall. He leaned against the desk in front of me exactly the way I'd expected him to.

"You haven't signed the contract."

"I know." And I knew this was one of the reasons he'd called. The contract was somewhere on his desk behind him. He wouldn't let me leave without owning me again.

"Is there something wrong with the terms? Something you'd like to change?"

It was the moment I took back my freedom. I'd walked away from my life before, but this time, I was determined to trade up. The words out of my mouth should have been, "I'm done. Goodbye. Go fuck yourself." Yet, a small, almost unrecognizable voice, said, "My attorney has advised me the current version is in line with the last several." I was slipping away and falling into the darkness.

Victor leaned down and took my face in his hands. "What's really bothering you, Isla?"

A painful chill traveled from his hands down my chest to the spot my legs met and touched the seat beneath me. A silent tremor shook my chest and turned all my breaths shallow. The first time he'd called me Isla was in his bedroom. He'd taken off my dress and made me believe him when he'd said, "You're beautiful, and from now on, you are Isla."

Where my life would be without him? Without the first orgasm I had in his house at the Hamptons back when I was practically a child and Victor was pretending to watch out for me.

I could never explain to Victor what was really bothering me. In his mind, he'd rescued me from a ditch on the side of the road in North Carolina and delivered me to heaven. He'd be more insulted that I'd leave this gift of a life he'd bestowed upon me behind than he would be if I never let him touch me again. The defeated ache of being trapped returned and brought with it my anger. "Am I permitted to be bothered by something?"

He dropped his hands and sat back annoyed with my petulance. "What's going on?"

I could leave. Just stand and walk out without another word, but that would tell him something I wasn't ready for him to hear. I would think this through. It would be my decision and my consequences. "You tell me. This is your meeting."

"Ramona said you want some time off."

"The Ramona I pay, and whom you do not?" I practically spit the words in his face. No one was worth trusting in this business. Ramona was my employee, and I thought, my friend. "Or are you paying her, too?"

"Of course not. She's worried about you."

"She should be. Don't you think?"

Victor's spine straightened as he sat up straight in denial of my accusation. He didn't like being questioned—his authority or his decisions. He was going to will me to believe whatever he told me. "You're safe . . . with me."

"Your security detail is useless. I could outrun all of them." My best friend, Dick, was eating a chocolate donut and smoking a cigarette at the same time the other day. They were unathletic goons. "Things are changing too fast. Mistakes are being made."

"I assure you, you're fine." His jaw clenched, exposing the depth of his irritation. The conversation should have ended when he'd said I was safe. This debate and the unsigned contract behind him were scorching Victor's firm exterior.

I no longer cared. "All you're concerned about are my next tour dates."

"That's not true. I love you." Another man who would never understand what the word meant professing his love.

I didn't huff or roll my eyes. I stayed motionless. The same way I used to kneel in front of him as he touched me. "Stay very still, my Isla," he'd say with his penis against my face. "Now open your mouth," he'd demand and stick his dick down my throat. When he'd finally pulled it out and let me breathe, he'd say, "Now sing for me."

Ours wasn't the love affair of a young girl exploring her sexuality in the hands of her protector. It was abuse, but I'd been too young to know it.

When we were apart, it drove him mad. He hated the long months of travel associated with my tours. He couldn't keep an eye on me as easily. Dick and Alex were born of his discomfort with my absence.

"I'll always protect you," Victor said, but who would protect me from him?

Dick and Alex were reporting every move I made back to Victor, and apparently, so was Ramona. They were stalking me more than protecting me, and they were being paid to do it by the one man who I needed to be protected against.

"I'm done." I stood without taking my eyes off Victor. He was paralyzed by my words, and his lack of reaction was terrifying. "With all of this."

"You're not going anywhere." He swung me around and forced me onto my back. His hot breath in my ear flexed the muscles in my thighs where his hands roughly grabbed my leg before hauling my skirt up and ripping my knees apart.

My breath caught. The heat from Victor's body poured over me as he slammed my head against the desk with his hand over my throat.

I gasped for air. I'd pushed him too far. The power I'd felt ending things with Cruz this morning slipped away and was replaced with the compliant silence of the hollow teenage girl Victor had created.

"Is this how that little tool, Cruz Allen, fucks you?" He forced two fingers into me.

My back arched against the pain that seared through me.

I would not live this way.

Ever again.

"Is it, Isla? You think I can stand the thought of him touching you? Ridiculous prick."

"Victor—" He was crushing my windpipe against the desk beneath me, but he didn't care. There was no safe word with him, no signal. "Stop!" I managed to get out. I raised my knee against him. "Get off me," I said with the authority over my body I deserved.

Victor paused. A rare moment of surprise colored his expression.

I pushed his hand away and sat up. "Cruz Allen and I are done."

Victor took a step back. He was recalibrating in the wake of my rejection. He stood straight and squared his jaw; I knew I'd just launched us into an ugly new reality.

"I'm sorry to hear that." His words were cold and distant. Victor was staring at the desk I'd just been assaulted on. He was still trapped in his thoughts.

I wanted to be away from all of it. Victor, Ramona, Dick and everyone calling my name. "I want the security team fired," I managed to say because the other words were trapped somewhere between Victor's office and a ditch in North Carolina. "They're useless."

"You're wrong. They're keeping you safe." There was a frightening weakness to his voice.

"I'll take my chances."

Victor's blank stare hid the intricate workings of his mind. "As you wish," he said. His frigid agreement scared me more than his dramatic yelling. Victor never gave in. Even when he let me believe I'd won.

I stepped back onto the floor and straightened my skirt he'd just forced up to my waist. Victor watched as I smoothed down my hair in the back. A lump was forming in the back of my throat. I fought the urge to spit it at him.

"Call me . . ." His gaze lingered down the front of my body. I'd call him when I was ready to. Victor leaned against his desk like a beast that was unaware its treasure was about to walk out the door. "As soon as you need me, call."

I stopped fixing myself and studied him one last time.

"I'll always protect you, Isla."

He sounded so sincere. As if he almost believed it.

CHAPTER 4

Isla

THREE SUNSETS IN A ROW I'd watched from inside my apartment. I moved a chair over to the glass door and sat back with my feet resting on the wooden star-shaped table next to my bed. It was as close as I would get to the outside world right then. The fresh air and warm sunlight were on the other side of the door with the empty patio I could be photographed upon. I'd let them take the sunset and the night sky and the morning breeze, but they couldn't have me.

"I'm sorry, Isla," Victor's message had said. "You need me as much as I need you. For your safety . . . come back to my office so we can discuss this. All of it."

I didn't call him back. I contemplated only one thing through breakfast and my ride to the gym. I missed a kick and fell to the ground during training because I couldn't solve it in my mind. How was I going to tell Victor that I was leaving? Based on our last meeting, my taking some time off would be impossible.

As my trainer and I exited the gym, I laughed aloud at the brilliant idea of writing him a song about it. The mental vocals were soft and cooing, but the words themselves were harsh and cruel. I was so engrossed that I didn't see the crowd gathered until they started screaming.

"Isla, let us see the ring!"

"Isla!"

My trainer moved to stand in front of me, but the crowd surged next to us and almost knocked us to our knees. For the first few years, I couldn't get past the terror that someone would touch me or tear my hair out while I was trying to escape, but at some point, I came to accept it as the way I entered and exited buildings. The unreal became real.

"Isla, when's the date?"

"Are you pregnant, Isla?"

"Isla, over here. Isla!"

There were at least fifty of them crowding the sidewalk outside my trainer's gym. A place they rarely followed me. I climbed into the SUV and locked the door behind me, operating on the outrageous fear that they'd open it and rip me from the car.

"What's going on?" I asked the driver. He was the same man who drove me to Derek's every morning I was in the city. Mixed martial arts training began two years ago and continued while I was on tour. Another gift of my new life—a need for self-defense.

"Haven't you heard? You're engaged." The driver drove away from the curb with two photographers leaning across his windshield still taking pictures. "Fleas."

"What?"

"It was on CNN this morning. Isla Monroe and Cruz Allen to wed."

The anger boiled down deep in my stomach until it erupted and reached every inch of my body and my brain. My chest heaved instead of the deep calming breaths I needed.

"Ugh," was the guttural sound I released as I found my phone from my bag and dialed Ramona's number. When the call connected, I asked, "What the hell is going on?" without letting her say hello.

"Calm down. This is not a big deal."

"What planet are you on that getting engaged to a person is

not a big deal?"

"Isla."

I wanted to scream at her, *"My name is not Isla!"* but instead, I said, "I told you three days ago that Cruz and I were done."

"I know, but first you need to be engaged. You can't just breakup. Where's the headline in that?"

"It's not news. It's my life. We hung out, and now we're not going to anymore."

"You know, you could be a little more grateful. Being your publicist is not easy."

Grateful was not the emotion I was fighting through.

"You don't smoke, barely drink, no sex tape, no rehab, no scandal. What am I supposed to work with here?"

"Talent?" I screamed into the phone.

Ramona laughed a little. "Please."

I hung up and leaned into the front seat. "Arnold, would you mind if we make a few stops before going home?"

"I'm all yours, Ms. Monroe."

"Thank you."

I was a young woman navigating a world full of older men who swore they knew what was best for me as they imagined climbing on top of me. They were loathsome, but I was cordial every time I was near them. Before I left North Carolina, Mama had said, "Always be polite." She hadn't realized that would extend to Victor Addario wanting to own me. He'd seemed like the perfect mentor when he'd flown to North Carolina to meet her, so I seriously doubted she knew what kind of beast she was letting me leash myself to.

I stopped at my accountant's first. He wasn't seedy and actually seemed like the one decent human being in the entertainment industry. This was evidence enough that he was twisted beyond comprehension. He confirmed every detail I already knew about my finances. Living frugally was a gift of my childhood. When you never had any money, choices were easy. I'd lived the last decade meagerly compared to my peers. "Predictable," was the term my accountant used for my spending habits.

My assistant called my lifestyle boring. I'd never felt any allegiance to her, either. She'd been hired by Victor, so I assumed she was more of a babysitter than a business partner. I also suspected she'd leaked the story of Cruz Allen meeting me in Rio while I was on tour.

"Oh, oh . . . I didn't know . . ." she'd said when she'd walked into my hotel room and found Cruz lounged on the couch. Her eyes filled with dollar signs as she replaced her shock with utter joy. I'd assumed it was just Cruz. He had that effect on women, but when the story was all over the tabloids the next day, I couldn't shake the feeling that it'd come from her.

My attorney was next. We discussed First Right of Refusal, Transference of Ownership, and Length of Term . . . again. He was used to starlets and wide-eyed singers signing on the line he pointed to. I was used to being screwed, so he had to earn his money when it came to representing me.

"Why all these questions now?" He leaned down and caught my attention as I was reading through my last contract again. The question cracked open the door to a room full of inquiry behind it. He was prying because he was being paid to do so, and there was only one person in the world he'd risk his license for. He feared the consequences of disappointing Victor Addario more than he feared unemployment.

"I've just come off tour." I tried to sound nonchalant even though we both knew there was more to this than general education. "I'm getting older. Most people my age are already contributing to a 401K or something similar. They're getting married and having children, saving for college, buying homes."

"You're not most people, Isla," he said and stifled a laugh.

I wanted to be.

"Well, thank you for your time." I stood to leave. "Any plans for the rest of the summer? Traveling at all?" We should have been talking more about him. Anything but me.

"We're taking the kids to Disney, God help me. You?"

I left the smile cemented to my face. "No plans."

The way he paused before nodding his head told me he didn't believe me. It didn't matter. He could tell Victor whatever he wanted. As soon as I knew when I was leaving, I was going to tell the man myself, even if the idea of the conversation terrified me.

When I finally returned home, I dropped my things on the floor of my condo. The messenger bag I'd brought with me to New York City ten years ago was in the bottom of my closet. It was an army green color with patches sewn onto one side. It was the coolest thing I'd ever owned back then, and it meant more than the Louis Vuitton and the Valentino bags that littered my closet. Only my brother understood the litter of luxury.

"You can just leave it all behind," my brother had suggested when he and his wife met me on tour in Nashville. He'd said it as if it was an actual possibility. The three of us were perusing the room service menu in my hotel room because we didn't dare attempt eating out in public. The words had been uttered in the same context as, "Maybe the pasta and then the tart for dessert."

"That's crazy," I'd said. He examined every inch of my room before meeting my gaze across the table.

"Is it? The crazy part?" He held me in his stare. In all our years of being victims together, he'd never been more serious than that moment. "A man threw himself on the hood of our car today to take a picture of you. We only get to see you a few days a year. People are paid a salary to make up stories about your life and print them all over the world."

"It's complicated, I'll admit."

"That's what Mama used to say after she'd been punched in the face."

I lowered my head. Her shame was mine. She'd dragged my

brother and me through the river of self-loathing with every injury she'd sustained.

"Just because she couldn't make a good decision to save her life, doesn't mean we can't."

"I don't need to be saved," I said. I wasn't Mama.

My brother pushed his menu back a few inches and rested his hands on the tablecloth in front of him. "That's my point."

"I don't understand." I stared deep into his eyes, willing his thoughts to penetrate me.

"You're smarter than her. You're stronger than all of us. Stop letting yourself believe what everyone else is saying and listen to the voice inside you."

I laughed a little. Not that anything he said was funny. "Mama was a wreck."

"You don't have to be."

Our whole lives, he'd spoken words that had meant something to me. Mama'd said he was the thinker and I was the doer. He never accomplished a thing but had everything worth having, and I screwed them all up and had nothing.

Today, I would think. I put the snow globe in the messenger bag and rested it atop the coffee table my fake fiancé had sniffed his coke off. I'd pick a flight and call Victor. He'd let me go for a few weeks. He'd give me time to renew, especially after the scene in his office the other day. Victor wasn't comfortable being defied. He'd do whatever was necessary to restore his reign of power.

The Bible my mother gave me was on the kitchen counter, and next to it . . . was a paper . . . folded into thirds. My heart stopped with my paralyzed footsteps. I became aware of every sound, the particles of air moving around me, and all the shadows seeking the light. I inhaled deeply the silence of my apartment.

The paper was off-white, almost yellow. The color of a smoker's stained teeth. Without touching it, I knew it had the same grainy texture of the thick paper you could buy at any office supply store.

It meant a great deal to the author. To me it was a death notice.

I ran my fingers across the top of it. I'd read this last one and then never again. My plans had changed.

CHAPTER 5

Dalton

"ISLA MONROE IS RATHER UNPREDICTABLE, Mr. Dalton," Victor Addario said with a controlled lightness that, based on his taut jaw, appeared to be a struggle.

I wouldn't let the utter boredom show on my face. I hated Hollywood and the entire entertainment business, but Victor Addario didn't need to know that.

"She's . . ." Addario glanced down at this desktop as if running through his memories to find the right word. "Willful." I wasn't sure if we were still talking about the pop princess I'd barely known the name of before the trip over to his office. It took twenty minutes on Google to get a handle on Isla Monroe, and nothing made her seem compelling to me.

"Mr. Addario, it's not that I'm not interested in working with you and your company, but what you're requesting is less of a security detail and more of a private investigator's role. You'd be wasting your money employing me." And I'd be squandering my life. I was a West Point graduate and Special Forces in the United States Army. Just because I currently worked for a civilian firm didn't mean I was going to follow around Isla Monroe while she got her nails done.

"Your director, Mr. Wright, assured me you were the perfect man for the job."

"Perhaps he misunderstood the request."

Addario stood and walked around to the front of his desk. He wasn't a typical CEO. He still had his hair. Even beneath his suit jacket, I could see he could kick some ass if he needed to.

"I'm going to level with you," he said and immediately clued me in to his coming lie. "Ms. Monroe means a great deal to this label. We found her, we cultivated her talent, and we launched her career, and we want to make sure our business relationship continues." He turned to stone on the word "business," and it was another clue. The man was obsessed with her, which was the worst type of security detail I could possibly be involved with. "She's young and rebellious, and I'd expected her to sign her contract when she was here on Friday, but she didn't." He faked a laugh. "A bit of a handful if you know what I mean." I remained perfectly still, waiting for him to hang himself, but he didn't stumble. "And while I'm sure the assignment will be elementary for you, I believe it'll be a short one."

A short one. I'd just left Libya, which was also supposed to be a quick in and out assignment. I'd wallowed in a hotel for almost six months waiting for the name and location of the target, but it never came. Work was rarely executed exactly as it was planned. I'd spent the entire time reading. Fiction, biographies, and every detail of the world events occurring around me that I had absolutely nothing to do with since I was locked up in a hotel on the outskirts of Tripoli. I preferred the food in New York, but nothing else about this assignment held any appeal. I'd rather eat mutton everyday alone than follow Isla Monroe around.

Plus, this assignment didn't even make sense. Wright said two weeks tops. I begged him. Literally pleaded with him to assign Evans to it, but he was in Israel working on something that I could only assume was stimulating and worthy of his skill set. My schedule had rendered me available to follow Isla Monroe around. I'd be mentally bankrupt by the time she dragged me into Sunday.

"Why the short term?"

"Because as soon as Ms. Monroe signs her contract, she'll be back in the studio, and things will return to normal, I'm certain."

"What's normal?" *And why the need to follow her?*

Addario didn't answer. He handed me a black matte folder. Inside, the two pockets held every detail of Isla Monroe's life I could live without knowing. "I'll expect an update within a week. My private cell phone number is listed on the card."

I shook his hand. His grip held just the amount of excess force to hit home the point that he was in charge. Addario was used to being the Alpha male in the room.

"Make sure you keep your distance from her," he added as I was about to leave. The directive, and the reason behind it, left me cold.

"Of course. In this type of assignment, no contact at all will be made."

Thanks, though, dickhead, for telling me how to do my job. Or at least, how you'd like me to do it.

Victor Addario made my skin crawl, and that instinct was never wrong. As soon as I cleared the front door of the building, I hit Wright's number on my phone.

"Yes?" he answered as if I wasn't going to beat him the next time I saw him, which I might.

"You've got to find somebody else."

"There's only you. This firm billed seventeen million in services to Addario last year. If he wants you to follow around Isla Monroe, you're following her."

"Why me? I can't even stand pop music, and I hate teenagers."

"Have you read her profile?"

"Why?"

"Because she's not a teenager. Don't make assumptions."

"I want to kill you."

"I know. Just do your job, and you'll be handsomely rewarded. The next coup attempt or assassination, I promise, is yours."

I took the subway downtown and found Isla's apartment building.

It was only eight stories and in the heart of the East Village. Not what I expected. There were several doors on the first floor that led to either emergency exits or retail space. I tried them and they were all locked, except for the front door where the doorman stood guard.

I met her recently fired security detail in front of the building. The two men were dressed in all black. Black suits, ties, and shirts. They were also both smoking cigarettes. They looked better suited for a low-budget comedy than a protection detail. I walked up, and they didn't even move. The large one sneered, but it appeared only because our conversation was going to be an effort. The smaller one smiled. I thought it was genuine.

"Hi. My name's Dalton. Victor Addario suggested I speak to both of you."

"Yeah." The big one grunted the word. "He said you were coming."

"How long have you guys been on her?" I softened my facial features. They needed to believe we were on the same team, but if this were fifth grade kickball, I'd pick the big one last.

"We just got back from her tour. She's been on the road for over a year," the angry one said. "And now we've been dismissed."

Addario had said she'd fired them, but he didn't say why. I didn't really care to ask, either. "Well, that's a long assignment. You guys must have been getting tired of following her around."

"I'm ready for a change," the smaller one said.

Fatty grunted again.

"Well, I'm planning to be in and out on this one. Anything I should know? Any strange comings and goings for our little pop star?"

"She's sweet," the little one said.

"A sweet asshole," fatty added, confirming my initial impression of him.

"Oh, great."

"She's just difficult." He remembered he didn't know me and

softened his tone.

"Addario pretty much said the same thing."

"It's true." He smashed out his cigarette and left the butt on the sidewalk near my foot.

"How, though? Addario didn't give me any examples."

"Our last job was Tiffany Snow," he said as if I should recognize the name. "She loved having us around. Just the look of us." I hid the confusion on my face because the "look" of him was a deterrent for sure. "She was *easy* to work with." He lit another cigarette. "Isla Monroe hates us following her around. She thinks she's better than everyone else. She's a bitch."

"Oh. This is going to be fun." I fake-laughed. He was an idiot, I was sure, but Isla Monroe probably was a bitch. She was a pop star for God's sake.

The smaller one smiled at me without speaking another word. He didn't seem to be in charge of anything, not even of his own speech. I left them and walked across the street. I sat on a bench in the park and listened while the paparazzi talked about Isla and some douche named Cruz. Who names their kid Cruz? I flipped through the pages in the folder as the men around me debated her day's schedule like her personal assistants instead of standing outside in the sweltering sun just watching her.

Ida Malone, DOB 3/21/90. An old headshot showed Isla with long, light brown hair and green eyes. Neither of which I could reconcile with the pictures I saw on the subway ride into Addario's office this morning. Her glow in the dark hair skewed every other feature.

"Cruz left last Friday and hasn't been back since," one of the men facing the front door of her building said.

"I saw him last Thursday, too. They were together the day she got back, but then, all of a sudden, he was gone."

"Is he on a movie?"

"No. Walt's on him and said he's still going out around here. They're done."

I actually liked the idea of the breakup. Following Isla Monroe around would be bad enough. Cruz what's-his-name tagging along, I was sure would be intolerable.

Her doorman whistled for a car, and an enormous SUV drove up from a spot at the end of the block. The men surrounding me and several spanning from corner to corner ran across the street, pulling their cameras from their bags as they went.

Isla paused at the top of the three stairs to her front door. She stared right at me, or so it appeared through her dark glasses and scarf. After the brief hesitation, she climbed into the waiting car without a hint of what she was thinking. The SUV drove off while I scanned the area. Behind me stood a guy staring toward the street. He had no camera or obvious purpose for being there, but he never took his eyes off the car Isla was in. When her vehicle made a left at the light, he noticed me.

"What's up, buddy?" I asked him. The bottom two buttons of his dark blue shirt were mismatched. It was velvet with long sleeves, which was an odd choice for a humid summer day. His lips were pursed shut, but I couldn't tell if it was to keep from screaming or crying. "Everything okay?"

He glared from the top of my head to the concrete below me before walking away without a word.

"Don't mind him. He's harmless," one of the returning cameramen said to me.

"Is he here a lot?"

"Who's not here a lot?" He tipped his head, signifying how arduous hunting a pop star was. "Where's your gear?" he asked, but I was already following the guy in the blue shirt down Avenue A.

His pace quickened. I had to dodge through irate traffic to stay with him. He sensed me closing in and sped up. I had one last glimpse of him before he hopped on a bus that was driving away. He stared at me through the window as I memorized every detail I'd learned about him. People who didn't want to be seen were always the ones you should watch.

CHAPTER 6

Dalton

ISLA MONROE WAS ORDERING ICE cream, but she couldn't make up her mind as to what she wanted. She kept having the girl behind the counter go into the back freezer and check for flavors that weren't in the cooler.

"Whatever you want, we can make it," the owner said, and I wanted to pull out my piece and shoot him. Or maybe I wanted to shoot myself. I couldn't really be following this woman around. I hated her and everything she stood for.

The ringing phone blurred the images in my mind. The sound was coming from the back room, or next to me.

I opened my eyes in my apartment, not an ice cream parlor. Isla Monroe was already ruining my dreams. The phone rang again. I answered it without saying hello.

"She's in the wind," Paul said. I shook myself fully awake and sat up.

"What?"

"Isla Monroe. She's moving."

I held the phone in front of my face and pressed the home button. It was three fifty in the morning on Wednesday. I hadn't even had this assignment for twenty-four hours. My counterpart, Paul, was also being tortured by mind-numbing shifts. The excitement in his voice at the location change of Isla Monroe was sufficient evidence of his boredom.

"Where is she?" I stood and searched for my pants.

"The airport."

"What? Where the hell is she going?" I was fully awake. "Let me guess. North Carolina."

"How'd you know?"

"They always go home."

"Stay with her. I'll meet you down there." I looked around the room for my backpack and stopped as dread invaded me. "How much luggage does she have?" Large suitcases meant extended travel. This was a short-term assignment for me.

"Just a purse. She's sitting alone by the windows with her head all wrapped up and a bible in her lap. It's really creepy."

"Why didn't she fly private? Surely, there's someone out there with a plane to lend her."

"I don't know." Paul's voice dropped. He truly sounded sad just from being within twenty feet of her. "Did I mention we're in Philly? We're booked on the five fifteen to Wilmington with a stop in Charlotte."

"Not even direct? Stay with her. I'll take over for you when I get to North Carolina."

"How do you know where she's going?"

"There is a zero percent chance she doesn't end up in Swansboro."

I hung up and switched to military mode. I was booked on the nine ten out of Newark, but traffic around the city would increase as soon as the sun rose. I had to get out before the day started.

I had some clothes, my phone, laptop, power cords out the wazoo, and my folder on Isla Monroe that I'd already memorized. Upon landing, my Mid-Atlantic counterparts picked me up at the airport, outfitted me with several handheld weapons, a new ID, and cash, and then they delivered me to my waiting car and Paul at the Icehouse Waterfront Restaurant.

I wanted to tell them it was unnecessary. This wasn't going to be a challenging assignment. I could have rented a car to follow Isla Monroe, but there was only one standard to complete a mission. The right way.

Paul ordered the clam chowder and a beer as if we were a gay couple from the Midwest vacationing together.

"Well?" I was impatient with my boyfriend.

"You're not going to believe it."

"Try me." I stole the crackers from his saucer and ate them both at the same time. Isla Monroe had already fucked up my breakfast.

"She's at a hair salon up the street."

I nodded.

"You don't think North Carolina is a little far to get your hair done? Rich people are crazy."

What Paul didn't know was that Isla's sister-in-law worked at the salon. "I'll take it from here." Isla Monroe's daybreak departure had piqued my interest in her, even if she landed exactly where I assumed she would. Being right was so satisfying. Isla'd relax, spend some time with her family, cover up her roots, and hop a plane back to New York. Maybe she'd even go to the beach for the day. The assignment was starting to please me. A few days in the sun would be good for me. It'd been too long since I sat on a beach or swam in the ocean.

Not that I wouldn't be able to spot her with the glow-bright hair, but I asked, "What kind of car is she driving?"

Paul lifted the bowl and slurped the rest of his soup. "She took a cab from the airport right to the salon."

Why didn't someone pick her up? Wasn't she expected?

I left Paul chatting with the bartender. He was in no rush to get back to New York. North Carolina had a way of sucking you in. Like the corner of a sectional sofa at the end of a long day, you just sank down and didn't realize how comfortable you were until it was time to get up. I half expected him to say goodbye with a

Southern drawl.

The hair salon was a pole barn nestled between a used car dealership and a storage facility. The shared lot between the two was perfect for me to park and wait.

By noon, I thought we'd screwed up somehow and searched for Isla's brother's address in the folder. She must have gone back to his house already. She was probably sipping wine and eating pulled pork while I tried to be inconspicuous in the storage facility parking lot.

At one forty-five, two women emerged. One was Isla's height and build, but her hair was light brown and at least six inches shorter. The other woman was taller than Isla. She hugged her and gave her a set of keys. The two women walked to a car in the back lot, which was diagonal to where I was parked. I leaned down in my seat and listened through the opened windows.

"Take care of yourself."

"Always."

There was a long pause I assumed was a hug. "I know you want to be invisible but don't hide from love."

I concentrated on her words and memorized the cadence of her speech. She laughed and said, "I'm not twelve. I've been in love before."

"No you haven't. If you find someone amazing . . . someone you'd never be able to leave . . . someone who'd *kill* for you—don't run away."

"You're very theatrical, and I think the ones who would kill for me are the ones I'm running from."

She's running?

"Your brother's gonna have my ass for doing this."

"Tell him it was his idea."

"You know this isn't what he meant."

"I think it is. He just didn't know it."

Isla drove off in a Honda Accord with me trailing behind her. Instead of turning toward her brother's house, she traveled north and picked up Route 50 to Raleigh. Isla and I were leaving town. She exited the highway on the west side of the city and pulled over on the shoulder of a country road. I had no choice but to pass by. There was no place to stop without being seen. I waited fifteen minutes and circled back. Isla was talking to a man about a car for sale on his front lawn. It was an old Chevy Trailblazer with a sign in the windshield that read: $6500 or BO.

I picked up the phone and called Paul. "I'm going to need some help," I said when he answered.

"Having trouble getting a pedicure with the pop princess?"

He annoyed me one hundred percent of the time.

"She's on the move again. Right now, she's buying a used car off the side of the road. I can't stay close to her or she's going to make me. We've got to switch out until she gets where she's going." I parked the car on the far edge of the shoulder with the front facing the direction she'd be driving from. Then I raised the hood and sat in the passenger seat.

"All right. I'm at the hotel. I'll get a car and catch up to you," Paul said and hung up.

A round fired in the near distance. I got out of the car to listen for a second shot. Did she somehow get herself killed while I was watching her? I shook my head in disgust, lowered the hood in the car, and drove back toward the used car.

Isla appeared tiny, almost cuddly—I rolled my eyes at the thought—as she shook the old man's hand before he handed over the keys to her. She drove off past me without a glance in my direction. I turned the car around when she was out of sight and sped off after her. I didn't relax until she checked into the Hampton Inn in Raleigh, yet another odd choice for a starlet. The second she left her car, I put a GPS unit under her bumper.

The next two days were grueling. Isla barely stopped for gas and water. Her stamina was remarkable. Even if she'd been pampered in her present life, she apparently knew how to go into battle, and

I wondered—not for the first time—what exactly she was battling. She stopped only to sleep when Paul and I wanted to collapse. From Raleigh, she hit Knoxville and drove right through to Nashville. Isla stopped at The Mall at Green Hills where she bought a suitcase and rolled it around the mall, filling it with clothing purchases. I heard her tell a saleswoman that there'd been a fire. No one was hurt except her undies. She enchanted the saleswoman with her authentic accent and kind demeanor. I watched her check out in Carmella's and called the office.

"Can you hack into a store called Carmella's in The Mall at Green Hills and find credit card and identification for a recent sale that took place at"—I twisted my watch toward me—"one fifteen PM?"

"I'll run it now and send it to you." Ty could find out your favorite salad dressing from a hotel room three continents away. "How's it going?"

I thought about that for a second. Annoying? Isla Monroe was nothing if not unpredictable. "It's interesting. Let me know. If I can find out what name and credit she's working with, it'll make my job easier."

She picked up a new cell phone and checked into another hotel room. Paul took over and let me sleep. We ditched one of our cars. We'd pick up a new one in the next town if she stayed long enough for us to switch it out. The next morning, before the sun came up, Isla was on the move again.

"This is so much better than driving," Paul said and put his feet up on the dash of my car. He was taller than I was, and the two of us looked ridiculous driving across country in this little Honda, but that was what the office had delivered to us. I could see Wright laughing back at his desk. I was being punished for something, I was sure.

"You're driving next. So, don't get too comfortable."

"I'm six-three in a compact Honda. 'Comfortable' is going to be a stretch." Paul leaned his back against the car door and folded his one leg in front of him on the seat. We called him the contortionist because his flexibility had gotten us out of more than one jam before. He claimed the ladies were equally impressed with his flexibility, but Paul swore women were enamored with everything he did sexually.

His phone dinged before a German song played from it. I raised my eyebrows at him.

"She's got the best tits I've ever seen."

"Lovely," I said and fell two cars behind Isla.

"I've seen a lot of tits."

"I think I've had to hear about every single one of them."

"I can't help it. This is how God made me. Don't try to tell me you haven't noticed Isla Monroe's rack."

I shook my head. "You're unbelievable."

"I'm a hot-blooded male, born to travel the earth and find fertile ground to plant my seed."

"What does that have to do with tits?"

"Well, I'm no farmer, but that's how I determine whether the ground is fertile. How great their tits are."

Paul would be fourteen forever. "I think talking to you lowers my IQ."

"You need to get laid."

I stopped listening. In my head, I was trying to calculate how long we'd been on the road and how much longer I'd be stuck in this car with Paul.

"Seriously. I know you've had a tough run, but it's time to get back into the race." He was quiet for a minute. I braced myself. Giving Paul time to think was never helpful. "Do you even remember how to talk to a woman?"

I sighed. Why was I trapped here with him?

He just kept talking. "Next stop. You should go out and get some. No one ever forgets how to do that. I'll help you out with the talking."

"And what happens when Isla Monroe takes off at four AM?"

"Oh, you'll be done by then." Paul laughed hysterically. Cracking himself up was his second favorite thing to do. Right behind getting laid. We'd been working together for almost ten years, and he hadn't changed a bit. I envied him of that.

"Next time she pulls over, I've got to call *fräulein* back."

I had no one I needed to call. The last woman I'd had sex with had called me cold and certainly wasn't blowing up my phone. Maybe that was what shifted my opinion of Isla Monroe into the intriguing category. Since her sister-in-law, she hadn't spoken to anyone, either.

"Do you remember the time we met those girls in London and they believed we were American spies?"

"It wasn't completely a lie."

Paul stared out the window whimsically. "Man, I miss London."

"I thought you missed Germany."

"That London girl sucked great cock."

"You make me want to never have a daughter."

"What? I'm a complete gentleman with these girls. And believe me, that English girl would be proud to hear I told you she sucked great cock."

"Yes. Very proud."

"It's getting harder and harder to have fun with you. I think you need a vacation."

"Maybe." I switched lanes and sped up just enough to still see her.

"Maybe London when this shit show of a job is over. How far can she go? For how long? We've got the identity she's using, so all she has to do is settle in somewhere. Then we're home free, or London bound." He bounced his eyebrows at me.

Isla drove her Trailblazer seventeen hours to Denver all by herself with Paul and me trailing her. I'd never been as grateful as when I got the message that Danielle Morris's credit card had been authorized for three nights.

When Paul had taken over driving, I'd spent the hours searching the Internet for information about Isla Monroe and Danielle Morris. There was nothing on the latter, but the former was literally everywhere. Entertainment, gossip, and legitimate news sites all covered her comings and goings. According to search engine data, she was the most searched celebrity last year. By the time we'd crossed into Colorado, I'd listened to her last album in its entirety, read every review I could find, and analyzed her latest interviews. There was nothing about her personality. No evidence of scandal I'd been expecting. No sex tape or arrests of any kind.

"What do you know about Isla Monroe?" I asked Paul.

"She's hot. That's really all I need to know."

This was futile, but I continued. "What's her reputation? Is she a spoiled drama queen?"

"I don't think so. That type of behavior makes them globally known, but to work in this business for this long, she must be good. Like, professional good."

"How long's she been around?"

"I don't know. Ten years?"

"The report said eleven."

"Yeah. That's like fifty years on the job at a corporation. Stars can't shine bright forever, especially not the female ones."

Isla showed no signs of slowing on her road trip from hell. I hoped her intention of staying a few days in Denver hadn't changed. I feared she might drive all the way to California and then right off the coast into the ocean. She exited onto I25 South and headed toward downtown Denver, and I exhaled. I was exhausted.

She stopped at the hotel valet and stepped out of the car. Paul let me out a half block away. I entered the hotel and found the restroom. I waited in the corner of the lobby until she and her new suitcase entered the building. She walked up to the front desk and practically rested her head on top of it. Isla's shoulders sagged as she offered a labored hello and took out her credit card and license for check-in. Or Danielle Morris's. As they were finishing up, a woman walked in, pushing a stroller and carrying the child that should have been in it. The kid threw his cup down, and it bounced off the ground and hit Isla in the back of the knee.

"Oh my God. I'm so sorry," the mother started to say as she rushed over to Isla.

Isla bent down and picked up the cup. She handed it back to the child, who threw it on the floor again in a fit of rage.

"Oh my God," the woman said. She rubbed her forehead with her free hand.

Isla picked up the cup again and handed it the mother. "It's okay." She smiled. The child stopped fussing and stared at her. "I feel exactly the same way. If I had a cup, I'd throw it, too."

I thought the mother was going to hug Isla. She reached out and rubbed her arm. "Thank you. It's been a hell of a day."

"Good luck," Isla said and made her way to the elevator. I strolled over and timed it perfectly to arrive at the bank as the doors closed. I watched the numbers above me and her elevator stop on the sixteenth floor.

Paul walked in and met me at the front desk to check in. He stretched, raising his arms toward the ceiling to try to adjust his spine that'd been shoved into our compact car for too many hours. He couldn't fix the dark circles surrounding his glassy eyes. We needed sleep, and we were working as a team. Isla was alone.

CHAPTER 7

Dalton

"WHERE IS SHE?" VICTOR ADDARIO'S voice was tight. The words, he shoved past gritted teeth.

"Well, she's in motion."

"I can see that. She's cut off her manager, publicist, accountant, and her makeup artist claims he hasn't spoken to her. Her money's gone. She left a note in her apartment that every item in it can be donated. Where . . . the *fuck* . . . is she?"

I was impressed with her ability to cut all ties, especially the ones to her career. While some celebrities drowned themselves in pills and alcohol to deal with the fame and the fear of losing it, Isla Monroe had run away in the middle of the night without looking back. Meanwhile, Addario was losing his edge with every word he spoke of her. It made me think she was running from him. The thought of petite little Isla Monroe being afraid of Victor Addario surfaced a buried instinct to protect her.

"Don't you think her actions seem a bit extreme?" I asked. "I mean, you described her as unpredictable, but exiting her entire life . . ."

Addario exhaled loudly into the phone.

"I think—"

"I'm not paying you to think!" he erupted. "Where the fuck are you right now?"

I admired the Denver skyline I'd woken to this morning from my window at the Four Season hotel. "I'm at a Hampton Inn in Houston." He sure as fuck wasn't paying me enough not to think. "I'll be in touch."

Addario hung up. This was more than a contract negotiation, and Isla's disappearance was more than a vacation.

"What the fuck are you doing?" Paul asked from behind me.

I didn't turn around. Even though I couldn't stand Addario, I knew I was ignoring protocol. I could be pulled from this assignment, which in that moment I realized I didn't want to be. I wanted to know where Isla was going and what, or who, she was running from.

"You realize you could get taken off for what you just did."

"Yeah." None of the pieces lined up on this assignment. "Have you ever been on a job like this? *Watching* someone because they didn't sign a contract? There's something more to this. It's too extreme."

"What do you think? That we're the A-Team? We follow orders. Period."

"I know. I just need some time."

"You do? Or she does?"

Maybe both of us. It wasn't fair to involve Paul in this. "I've got it from here. You can head back."

"You don't have shit. You're going to fuck this up so bad that I'm not going to be able to help you." I didn't move. "She's not worth it." Paul didn't know that, but neither did I.

"There's more to her than what Addario told us." There was so much more just based on our road trip across the entire United States. "Don't you think it's significant that he hired us to follow her the day before she flew the coup? Addario knew she'd leave, because she's running from him."

Paul only shook his head in disbelief.

"Something about Addario doesn't sit well with me."

"None of that matters. If Addario paid us enough, we'd kill her."

"That's not true."

"It's not?" Paul raised his eyebrows at me. He was a mirror to my moral compass. Paul stared at me. I wasn't myself. This particular job was doing something to me. Exactly *what* should have frightened me, but instead, I felt more alive than I had in months. Maybe years.

"I don't know," I said, but I wasn't letting anyone near her until I found out who she was afraid of.

"That's what I'm saying. You don't know what the fuck you're doing. She's messing with your head."

"I just need a few more days to figure out what's going on. She'll meet up with someone soon. There'll be a conversation . . . some form of contact."

"What if there's not?"

"Please. She's a kid. She's not going to run away and spend the rest of her life alone." That type of behavior was reserved for retired military in elite security operations.

"You're playing with fire."

"That's why I think you should go. Besides, I might need your help later. I don't want you to wear yourself out."

"You're an idiot," he said, and it sounded like something I would say to him.

"Thank you. Take the car." The office would track it. I'd have to get another.

I walked Paul to the lobby and stopped in the gift shop to get a better view of the side street. Without Paul, Isla's next move was going to be even harder to follow, but I couldn't take the chance of word getting back to Addario about her location before I was ready to tell him, so it was going to be just me and Isla.

I picked through the candy on the shelf, letting my fingers run over all my childhood favorites until I stopped on the large yellow bag of peanut M&M's.

"Can I sneak in here?" she said and reached across me for a

bag. It was Isla in a bathing suit and cover-up. The black straps tied behind her neck and ran across each of her collarbones before the long white shirt covered it. My gaze lingered at the spot where her neck met her shoulder a half second too long. "Sorry."

"No problem." I took a bag for myself as Isla put a novel with the ocean on the cover, a bottle of water, and the candy on the counter. The woman at the register rang her up.

Shit! Now there's been contact, and I sent Paul packing. I was *fucked* with this assignment.

"Going to the pool?" the cashier asked.

"Yes. Is it nice up there?"

"Oh, yes. Very relaxing. Are you traveling alone?" She handed Isla the receipt to sign.

There was a miniscule pause before she wrote a name, but it was shrouded in Isla's pleasant chatter. "Actually, I'm alone for a few days, but meeting friends later."

The cashier handed the bag to her. "We all need a little time to ourselves . . ."

"Amen," Isla said. *Yum*, she mouthed as she held up the M&M's and brushed by me to leave.

When I got back to my room, I threw out the Villanova cap, the sunglasses, and the rugby tee I'd been wearing. "I loved those sunglasses," I mumbled.

I walked the seven blocks to Enterprise Rent-A-Car and picked up a new sedan. Something a little bigger that didn't "crush my balls," as Paul had put it. The next three and a half hours I spent in the lobby while Isla was lounging at the pool. I knew every inch of the interior, from the floating fireplace in the center to the extensive amount of leather seating near the giant windows that looked out onto the street. I had a book to fake-read and a newspaper to hide my face when necessary. I moved to seats next to women whenever possible to give the appearance that we might be traveling together. There was a precise rhythm and timing to this. Women in general had very good instincts about who sat near them, but since I was completely safe, most were intrigued rather than disturbed by my seat choice.

Isla exited the elevator and spoke to the concierge for a few minutes. She was wearing the long blue dress I'd watched her select off the sale rack at Ann Taylor Loft. It was soft and clung to her body, but still innocent and respectable. It and her silver flip-flops were a far cry from anything I'd seen her wear in the hundreds of pictures I'd studied of her.

When she stood still and didn't smile, which wasn't often since we'd left North Carolina, I could make out a resemblance to her celebrity persona, but as she warmly thanked the concierge I was certain he had no clue who he was actually speaking to.

She exited the hotel and walked left onto 14th Street. The stifling air and the torrid sun were a welcome respite from the frigid air conditioning inside the lobby. I could have spent the day at the pool, too, if Isla hadn't made contact over a bag of M&M's. We followed 14th to Colfax and strolled past the capitol. Isla stopped and admired the building before starting again with seemingly no destination in mind. That was, until she made a left on Logan and entered the Catholic Church that towered in front of her. The Cathedral Basilica of the Immaculate Conception listed their mass time at six thirty this evening. It was currently twenty minutes to six.

I waited after she entered. I wanted her seated and staring toward the altar when I walked in, but when I finally stepped inside, Isla was nowhere to be found. The sanctuary was filled with candlelight and echoes. The soft lighting was good for me. The empty pews were not.

Two elderly women came and sat midway up the aisle together. I chose a pew two rows behind them. If she made me again, I'd have to take myself off the job. The confessional door opened. Isla stepped out without looking in my direction. She was grabbing the side of her dress and raising it up so she didn't step on the hem.

"Baptized Catholic. Attended religious education through confirmation," was what the report had detailed about Isla Monroe's religious affiliation. I hadn't been in a church of any denomination since . . . I pushed the last time back down in my memory.

Isla sat in the last seat of the third pew back. She was alone and silent until a woman came and held out her hand. Isla took it. I couldn't tell if they'd ever met before, but Isla followed her to the back of the church. I was trapped. The silence of the room would draw too much attention to me if I attempted to stand or follow.

The two women in front of me whispered a conversation to each other without any regard for the people around them.

"No. She didn't?" the one asked a little too loudly, and the other woman shushed her.

"Keep your voice down. It's between her and God."

"And the entire ping pong team at the senior center, apparently."

They both laughed, and my impatience grew. I needed to find Isla without anyone noticing me. The organ note pierced through the peace and echoed off the marble surrounding me. I had to get out of here. I wasn't confessing a thing, but then her voice—that of an angel—rang through the church, and people filled the pews around me. I slid over behind a pillar where I could safely watch Isla sing songs I didn't know and could barely make out the words to. This little being, eclipsed by the bronze background of an ancient organ, captured the entire congregation by the time her song was done.

She sang one more and then nodded to the crowd before our attention was drawn back to the front of the church by the priest clearing his throat. Isla returned to her seat in the shadows near the front. I tried to make sense of the sounds I'd just heard. She wasn't just talented, she was gifted, and you'd never know it by the music she made and sold to millions of teenagers around the world.

Church filled me with a sense of finality. I knew she was leaving in the morning. I was starting to sync with her. She'd come all the way to Denver to sing these songs. I didn't know where we were going next until four in the morning when I got the notification that she'd moved her car.

Twelve painful hours of driving ended at The Riverside hotel in Boise. Isla went to her room for twenty minutes and then relocated to a bar stool at the Sandbar Pub. The bar was outside and gearing up for happy hour. Children ran on the lawn while their parents sipped drinks and half watched them. Isla ordered a glass of champagne. "Whatever kind you have," she said, reminding me that she wasn't difficult.

"Celebrating something?" the bartender asked. He poured the bubbly liquid into her glass.

"Freedom."

His eyebrows rose. He was already counting on the fact that she'd still be sitting there at the end of his shift. Her declaration had made it sound like she'd just finalized her divorce.

A man playing a guitar and a female vocalist began a set at exactly five in the evening. Isla ordered two more glasses of champagne. She should have just ordered the bottle. It would have been cheaper, but I doubted she cared and the bartender's pours were heavier with each order. Her eyes closed a little as she moved back and forth to the music.

I ordered a hamburger and watched her from a table. She needed to eat something or she was going to want to die tomorrow. These were the first drinks I'd seen her consume, and she wasn't slowing down. Something had changed since we'd left Denver. The need to know *what* ate away at me. Again, I went over every detail about her and this trip in my mind.

A family of five rode by on their bikes, the misting machine above me attempted to cut through the heat, and Isla Monroe ordered another drink. By eight, the bartender was leaning on the bar talking to her. I was ready to take her home, or wherever else she wanted to be. This guy had no idea who he was dealing with. In Isla Monroe or me.

She stood, caught the stool she'd almost knocked over, and left cash on the bar. I followed Isla back to the hotel, making sure she got there safely. She didn't notice me as she entered the lobby and headed for the stairs to the second floor, still I waited long enough for her to be inside her room before following.

When I opened the door to the hallway, she was still fumbling with her key. She finally got it to work and walked into the room right beside mine. I practically tiptoed to my door, opened it, and locked myself inside. Isla was drunk. She shouldn't be out by herself. I'd had similar months of celebrating my freedom after my breakup. There was nothing happy about it. Only lonely drinks and unanswered toasts.

I listened through the wall for sounds of conversation. Everyone called someone when they were drunk. Tonight was the night she'd make her first mistake, and there was no way for me to help her. The door between our rooms had only a lock on the handle. I could be in there in half a second if I decided I wanted to be. As if she'd heard my thoughts, I could hear her moving furniture against the door on the other side of the wall. I searched my own room. She must have been moving the entire dresser her television sat upon. Even drunk, she still impressed me.

I dropped and did a hundred push-ups. I ran in place and did jumping jacks. Sit-ups. Lunges . . . anything to take my mind off her next door to me. She'd sleep tonight. She was going to feel awful tomorrow. A full bottle of champagne on an empty stomach was going to injure her. She couldn't have weighed a hundred and thirty pounds.

At half past four in the morning, my GPS app went off on my phone. She was driving again. I rolled over and cursed her. "What the fuck is wrong with starting your day at eight, Isla?"

I got up and threw my things in my backpack. I brushed my teeth, the whole time watching the blue dot move across the highway. We were heading west. Again.

Seven more hours to Portland ended with her driving in circles and me trying not to be noticed. For the first time since I sent him on his way, I wished Paul were with me. I admitted to myself that he was right. If Isla went farther on this adventure, I'd need to bring him back into the fold and follow the rules. At this rate, we were just going to drive around a single neighborhood north of I-84 for the rest of our lives.

She slowed, pulled into a driveway, and got out of the car. She wasn't interested in the street. No, she just examined the house as if she'd been there before and was trying to remember if this was the one. A sign in the front window read: For Rent.

Thank you, God. May this be her new home.

I parked down the street and read the Isla file again. I knew there was nothing in there connecting her to Oregon, but it seemed like an odd choice, considering her North Carolina upbringing and her insistence on not moving to Los Angeles earlier in her career. One of the interviews I read about her described her loyalty to the east coast as "unwavering."

The house next to my car had a For Rent sign as well. Both sides of the quaint road were packed with bungalow type houses and overgrown front yards. The street was transient. There was a cafe on the corner and a marijuana dispensary directly across from where Isla had parked.

A man exited the house across the street from Isla's location. It was a two-story bungalow.

I got out of my car and asked, "Excuse me, is this house for rent?"

"It's about to be. I'm moving out tomorrow morning." He had a box in his hands and two backpacks hanging off his shoulders.

"Do you have the owner's number?"

"It's me." He put down the box next to his car. "Rob Walcom." I shook his hand. "I'm getting married, and my fiancée just picked out a house. We can't afford both, so I'm moving in tomorrow." He rolled his eyes in frustration. "Six months ahead of time."

I felt bad for the guy. He was mourning the premature death of his single life. "Time keeps on ticking . . ."

"Yeah. It's one bedroom, one bath, furnished and fourteen hundred a month."

The door to the house across the street opened, and an elderly woman stepped out.

"Can I see it?" I rushed Robert toward the door in hopes of disappearing before Isla emerged. Once inside, I acted interested in the surroundings and paid cash for the first and last month's rent and the security deposit.

"Must be my lucky day," Rob said and counted the cash. "Maybe it's a good sign for this marriage."

I signed a lease, let Rob take pictures of my identification, took the extra set of keys, and promised to be back with my stuff the next day. I had no belongings, though. Isla, across the street, was my only possession.

CHAPTER 8

Dalton

ISLA OPENED THE CURTAINS A slit and peered out. No one walking on the street would even know she did it. I just happened to be staring at her windows for the last five hours. I leaned back, letting the wall hide me from her before I stepped farther into the dark room, hiding myself in the shadows as I watched her.

She reminded me of a cat—silent and cunning. Not that I'd ever had a cat, but this was how I imagined it would be to live with one. Constantly spending time with someone, or something, that didn't seem to care if I left it completely alone for the rest of eternity.

Either someone would come today or Isla'd go out. Surely, she'd dragged me all the way across the country to meet with someone. There was a loved one at the end of this journey. A best friend from high school, first love, bandmate . . . someone Isla cared enough about to tell them where she was.

After a few minutes, she emerged from the door on the side of the house. The place I'd rented was a whole house. Isla only had the top of hers, and an old man occupied the bottom apartment. She surveyed every direction before gingerly stepping onto the small stoop. The storm door rested against the back of her as she went to work locking the three extra deadbolts she had installed on the door within hours of arriving the day before. Each one was a different key, and she was still getting used to the sequence.

She had on a pair of the yoga pants she'd bought in Tennessee and a tank top that did little to cover her ass. Her black striped sports bra stuck out from the sides of her shirt. Apparently, the shirt didn't cover anything. My sight lingered down the front of her, and I had to admit—if only to myself—that she did have a great rack.

I was no better than Paul.

Isla grabbed the handle and shook the door to test its security. If someone wanted to get in badly enough, a set of locks wasn't going to keep them out. It wasn't a petty burglar she was afraid of, though.

I needed to get my wallet and hat so I could follow her, but she paused, facing the door, and I was captured by her lack of movement. Through the binoculars, I could see her sullen expression hidden behind dark blue sunglasses and light pink lip gloss. If she'd just smiled, I'd have been able to shake the eerie feeling I had when I watched her lock the door. She transferred her terror to me somehow, which was insane because I wasn't afraid of anything.

Isla rested her forehead on the door. Her shoulders sank. I leaned on the wall next to me while she stood motionless across the street. The urge to pick her up and let her rest gnawed at me. I was exhausted just watching her.

What was happening to me? Isla Monroe was torturing me. I dropped the binoculars as my phone rang. Wright's codename, Mountain, lit up the screen.

"Hi," I said. I tried to keep it light with him. Anger was his favorite emotion.

"I just got off the phone with an irate Victor Addario. I thought you said you'd know what was going on a few days ago."

"I know."

"I know . . . I know . . ." he mocked me. "Do you *know* what the fuck is going on? Because it seems like you're wasting a lot of time and money on a job you didn't even want in the first place."

"It's not that easy. She's guarded. This is much more than

avoiding a contract negotiation."

"Like what?"

"I don't know yet."

"You're an expert in tactical operations, surveillance, and inter-rogations. What could possibly be 'not that easy'?"

"I need a week."

"One week. Not one minute more." Wright hung up without saying goodbye—or yelling it.

I followed Isla to the furniture store off the highway that adver-tised two-day delivery. I waited in the car since the parking lot was half full and I could see the door without the threat of her seeing me. Thirty minutes later, she walked out carrying a lamp, and an employee followed her carrying two more.

She stopped again at a sporting goods store and bought a cart full of stuff. The only items I could see were the pillow and sleeping bag billowing out of the top. She had enough money to buy whatever she wanted. She could hire someone to do all of this for her, but Isla trudged to three more stores. Her last stop was at a Goodwill Superstore on Halsey Street. I couldn't imagine what she'd buy sec-ondhand. There was no mention of her being a recycling advocate of any kind in the information I'd read about her.

A man carried out an old television. Isla held a record player in her hands. A bag hung from her elbow with God knows what in it.

"Enjoy your new apartment," the man said.

"Thank you. Good luck with your new truck," she answered, having already heard his life's story I was certain.

Isla hopped in the driver's seat of her used car and drove back to her second-floor apartment. I parked a block away and walked back to my house, watching her the entire way. She was unloading the car, one bag at a time, and scanning everywhere around her before she entered the house. She relocked the three deadbolts with every trip to her car. No one was getting into Isla's apartment without her knowing about it. Her last trip was for the television.

It was an old set, the oddly shaped kind that were always at least thirty pounds heavier than they looked. It wobbled in her arms until she almost dropped it. I could carry that upstairs for her without losing my breath. Her arms weren't even long enough to get a proper hold on it.

I stopped myself from running over and assisting her as she set the television down, locked her car, and picked the set back up. Instead, I forced myself up the short walk to my own door and into my house, pretending the whole way as if I hadn't noticed her. From the safety of my living room, I watched her lift the set up the three steps to her door. She stopped and rested the television on each step above the last one. She couldn't carry the weight in one continuous movement, and she had an entire flight of stairs to go.

When she got to the top of the stoop, she unlocked the door and ran upstairs. She returned with a large sheet that she wrapped the television in before tying a knot at the top of the fabric. Then she dragged the sheet-covered television through the side door, using the bundle to combat the odd shape of the television.

She locked the door behind her.

I didn't see her the rest of the afternoon, and I didn't hear any horrendous crashes of a television being dropped down a flight of stairs. Whatever she wanted to watch must have been important, because she worked hard to get that set inside.

I lit a cigarette and held it near my mouth, even though the smell of it repulsed me. I needed a reason to be outside. Isla's windows were always covered with drapes. She had always been careful not to let anyone see inside, but tonight was cool and she had the windows off the front of the house open. Through them, I could hear her voice as she sang. The hair on my arms stood at the perfect pitch and the emotion brimming from her words.

As if she felt my intrusion, she closed the window and locked it. She was well suited for my line of work. I might ask her to join the team when this assignment ended. The idea made me laugh until the thought of not being with her left me cold on my front porch. She'd worked her way into my psyche to the point where I'd miss her when she was gone. I told myself it was only because I was forced to watch her, but I knew that didn't explain why I wanted to know so much more about her. I put out the cigarette in a can by the railing and went inside.

Isla, my love,

The holidays are about celebrating and spending time with the ones we love. That's all I want from you. Your time, your love, and to share your life. The tree in the center of the courtyard was different with you staring up at it beside me. I'd been waiting for your arrival next to that tree for almost an hour. It was just a tree until I saw you standing by it. When you lingered there . . . you wanted to go home with me. This is our first Christmas together and our last one on the road. Next year, we'll have our own home.

Finally, the chaos of your schedule will halt for a few days so you and I can be together. Last year was difficult. I hated that I couldn't have you all to myself. I know it's your career and what you've dreamed of doing your entire life, and because of that, I'll support you. I'll always be here for you, but these people are relentless. All those strangers, reaching to touch you as if you were a toy designed for them to play with. Screaming your name as if they know you and you owe them something—a piece of yourself they were never meant to have. They're sick, but I can almost understand them. If I didn't have you in my life, I don't know what I'd do. You're my inspiration. We'll be together soon.

Love,

Ian

CHAPTER 9

Mae

I HADN'T HEARD THE NAME Isla since I left the city over a week ago. The driver had asked for my autograph on the way to Philadelphia. He must have been new because that was completely against the rules. I handed it to him and told him, "Hold on to it. It might be the last one I ever sign." He promised to cherish it. I'd sat back in my seat and closed my eyes. Philly to North Carolina to God knew where. Far, far away from there.

My back was killing me from driving across the country in only a few days and sleeping on the floor. I should have just hid out at the Four Seasons a little longer, but it was too risky. Someone I'd met in the last decade could be staying at the Four Seasons at any given time. I'd taken a chance staying for two of the three nights I'd reserved, but I'd needed a moment to rest.

I pulled the curtain back a half inch and peered out, leaning forward just a bit more so I could see down both sides of the street. I counted the cars on the road and wrote down the makes and models. People, normal people, were creatures of habit. They liked to park in the same spots day after day. The routine provided some sense of security. I'd keep track of who was around me for my own sense.

I surveyed my new apartment. With the new locks on the door downstairs, I felt better about the place. It was the only one on the street for rent that was on the second floor. I needed to be up high to defend against intruders. One of the windows was above an overhang, which wasn't ideal, but it was the best-case scenario. If I ever built my own house, I'd have even the first-floor windows seven feet off the ground.

The apartment was sparse, which was fine. There was no reason to elaborately decorate. I'd leave this all behind, too, as soon as I needed to. I wasn't interested in a home. I needed a hideaway, and this was just as good as anywhere else. Besides, this street was full of rentals that were in the process of turning over, which probably had something to do with the pot shop called Jack 'n' the Weed Stalk in the middle of the street. I'd never done a drug in my life, but I'd certainly spent time with people who had. Pot smokers were the least offensive. The shop didn't bother me at all, and it probably had amazing surveillance.

Which was the benefit that led me to walk into it the day my bed was delivered. Shopping, talking to people, and hearing their stories made me miss the human race. Not the part of it I'd left behind in New York, but the people of North Carolina with their unflappable demeanors, their love of pulled pork and drinks in mason jars, and most of all the way they spoke to me no matter what they thought my name was.

The shop was similar to how I imagined the first-floor apartment of my house. The front room was filled with bookcases with glass shelves floating in the center of the room. The light from the windows beamed in and illuminated the endless selection of glass-blown bowls and bongs on display. Camera bubbles decorated the ceilings in each corner of the room and filmed no one. The shop was empty and, based on my observations the past few days, had a slow but steady cast of visitors throughout the day that wanted nothing more than to get high. It was a good place to work for someone who didn't want to be seen.

"Can I help you?" a woman asked. She was thirty-five, maybe

forty years old and scrutinized me the same way she would if she'd caught me stealing.

"I was just looking . . . for a job. Any chance you're hiring?"

She stepped back and examined me. "Where are you from?"

"North Carolina."

"Hmm. Charlotte?"

"No. Out on the coast."

She tilted her head to see me better from a new angle. "Not Nags Head, I hope."

"No." I shook my head, agreeing that the thought of it was awful but having no idea why. "Off Emerald Isle."

"Oh." She walked into the other room.

Commercial refrigerators with drinks and perishable items lined the wall behind the register. Displays counters held pot, joints, and vaporizers. Oils were hung on the wall behind her. I'd been in a pot shop once in Colorado with Cruz. He'd been giddy with the selection. I had to stop him from posting a picture of himself making his purchase on the Internet.

"My stepfather had a house in Nags Head," the woman said a moment later as she came back through the door and sat on a stool behind the counter.

"Oh," I said, not knowing what my other options were.

"He killed himself, though."

It'd been almost two weeks since I'd talked to anyone about anything real. My attorney. My accountant. Had things changed? She was so matter-of-fact. Flat. She was void of any emotion. "I'm so sorry."

"I'm not. He was a bastard, but the house was magnificent."

Victor's East Hampton residence flashed through my mind. "I know what you mean. A bit of a waste."

"Completely." She almost smiled. It was a moment of under-standing. "So, what do you smoke? You seem more like an edibles person to me, but I've been wrong before."

"Oh, I don't do drugs."

"We all do drugs." She sipped her coffee. "What's your pleasure?"

"Well, I've never smoked pot or done any other narcotics."

"That's hard to believe."

"You have no idea." Not a soul would believe Isla Monroe didn't party. "I guess I'm afraid if I start, I'll never stop. We've got some addiction history in my family." At least I assumed. Why else would a man drink until he punched his wife in the face before he passed out on the couch and then shit himself?

"Do you know anything about the product?"

"Plenty." I smiled, happy to leave my childhood memories behind. "I seem to be attracted to people who love to smoke pot."

"They're a friendly bunch, for sure." She laughed. The cackling sound was almost more disturbing than her original demeanor. "I guess we wouldn't have to worry about you stealing. What's your name?"

"Danielle, but everyone calls me Mae."

"Well, Mae. I'm Rita, and I only have the worst shift available. We keep losing people because of sticky fingers."

"Maybe you're hiring the wrong people. What's the shift?"

"Two to ten every day but Sunday."

"That is terrible." We both laughed. "I'll take it, though."

My old employer took every second of my life from me, and it wasn't as if I had better things to do. I wanted to go to church and I wanted to be left alone.

***

Jack 'n' the Weed Stalk proved to be perfect. It was a slow pace with friendly neighborhood customers. Some tourists stumbled upon us. Once in a while, an overly chatty customer caused me some alarm, but I rarely worked alone, and the constant surveillance of the facility made thieves wary.

Rita was with me most of the time. She owned the shop with her brother who was too busy with his accounting firm to ever stop by. I think she took some responsibility for me since I'd been hired without his approval. After a few days, she realized I wasn't there to rob her and was actually pleasant. Most days, she sat in the back room watching reality television and working through the sales numbers. When she manned the counter with me, I waited on customers while she devoured trashy magazines.

"Look at how fat she is!" Rita was referring to my old friend, Simone, who always ate pizza when she drank too much. Judging by the thick and pasty appearance of her skin, she'd been on a bender lately. I should talk. I'd had pancakes every day before work since I'd moved here. My new clothes were getting tight.

I wiped down the counter that was already spotless. "Why do you read that stuff? None of it's true."

"What's not true? She's fat."

I shook my head and ignored her. The bell above the front door jingled, and a tall man walked in, looking more out of place than I probably had my first time.

"Hi," he said and stood six feet away from us. His hair was slightly longer on top than on the sides. I tried to decide whether he'd styled it or had just woken with it falling perfectly away from his face, but his squared jaw, light mustache, and scruff stole my attention from his hair.

"Can I help you with something?" I put the cleaner in the bin on the floor and walked around the counter to him.

He didn't take his eyes off me, and a vague sense of recognition made my steps slow. "I need to buy a gift," he said and exhaled the burden of his visit. "For my college roommate who smokes continuously."

"Oh, how nice. Were you interested in a bowl? We have some beautiful hand-blown ones." I moved into the front room, and he followed. I picked up my favorite piece. The weed sat in a bird's beak, and you smoked it through the tail. Blue feathers were intricately woven into the glass.

It was only after I turned to show it to him that I realized how big the guy was. He towered over me as I held the blue bird bowl. He smelled of hickory. At least that was what I told myself. In reality, I had no idea what hickory smelled like, but this guy smelled of man and that was how I imagined hickory. I inhaled him and placed the bowl back on the shelf.

He picked it up. I watched in wonder as the light shone through it. He placed it in his palm so his fingers didn't block the light, and blue and white beams shot around the room.

When I returned my attention to him, he was staring at me. "What do you smoke out of?" he asked.

I put some inches between us so I could think about something other than his shoulders. I wasn't typically attracted to a man's shoulders, but his were particularly noteworthy, like his brown eyes, which were so dark that they reminded me of the night sky minus the stars. I inhaled deeply and listened for the little voice in my head to tell me to run. Surely, I hadn't lost all precautions at the sight of his shoulders.

"Well, most people rave about the oils and the waxes," I began after hearing nothing but silence from within. "But there are still plenty of others who love the earthy aromas of weed." I'd practiced this pitch a dozen times, but we rarely got customers who had no idea what they wanted to buy. The majority were repeat patrons.

"Most people . . ." He strolled around until he was behind me again. My instinct to flee should have kicked in, but it was still quiet. Maybe I'd neglected it for too long, and it had abandoned me. I didn't feel anything but that whips of familiarity and a sense of safety as he took another step closer to me. He was that high school friend you barely spoke to, but you knew where he came from, so he was safe. Although, nothing about the way he made me notice him felt like a friend. "That's a bit evasive."

I warmed at his statement. It'd been forever since a man listened to a word I'd said, let alone challenged it.

I don't smoke, I mouthed to him. His eyebrows rose. "But that's bad for business," I whispered.

He nodded and glanced over at Rita. "I'll take the blue bird one."

As much as I hated to see the bowl go, I was glad it was leaving with him. "Wonderful choice. It's my favorite. Would you like it wrapped?"

"You guys wrap?"

"Not typically, but I can figure something out."

While Rita rang him up, I searched for a paper bag to use as wrapping paper. She shamelessly flirted with him while I worked. "Do you need any other gifts? Perhaps something for a girlfriend or your wife? Women love the oils?" She waved her hand in front of the back wall. I couldn't hear what he said over my scissors cutting the paper. I found the red twine Rita had used to tie the patriotic stars to the mailbox out front and tied it around the box.

"Here you go," I said and handed him the box.

"Thanks. That's great." He took the box from my hand and stood awkwardly still in front of me. His uncomfortable stance must have been infectious, because suddenly, I didn't know what to say, either. Some other instinct was taking over. I could feel the heat rising to my cheeks. I used to command fifty thousand people in an arena, yet this guy had rendered me speechless in a converted living room in Portland.

"Dalton, here, is new to town." Rita saved us.

"Oh."

"I told him you hadn't been here that long either. Maybe you guys could explore together."

"Oh." Absolutely not. There was no way I was going anywhere with him, his shoulders, or anyone else for that matter. Admiration at my place of employment was one thing. Alone in a car or behind a closed door were completely out of the question.

"It's okay," he said softly and put me at ease.

"I know." What did I know? My gaze darted around the room.

I wanted to walk out the door instead of finishing this ridiculous conversation. "It's just . . ."

"Strange. Forward. Uncomfortable."

I shook my head, trying to come up with any other word besides "terrifying."

"I live next door, and I've been meaning to come in here for a while now. I'm sure I'll see you around."

I wasn't sure if I was more surprised by the fact that he lived across the street from me or the delight I felt because of it. That was why he seemed familiar. We'd probably passed on the sidewalk before. It was impossible that I wouldn't have noticed him, though. I was currently hyper aware of everyone around me. This man would never have slipped my attention.

Rita was behind him, beaming from ear to ear. I'd never actually seen her joyous, but somehow, this guy and I together was brightening her day even more than when the heart surgeon had come in and bought four bongs.

I couldn't deny a similar reaction.

"Maybe we can do breakfast sometime," he said and started toward the door, but then he glanced back over his shoulder and added, "I'm an early riser. Something tells me you are, too."

I started to say something but stopped. It'd been over two weeks since I left New York and Cruz's fake engagement and Victor and his threats. Before Cruz, I hadn't been with another man in over eighteen months. Dalton made me realize I was lonely. All the books and all the songs in the world weren't enough to replace other humans. Try as I had.

"I'll see you later," he said and winked at me. At first, I thought I'd imagined it. Maybe he blinked, but a woman knew when a man winked at her. I had to let myself trust my instincts. They were all I had left.

When Dalton was completely out the door and I could see him on the sidewalk, I asked, "Hey, Rita, mind if I go to dinner early?"

"No. Why, what's up?"

"I need to go see an old friend. It shouldn't take me long. Is that music shop still open on the other side of the supermarket?"

"Do I look like a musician?"

"You kind of do . . . but you're prettier."

"God, I love you, kid."

I walked out of the pot shop and to the music store a few blocks away. I'd left the guitar my mother had given me behind in my apartment because it was too much of a hint to my real identity, but no one knew me here. I was just Mae, and Mae always had a guitar with her back in the day.

"Can I help you with something, miss?"

I cradled the Martin Custom D in my arms as if I'd just given birth to it. I hugged it to my body and rested my hand across the strings. "May I?"

"Of course."

I played the first chord, and something ignited inside me. I could leave Isla Monroe behind but not the music. It wouldn't die, no matter how hard they tried to kill it with synthesizers, sequencers, and soundscapes. I tinkered on the strings and finally settled into the final coda of my favorite Pink Floyd song.

I leaned back and sang, switching from Floyd to Blues Traveler to Marley.

"You're good," he said and startled me.

"Thank you." It meant more to me than every word Victor Addario had ever said. This guy had nothing to gain from me.

"Once in a while, we get calls for local performers. If you want leave your name, I'll pass it around."

"No. Thanks, though."

"Seriously. You could make some cash."

I held the guitar away from me and let my sight fall over every line of it. "I'll take the guitar, though."

"You got it. Bring it over, and I'll ring you up."

CHAPTER 10

Dalton

WRIGHT CALLED WEDNESDAY MORNING WHILE I was doing push-ups on my dusty wooden floor. I wanted to throw the phone out the window. The window that faced Isla's house across the street. The one I watched her from every minute she was inside.

I still had no information that would explain why Isla Monroe was in Portland. I was equal parts frustrated with my lack of progress and worried that Wright was going to pull me off the job. None of it made sense.

"Well?" Wright asked with the patience of an irate toddler. He was as impressed with my delay as Addario was.

"I need more time."

"For what? Tell Addario where she is and what she's doing. That's what you were hired to do."

"I can't do that yet. I think he's involved in this somehow."

"In what?" Wright roared. I was thrilled this conversation was taking place over the phone.

"I don't know. I realize this sounds crazy, but you have to trust me on this. There's a lot more going on here than what we were originally told."

"None of which we were paid to know about. That makes you completely out of line and soon to be out of work if you don't get off this phone right now and deliver your report to Addario." He hung up.

I went for a run. The last ten blocks I ran full out and tried to sweat Isla Monroe from my mind, but every detail of her road trip west had left a mark. I went through each stop as my feet hit the pavement and my thighs burned. I slowed two houses down from my rental and eased into a cool down, running in circles until my heart pounded in my chest. I leaned over to catch my breath and wiped my brow with my T-shirt.

Isla was standing on the front porch of her house watching me. I lowered my shirt and waved. She stared at me for a second longer and finally waved back. The old man who lived on the first floor of her house walked out onto the front porch, too, and handed Isla a stack of papers.

"Morning, Bob," she said in the same way she'd greet an uncle she'd spoken to every morning of her life.

He pointed to different lines and leafed through the sheets until he showed her a detail on the last one.

Isla nodded and spoke to him while she concentrated on whatever Bob was showing her. I couldn't imagine the details. Bob's main priority was getting high. At least according to my observations.

She reached for a bakery box off the railing and handed it to him. Bob chose an éclair from the box and shoved it in his mouth without hesitation. He shook his head and closed his eyes signifying the mere taste was heaven. Isla took the papers with her to the pot shop and left me in my front yard, sweating and wondering if she'd known Bob before she'd come to Portland. Maybe he was the reason she was here. *We* were here.

I showered and paced around my apartment for most of the day. I wasn't getting any information from watching Isla Monroe. She was meticulous in her efforts to not provide any. I was going to have to inject myself into her life or send the report through to Addario and hop a flight to the next job.

I emailed a report. It was full of fictitious locations and believable details to keep him at bay. For all Victor Addario knew, Isla was currently holed up at a resort in New Mexico. She hadn't been in contact with anyone and was reading a lot. She seemed to be relaxing.

"What else is she doing?" he asked with the disturbing curiosity of a voyeur when he called just moments after receiving it.

"Just eating, swimming, and reading from what I can tell." I answered as I locked my door and headed down to the café to grab my peace offering.

"What bathing suit is she wearing?"

Not what did she have for dinner? Is she eating her vegetables? Has she called anyone? Nope. Addario wanted to know what she was wearing. I felt like telling Isla who I was and asking her to help *me* get away from him.

I shook my head and tried to release the memory of the way the hair on my arms stood on end when he'd asked. I was running out of time. As long as Addario was happy, he'd leave Wright alone. And Wright always left me alone on a job. There had never been a reason to question my intentions or my actions. Wright's business worked because each of us did our job without asking questions. But if Addario started bitching, and Wright compared the fake report to my expenses, he'd know I was lying, and that was a fate I wasn't able to consider long enough to even fear his reaction. I grabbed two cups of hot tea at the café and headed over to the pot shop. I'd exhausted my sales. It was time for a new tactic.

"I want them to get together," Rita said. She licked the tip of her middle finger and flipped the pages of the magazine in her hand.

"Why? You don't even know them," Isla asked.

"They're adorable together. Did you see *Time Thrust*? They were so in love in that movie. You'll never convince me they weren't doing it during the filming."

"He's married with three kids."

"So? She's beautiful."

"She doesn't look like that in real life," Isla said and finally noticed me holding the two cups of tea. "Oh," she said to me. "Can I help you?"

"Of course she looks like that." Rita was aghast, completely oblivious that I was there.

"No one does. It's all computer edited. You're wasting your time reading about them."

"It's my time. I'll do what I want with it."

"I brought you guys some tea," I said, and Rita finally let the subject drop.

"Well, how about you, bringing us tea." She tossed her magazine on the floor behind her and leaned on the counter. She was infinitely more receptive than Isla, who kept straightening the joints in the counter by the front window.

"It's black tea over ice since it's such a hot day. I wasn't sure what you guys drank."

"We'll drink whatever you're buying." Rita took the cardboard tray from me and lifted each cup out of its holder.

Something fell on the second floor above us or was thrown down a flight of stairs. The rumbling noise had a clang at several intervals as it went on like thunder in the distance. Then Rita screamed and ran up the stairs.

I turned to Isla for information.

"Her teenage nephew is staying with her." She closed the cabinet she was working in. "He's prone to accidents." Isla walked over and took a sip of her tea. "And he's driving her crazy. Thank you for the tea."

"You're welcome."

"Don't you work?"

"I'm actually between jobs. Waiting for the next one to begin. I'm a carpenter."

She nodded without much evidence she believed me.

Rita returned to her perch on the stool behind the counter and huffed. "That kid is going to be the death of me. How does one fall into the cupboard holding the pots and pans?"

Isla laughed and rubbed Rita's shoulder. "Maybe he has some equilibrium issues."

"Is that what they're calling it nowadays? When I was young, they said you were dumb." She tightened the messy bun of red hair on the top of her head.

"Things have changed a little."

At the same time, Rita and Isla seemed to remember I was still with them. They faced me and waited for some explanation as to why I was in front of them and not buying marijuana.

"My mother's coming to town next week. Do you have any recommendations on where I should take her?"

"The Rose Garden," Rita said without hesitation. "It screams, 'My mother is coming to town.'"

"Rose garden?" I hadn't heard of it.

"It was created during World War I because they feared all the rose plants in Europe would be killed due to the bombings."

"Really?" Isla asked. Her face lit up with anticipation of additional information.

"Really. This is the city of roses." Rita shamelessly raked her eyes over my chest and biceps. She signed heavily. I fought the urge to cross my arms and cover myself. "Why don't you take your dinner break," she said to Isla while still surveying me.

Isla was watching her, amused.

"I'd love to," I said, and Isla looked up at me. "Go to dinner."

"Oh." Isla had thought she was only an observer of my and Rita's conversation, but she was my center of attention. Even though the reasons she occupied that spot were beginning to blur. "I, uh . . . just. Well, I—" Her search for an end to her sentence was painful to watch. "I eat out back."

"I'll meet you there." I walked through the front door of the pot shop and down the side of the house. In the backyard, I found Isla sitting on the top step of the back porch with a paper bag in her lap.

I pointed at my house over my shoulder. "We can go into my house. Eat on a table."

"No. We can't." She didn't attempt to soften the statement at all. Just left it there for me to be clear.

She slid over to the side of the step, making room for me to sit down next to her. The light was already dimming, but the day's heat hadn't dissipated.

"I saw you across the street earlier. You know, if you're ever delivering sweets, I'll take some."

"I'll keep that in mind." She unwrapped a peanut butter and jelly sandwich and handed me half. "Here."

"Thank you, but I can't take your dinner."

"I insist. These last few weeks I have eaten everything. All my favorites. You'd be doing me a favor." She pushed it toward me with hope in her eyes.

I took half the sandwich, which was cold from being in the refrigerator all day, and bit off the end. "Why do you work here if you don't smoke pot?"

"I couldn't beat the location."

I waited, hoping that wasn't all she'd offer.

"And Rita's great. I like the people, and the fact that there are so few of them."

"Do you not do well with crowds?"

"And small groups," she said and laughed at herself. To hear her speak, you'd think she was the most awkward person walking. "I like how things move at a slower pace in the pot shop."

"It's a slower pace, I'm sure."

"They're really a lovely group of people."

I squinted my eyes and frogged my voice. "Do they talk like this?" I asked as if I'd been smoking pot for the past six hours.

"You seem to harbor some prejudices about marijuana users."

"Prejudices?"

"Yes. Your college roommate smokes."

"And he's wasting his life."

"Is he happy?" she asked and stared at me. "Because if he's living every day satisfied and content, what difference does it make how much pot he smokes?"

Isla didn't judge. "I guess it doesn't." I shook my head and took in the shape of her eyes, the deep green color against the pale background of the porch, and the way her hair fell across her forehead. "But I'm not sure how happy he is."

"Your mother's not really coming, is she?" she asked. I stopped chewing.

Paul was right. I had no recollection of how to talk to women. "No." I attempted the truth for lack of other options. I wouldn't have expected her to address my lie even if she'd suspected it. Isla Monroe was direct. "I'm getting kind of lonely. My job doesn't start for another three weeks."

"Oh." This threw her more than my lie. She tilted her head slightly and examined me with a critical eye from a new perspective. But I felt nothing but kindness and warmth when I was near her. Maybe some other things. My gaze drifted to her tank top, which read: Slightly Dark and Twisted, and down her legs to her ankles and the high-heeled sandals she wore that made her stand a few inches taller than usual.

"Pathetic?" I finally asked. It was more of a declaration about myself.

"I've seen worse," she said and put me at ease with a pleasant grin. Isla's eyes fell to my chest. She took another sip of her tea before saying, "You appear to be in excellent shape."

I wasn't prepared for the compliment. Heat rose inside me from her words. Some sort of masculine pride was taking over.

"You're blushing," she said and laughed at me.

"I'm not."

"You should join a gym. Go to a reading at a bookstore. Sign up for a tennis match. You'll find someone to hang out with."

I hung on her every word. "I already have."

Isla kept eating as if I hadn't spoken.

"Can I ask you something?" I asked to repair the awkward silence between us. I wanted to talk to her more than I wanted to watch her. She tilted her head toward me. "Why Portland? Of all the cities to move to, why did you choose Portland?"

She sighed while she thought. "It's as far away from New York City as I could get in a car." She smiled before she added, "And I was getting tired of driving."

I nodded. Sitting next to her in the evening air made me want to believe it was just that simple, but that would require me to erase every moment I'd been watching her from my mind. I was determined to find out why we were here and hiding.

"What about you?" she asked. She was studying me, trying to pry me open the way I wanted her to break.

"I go wherever the work takes me."

She was an amateur. I was the professional.

CHAPTER 11

Dalton

ISLA WAS UP AND OUT by eight thirty the next morning. She peered out the curtains first before boldly opening them. Her eyes darted from one end of the street to the next, but she was commanding in her movements. Isla was gaining strength in Portland, and I liked the sight of it.

She was writing something on a clipboard as she studied the street below her apartment. I dropped my binoculars and searched the road between us. No one was outside. Not one pedestrian. From the corner of my bedroom, I could see her perfectly. She pointed at the street, and I realized she was counting cars and comparing them to the list she'd created.

She needed to get out. She was too young to be sitting in her house all day watching the neighborhood. Those were the habits of a ninety-year-old woman, not Isla Monroe.

The curtains closed. She was gone. Three weeks she'd been absent from everything but my sight. I'd never spent this long following in a young woman's trail. It would have been intolerable except this woman was Isla Monroe, and completely unexpected.

She stepped onto her side steps wearing the long blue dress she'd worn in Denver.

"Church clothes," I said and grabbed my phone and keys off

the counter.

I followed as closely as I could without her making me, but she didn't seem completely sure of where she was going. Eventually, she stepped into Saint Andrew's Catholic Church for the 9 AM mass. Not one other person I knew her age went to church without obligation, especially on a Thursday morning. I walked home and watched for her out my window when the mass ended. I wanted to hear her sing again, but things were already too complicated. There was no way I'd be able to explain my attendance at the same church she'd just happened upon.

She went into work at two, and as I watched her lock her dead-bolts, I realized I would end up having to pick the locks she was so fond of. That I would have to do after dark when a neighbor wouldn't see me. Since the pot shop had a direct line of sight to her apartment, I would run the risk of her seeing a light on. Of course, she had those thick blackout curtains on the windows to help me.

I waited until the next night. After she'd taken her dinner break, and I knew she'd be in the shop for a while. She'd brought one bag with her from New York and that was the one I wanted to search. According to Addario, she'd left her cell phone, mementos, and everything else in an abandoned apartment in the city. He said it was so untouched that he'd originally thought she'd been abducted. I didn't ask him what the hell he was doing in her apartment or how he knew what personal items were meaningful to her, and I wasn't going to ask myself the same questions. At least I'd been hired to watch her.

Bob was smoking a joint and singing opera on the front porch. It was a musical house. I walked down the block and stealthed back through the yards of Isla's neighbors. A couple was arguing over a waitress the guy had paid too much attention to the night before, an old woman was talking on a landline, and the rest of the houses were pitch black. There was no easy point of entry on the back of Isla's house.

I held my breath and worked each of the locks on the side door. Part of my training was entries. Paul and I used to compete on speed and agility. Since he was rubber man, he usually won getting into tight places. The last lock clicked. I glanced behind me before entering Isla Monroe's fortress.

I slipped the lock kit into the pocket of my cargo shorts and put the rubber gloves back on my hands. Bob was still singing on the porch, completely oblivious to my intrusion into Isla's world. The third step creaked, and I wondered if she'd somehow loosened the wood to use as an alarm system.

The door at the top of the stairs was, not surprisingly, locked also. I didn't even need the tools for this one. A simple swipe of my credit card opened the door for me. I left it cracked a few inches and listened. When the silence defined the room's vacancy, I entered. There was a *whomp* sound, and I dropped to the floor before a baseball hit the door right above my head. Gear rotation noises registered before I dove out of the way of the second ball hitting the door.

I crawled to the back of the room and pulled the plug from the outlet on Isla's homemade security guard. A baseball pitching machine was loaded and aimed toward the door to the apartment. A mallet hung above the rocker power switch, and the knobs were set to "fast" for frequency and "midway" for height. The mallet was attached to rope that ran through a pulley system running from the ceiling to a chair to the counter by the door. Everything hinged on Command Hooks she'd strategically placed throughout the room. The final length was fishing wire twelve inches in front of the door. If it were opened, the mallet would drop, and the machine would engage.

I was falling in love with this woman. A sign on the machine read:
Say Cheese.
You're Hit.
Now Run.

I searched every inch of the apartment for a camera, but there wasn't one. If I was lucky, I'd be able to get out of her apartment without it shooting the—I counted—twenty-seven balls at me. I couldn't hold back the laughter. She drove across the entire country. She was worth millions of dollars, and to keep someone out of her apartment, she'd set an old-school booby trap.

The sight of the machine and the mallet dangling from the ceiling silenced me. It swung with the weight of her stare every morning when she peered out the windows.

Isla Monroe was absolutely afraid of something, or someone.

Plastic bins filled with paint sat beneath each locked window that was unlikely a viable entry point for a criminal. Not to mention a little paint wasn't going to keep someone from stealing her television. The paint and the pitching machine were there for another reason. If Isla couldn't keep them out, she wanted to know when someone came in.

Her apartment was—I scanned it from corner to corner—strange. There was no real color scheme, but rather looked like she chose the furniture by what was on sale, or more likely, what could be delivered the fastest.

I sped through the living room. No shelves, tables with drawers, or baskets and bins to hide stuff in. Nothing had been put away in Isla's apartment, because there was little in here that wasn't related to a creative young woman's take on home security. She'd left a single light on. Not one knickknack, photo, or greeting card was anywhere to be found. Her bedroom was just as void except for a snow globe on the table next to her bed. I picked it up and shook it. The little girl inside was singing to the sky, and it reminded me of Isla in the Denver cathedral.

The bag she'd carried from New York was lying on the floor next to her bed, not hidden at all. The outside pockets were empty except for a pack of gum and a casino chip from the Borgata Hotel in Atlantic City. Inside was an envelope holding a picture of a woman and a little girl. "Ida" was written on the back. Disappointment weighed on me. I sat on the floor against her bed. The linens were pulled straight with only a length of cotton sheet peeking out under the comforter. It was white with blue flowers all over it.

Under the pillow was a book. I thought I'd hit the jackpot with a journal or diary, but it was an aged leather King James Version Bible. Pieces of paper stuck out from the pages. I ran my finger across the folds. Reading whatever the papers contained felt like a violation equal to listening to her confession. Isla deserved better than this. At least from me.

I flipped through the pages to the only one with the corner folded down. Next to Timothy 2:26, Isla had drawn a little heart in blue pen ink. The scripture read:

And that they may recover themselves out of the snare of the devil,

Who are taken captive by him at his will.

I buried the sense that I was eavesdropping on her conversation with the God she so faithfully sought out. Because of what I did, I'd abandoned religion. It was one more conscience I couldn't afford to consider with my work. The job of Isla Monroe was forcing me into thoughts and emotions I wasn't willing to understand.

I flipped the pages to the first folded paper stuck in the binding. How much would I take from her today without her giving any of it to me? This was work, not a relationship. Isla Monroe was my job. I unfolded the paper and read a letter that began with, "Isla, my love," and ended with the name Ian. Nothing I'd read, heard, or been advised about Isla included a man named Ian. He described their fleeting love in a desperate way I couldn't reconcile with Isla's directness, but she'd saved the letters. They had to mean something. The second one was written over Christmas time and painted a more optimistic view on their relationship. There was no date, no markings that would suggest what Christmas it was from.

The ick feeling returned, and I skipped the last few letters. I tore through every item of clothing, checking every pocket and seam. Her drawers I rushed through. My glove-covered hands lingered a second too long over her bright-colored silk panties, and I closed my eyes, practically defeated. I was becoming Paul. God, help me. I slammed the drawer shut, annoyed with myself.

The only jewelry I found was an antique heart locket. It had no personal markings and no picture inside. She'd tossed it in her sock drawer, not even in a box, like it'd been an afterthought when she'd packed, or something that was in the bottom of her bag, and she hadn't even realized she'd brought it.

I checked every corner, lifted her mattress off her bed completely, the toilet tank, the back of her closet. Nothing gave away what Isla was running from.

Think, Dalton. If you were a girl in your twenties, where would you hide something?

The room was bleak, but there was no place to hide anything. No fake books or lock boxes. I started to leave, and the television caught my eye. The old set was sitting atop an antique table. Something about it was off. I stared at it from every angle and realized it didn't have a cord. It wasn't plugged in.

Nice, Isla.

I unscrewed the back of the set and removed it. The interior of the television was filled with stacks of cash. About the same amount that would fit into the bag she'd left New York with. Maybe she was crazy, or heartbroken, or depressed. Maybe my instincts were completely wrong about this one and she wasn't scared at all. Maybe she was insane.

I refilled the pitching machine. With each ball, I felt more protective of Isla. My chest scraped against the door on my way out of the apartment. I didn't dare open it any farther for fear of engaging the pitching machine doorman Isla employed. The sight of it burned into my mind. She wasn't crazy . . . she was terrified.

CHAPTER 12

Dalton

SHE GOT UP EARLY. I only knew that because she peeked out her window every morning and surveyed the street in both directions, making notations on her clipboard as she watched. She kept her apartment completely hidden from the outside. She had curtains before she had a fork. Isla Monroe was scared of something. Something Victor Addario hadn't mentioned. I went through her file again. Cruz Allen seemed like a tool. Hardly someone to be afraid of. Her mother was dead. Her father was absent with no known contact. According to the dossier on him, he was living a quiet life in Georgia with his new wife and daughters. Her brother and sister-in-law were law-abiding citizens.

I followed Isla throughout the morning. She went to the grocery store almost every day and never bought enough to have her hands full of bags. It was her daily routine. Buy food. Cook food. She was also predictable with takeout pancakes from the café every morning for breakfast.

I stared through binoculars at the house across the street. Bob sat on the front porch, rocking back and forth and smoking a cigarette. I could barely hear music coming from the upstairs, but Bob sang loudly along with it.

"Sing it, sister!" he yelled to the window above.

I was about to exchange the binoculars for my car keys and head out to buy some new damn sunglasses when Isla emerged from the side door. She leaned her arms on the bannister of the front porch and said something to Bob I couldn't decipher.

"You should be famous with a voice like that," he said too loud. Bob only had one volume.

They spoke for a few more minutes before Bob stood to go inside. He wobbled at first, but then steadied himself. Isla was walking away from the house when he fell right inside his front door.

"Oh, Bob!" She ran to his side and lifted him back to his feet. He towered over her.

"Damn legs!" Bob said and held onto her. They moved only inches at a time until she helped him through the door. I'd already had Ty run his background and knew he was only fifty-one, even though he looked closer to seventy. A freak pretzel plant accident left him with a limp, chronic pain, and the inability to work any job in which he'd have to stand or sit for extended periods. Bob had been one of Oregon's first residents to obtain his medical marijuana card.

When she emerged from the house, she paused on the front porch and stared directly at the window I was watching from. It was impossible for her to see me. I'd made sure of it, but her attention disturbed me. Isla saw things. She noticed the details.

She hopped down the three front steps and jumped onto the sidewalk before crossing the road and disappearing into the pot shop next door. I exhaled, and my phone rang. Victor Addario's name flashed across the screen.

"This is Dalton."

"Where is she now?"

"She's been moving very slowly across the south. Does she have any connections in Mexico? It's like she's preparing to cross the border."

"No." He was silent after he answered, and it meant something. He was thinking.

"I know she'd just recently gotten engaged to Cruz Allen. How were things with the two of them?"

"To my knowledge, they were fine." He spoke slowly.

"Was the engagement expected by Ms. Monroe, or was it a surprise?"

"I believe it was a surprise, but there were areas of her life that of course were not part of our business dealings."

"Of course." Like her choice of bathing suits. I paused before asking my next question. I wished I were standing in front of him to see his reaction in addition to hearing it. "Could she have been seeing someone other than Cruz Allen, someone on the side perhaps?"

"No chance," he said without hesitation, even though he'd just said there were areas of her life he wasn't privy to.

"None? Maybe a secret lover. Someone she hadn't shared with her family and friends."

His deep breath labored from his body and into my ear. I held the phone away repulsed. "Isla was not seeing anyone other than . . ." He swallowed. "Cruz Allen."

I wouldn't anger him further. I needed him to be patient, even if he was disgusting. "In the information you provided, I didn't see any other service providers. Hair stylist, personal trainer, chef, driver."

"Isla didn't have dedicated personnel like most people in her position. She was comfortable using whomever in whatever city she was in. Her makeup artist was the one exception. He traveled with her on tour."

"It sounds like I should talk to him."

"I've tried. I assure you he knows nothing. He would have told me."

Addario made my skin crawl long after we hung up.

Isla worked. She played the guitar. Sometimes, to my delight, with the windows open. She went to bed early. Isla was a complete yawn when it came to security details. At ten minutes to ten, I walked out to the back patio. She'd take out the trash soon and finish locking up for the night.

As my back door shut, a shadow moved and a hint of brush swayed against fabric. I shifted slowly, as if I hadn't noticed anything. Whoever it was knew I was there; he didn't need to know I knew about him, too.

I tilted my face to the moon and whistled. *Stay inside, Isla.* I willed her to stay in, to be late. Just a few minutes while I rattled this guy's cage. He could have been anyone. He was tall. The branch that swayed was high if you weren't standing on the step like I was. He was also quiet, which meant he probably wasn't drunk or on drugs. There was some control.

Isla moved through the bottom floor of the shop. She was completely visible from the side windows. The sight was an eerie contrast to her never letting anyone see her through a window in her own home. She picked up something off the counter and lifted the garage bag out of the can. I went back to my house, ran through, and exited the front door without making a sound.

The back door of the pot shop opened. Isla sang as she walked out. The shadow lunged toward her, and I leaped in their direction. Isla spun around and sprayed him with pepper spray before kicking him in the face so hard he landed flat on his back on the ground. He screamed in agony and writhed on the ground at her feet. The last few seconds paralyzed me. I stared at her from fifteen feet away.

"Oh my God. Ricky." Isla crouched down next to him and tried to lift his shoulders off the ground, but he was grabbing his knees in the fetal position.

"What the fuck, Mae?"

"Well, why are you out here in a dark alley grabbing me from behind?"

"It was funny," he wailed and rolled onto his side.

"Is this funny?" she said and stared at him.

I, for one, thought it was hysterical. I closed my eyes and recalled her roundhouse in my head. I nearly got a hard-on. When I opened my eyes, Isla was in a defensive stance again.

"It's just me," I said and walked into the light with both hands up.

She exhaled loudly and dropped the pepper spray to her side.

"What the hell is going on out here?" Rita asked from the window above.

Isla shook her head and pointed her hand at Ricky. "I was taking out the trash . . . and I pepper sprayed him."

"And she kicked me in the face. What the fuck?" he wailed.

"I'm sorry," Isla yelled at him. "You scared me."

"Good Lord. Go on home. I'll wash out his eyes. What an idiot . . ." Rita said and shook her head.

"Are you sure?" Isla said as Rita stared down at her nephew.

"Oh, Lord yes. It's not the first time he's been pepper sprayed."

Isla walked toward me with her shoulders slumped and her eyes on the ground. She'd traded the lethal power I'd just seen her command for guilt and uncertainty.

"I'll walk you home."

She hesitated with the fear I might hurt her, which was ridiculous, but I gave her some leeway after what had just happened. "Okay."

We strolled across the street to the side door of her house. I could see the staircase inside that led to her second-floor apartment.

"That's some serious stuff." The pepper spray in her hand was a fog type that law enforcement carried. It wasn't sold retail.

She considered it still clenched in her hand. "Do you think I'll need more? How many sprays are in this thing?"

"Expecting to use it often?" I asked. My heart broke a little for her. She was frightened her weapon had run out of ammunition.

"What's the point of having it if it doesn't work?"

"I saw you kick him. I'm not sure you need it."

Isla's eyes rose from the pepper spray. They dragged up my chest and inched her gaze to my mouth until she finally settled in staring into my eyes. "Were you watching me?" Her voice was level. I knew if I said yes, she'd spray me right here on her doorstep.

"No," I said with feigned shock but not too much. "I was taking out my trash and I heard you scream."

"I screamed?"

"More of a muffled yell." The sound would haunt me the rest of the night.

"He put his hands over my mouth. Who would think that's funny?"

"Only an idiot."

She shook her head, snapped out of it, and smiled at me. "I'm Mae, by the way."

"Dalton."

"I know. I just never gave you my name. In case you were wondering what it is."

"I was," I said. "Wondering." I didn't know if she'd introduced herself to Rita and Bob as Danielle Morris. I liked that she'd given them her real middle name. It made me believe the person standing in front of me was real.

"Well, good night."

"You, too." I needed to say more. Something to keep her talking. "If we ever go out, I promise not to gag you from behind."

What the *fuck* was that?

She stopped next to me and stared up.

"I mean . . ." I shook my head. The muscles in my stomach tightened until I was close to throwing up.

"It's okay." She laughed a little in an innocent way. "I would appreciate that." She unlocked her door, walked inside, and dead bolted the three locks before smiling at me and climbing the stairs.

That night I dreamed of Isla Monroe, but she told me to call her Mae.

CHAPTER 13

Dalton

THE BUSH NEXT TO THE window in my kitchen didn't completely hide the backyard of the pot shop, but it made it difficult to see. When the music started, I stepped onto the back porch. I knew it was Mae from just the guitar chords. She had a certain essence to her that transferred to her music.

Rita had placed a cheap fire pit from the big box store off the highway in the middle of the spotty lawn and circled it with plastic chairs. It was Fatty Friday. All pre-rolleds were ten dollars, and during happy hour, everyone congregated in the backyard with their thermoses full of liquor.

Mae covered Johnny Cash, Metallica, Elvis, and Taylor Swift. With each song, she changed the composition until its appeal was hidden in the familiarity and enhanced by its newness. She was a master with the guitar. The twelve-or-so attendees whistled and clapped when she finished each song.

I wandered across the hedges just as she played the first few notes of Pink Floyd's "Wish You Were Here." The crowd went silent. They were in church. Mae was their pastor. She reeled them in with her restrained performance and let the lyrics carry them away. While I couldn't bear to listen to her pop hits endlessly repeated on the radio, her gift was undeniable in this overgrown parcel on the outskirts of Portland.

She finished playing and wiped her face with her knuckles.

"Mae, are you crying?" Bob asked. He leaned over in his seat to see her better.

"Just a few tears of joy, my friend."

"Better be. Angels don't cry."

"No worries." She sounded like a proper pot smoker. "Music heals the soul."

Bob took a long drag off the joint in his hand. "And this weed heals the body."

"Amen," she said and rested her guitar against her chair. She touched Bob's shoulder when she walked by.

"That was some performance," I said as she breezed by me toward the back door of the shop.

"Oh, thanks. Makes me feel ten years younger."

"Bob, too." I nodded toward him.

Mae turned back to see Bob. "He only smiles when he's high." She stared at him. "I used to think potheads dulled their experience with life because they couldn't deal with the reality they'd created." I didn't say a word. Just let her go on. "But working here has taught me a lot about what I never learned about people . . . real people." She caught herself lost in her thoughts and shook her head with a smile. She noted the beer in my hand. "Are you smoking tonight?"

"No." The idea was absurd. I tried to make it seem not. "Just having a few beers."

"Come out with us," Rita chimed in from behind the door. "We're leaving at ten. Maybe even close up a few minutes early."

Mae smiled back at her. "Well, listen to you," she teased.

"I need a night out," Rita said. "This nephew of mine is driving me crazy."

"How long is he staying with you?" I asked.

"Just 'til the end of the summer. Thank God."

I listened from my back porch as Mae played a second set around nine. The crowd had ballooned. They stopped by on their way to the bars, high and wanting to hear the songs that were floating down the blocks. Fatty Friday sold out Rita's pre-rolleds because of Mae's singing. Isla Monroe tickets were going for over six hundred dollars in the aftermarket, and these few high people were seeing her for free.

Rita knocked on my door at ten, making it infinitely less awkward to go out with them. I preferred being with Mae to watching Isla. I tried to forget the name. I didn't want to call her it by mistake and ruin everything.

We drank. Probably too much. Much more than I should have, considering I was on the job. Even though I liked everything about her, I'd still been hired to watch her, not hang out with her. The second bar we went to barely had five people in it. It was quiet and dark. The televisions above our heads played reruns of nineties comedies and the only music was a jukebox, which Rita kept playing. She yanked Mae off her stool to dance with her in the empty bar. Mae twirled her without complaint until Rita almost fell to the ground, taking her with her.

She sat Rita on a stool and ordered her a glass of water. Mae leaned over the bar so the bartender could hear her without yelling. Her dress was loose and sleeveless. It was quite innocent until she leaned over something like the bar next to me, then it barely covered her perfect little ass. I inhaled and attempted to exhale the tightening in my chest caused by trying not to notice her.

"What the hell does that say?" Rita asked too loudly while she squinted at the small type running across the bottom of the television screen above us.

We all looked up to see the last few words disappear.

"Isla Monroe's in rehab," the bartender said, and Mae's smile fell from her face. Her bottom jaw fell open, fighting to obtain air, and her sight was glued to the screen. "She's a junky like the rest of them."

"Wow!" was Rita's input.

"You're surprised? All these celebrities are addicts," the bartender said, assuming his version affected no one in the room. Why should it?

Mae's eyes were fixed to the set. The news story came across the screen again. "Isla Monroe's people confirm she's checked into an unidentified rehab facility to focus on exhaustion and an addiction to prescription drugs."

I didn't know if she was going to cry. It was like watching her as she saw herself die in a car accident. She rested both hands flat on the bar in front of her and stood straight. A hint of a newborn laugh was sparkling in her eyes. "It's all a machine," she said with complete satisfaction covering her face. Again, she surprised me.

"What is?"

She thought about her answer for a few seconds. "The world, I suppose." She twisted her body until I could have easily pulled her against me. I clenched my beer in my hand and fiddled with the label with my other hand. I needed a task to occupy my mind other than the idea of touching her. She was light and air in the dim bar, or maybe it was in my veiled existence. "Rita's drunk. The bartender's a cynic. The news is all lies . . . maybe it'd be worse if it wasn't."

She may have been young, but she reeked of darkness, and no one knew better than I did how that type of past aged you quickly. I wanted to change some part of this so she didn't have to be alone. With that thought, a heat rose up the back of my neck and threatened to choke me. It was the first job I'd let myself feel something for the target, and it was scaring the shit out of me.

She touched my hand and halted my assault on the beer wrapper. "What's your last name?" she asked and disarmed me.

"Dalton."

"Then what is your first?"

"Dalton."

She took a sip of her drink. "Oh, like Cher or Madonna."

"Or Jesus," I said and hoped I didn't offend her.

"Yes. I'll tell you my real name if you tell me yours." She was letting me in. My pulse raced at the idea of it. Mae needed to tell me everything.

"It's not Mae?"

"It's Ida Mae, but I go by Mae."

"Something wrong with Ida?" I asked.

"Apparently, it was a few letters off, but my mama loved it."

"I agree with your mama."

"Well, then, she would have loved you." She drew me in with her eyes and added, "Dalton."

Rita's drink spilled and snaked across the bar, drenching everything in its path with vodka and a splash of cranberry.

"I need to get her home," Mae said. She picked the ice cubes out of the mess and placed them back into the glass.

"I'll help," I said. I wasn't just talking about Rita. I'd help Mae get out of all of this if she'd let me. As the vodka dripped from her fingertips, I searched my mind for a way to help her that didn't include my blowing this entire assignment. I felt as if I were trapped between her and my work. Work was losing. My priorities were shifting. The change was so slight I only noticed when I was near her.

We delivered Rita to her house. The walk was twice as long since she was incapable of navigating a straight line. Mae and I walked alone in silence across the street to her house. I didn't want to leave her. I thought, maybe with a few more drinks, she might open up to me about her past and then I could end this assignment, but that wasn't what I wanted either.

At the side entrance to her house, she stopped and faced me. Her hair blew across her eyes with the summer breeze that slid down the alley between the homes. She faced the wind and let it blow the hair off her face. She inhaled deeply and asked, "Did you ever land exactly where you dreamed of being, only to realize it was nothing like you thought it'd be?"

Her stare was stealing my cover. I wanted to tell her everything. "Worse."

She stepped closer to me. I fought to keep my hands at my sides.

"I stopped dreaming of where I wanted to be," I said.

She'd already gone deeper than I allowed myself to dive. The rose color of her lips stole my attention from the despair of my existence. Mae stood on her tiptoes and kissed me. She ran her hand up the back of my neck until I wanted to fall into her, but I stayed completely still. The muscles in my arms twitched against the heat spreading through me. This . . . *she* was against every protocol.

She stood down, and I waited for what she'd say. Her eyes flitted open. My chest tightened with the fear that I'd hurt her.

"I suppose I should be properly embarrassed," she said and stared at the ground between us. "I completely read *this* wrong."

"No," I managed to say before pulling her to me. My want for her unleashed as I kissed her. The depth of it surprised even me. I forced my lips onto hers until the thoughts of what I might do to her next paralyzed me. I stepped back and caught my breath. I needed some control before I broke down her door and carried her through it. "You didn't. It's complicated." It was the most I could give her, and I hated myself for it.

"You have an incredible warmth about you." She took a deep breath and exhaled the possibility of me. She stood stern in front of me and said, "But I just moved heaven and earth to leave complicated behind." She kissed my cheek. "And I'm never going back to it. Good night, Dalton." Then she disappeared into her house.

I was part of the machine that Mae just escaped. The realization sank down on me as I crossed the street back to the perch I watched her from.

Isla, my love,

Our last visit was a rough one. I thought we were on the same page. I thought you understood what you meant to me, but then I had to wait in line and be searched like every other person who'd paid their money to see you. I was treated like a criminal when my only crime was loving you.

I didn't complain. I know you have a lot of people to please during concerts. You're too busy to manage everything you have going on, but I need to be your priority the same way you're mine. Your security team didn't believe me when I said we were together. You should have informed them.

The hordes of children and their parents who waited back stage for a glimpse of you or an autograph. The press, the radio stations, and your crew. Everyone wants a piece of my Isla.

The crowd filmed you on their phones, but I just watched and waited for you to say my name. My name. Not anyone else's, because you belong to me. No matter what song you sang, it was for me.

The thunder roared in the distance. It came so close that it drowned out your voice on the microphone, and you knew the show would be delayed if not postponed.

"This is a sign," you said, "of great things to come. Those with patience are always rewarded."

The stadium erupted. They didn't realize you were talking to me and not about a concert.

Your loyal fans waited through the rain, but I found you in your dressing room. We were meant to be together. No person, no rain, and no distance will ever keep us apart.

Love,

Ian

CHAPTER 14

Mae

IT WAS EASIER TO AVOID Dalton than it should have been. I stayed in my apartment until my shift started at Jack 'n' the Weed Stalk. I walked to work without even glancing in the direction of his house. Okay, that was a lie. I peeked just once, but other than that, my eyes stayed locked on the ground in front of me. I worked. I went home. I went to bed and stared at the ceiling. Easy peasy.

The next morning wasn't quite so smooth. I didn't have to work. I couldn't sleep in. He'd somehow fought his way into my thoughts whether I wanted him there or not. There was something familiar about him. I couldn't figure out who he reminded me of, but whoever it was, he had to have been in my life before Victor Addario. There'd been no one since who was remotely like Dalton. He was an enticing mix of quiet warmth and formidable strength.

I woke early and went for a walk. I preferred daybreak to sundown. Always had. It was full of promise, not reflection on the day. "Never look back," that was what Mama always said. That, and "Get off your ass," but that was mainly directed at my brother.

Dalton seemed nice enough. Hell, he almost seemed normal, but the odds of me meeting someone who wasn't deranged had already been proven low if not zero. I walked to the café and scanned everyone through the window before opening the door. Dalton sat at a table near the front, staring at his phone in disgust. He put it down and glared at the wall opposite him, seeking the answers there. He picked up his phone and checked it again before glancing right at me through the window.

I froze in his stare. I couldn't do it. I couldn't just go in, say hi, sit at a table like a normal person, and talk to him. No matter how much I wanted to. My feet followed my heart in retreat, but before I even made it a few yards away, he yelled, "Wait!" behind me. I stopped until he caught up and stood in front of me, almost as close as he had on my stoop.

"There's nothing sadder than eating alone," Dalton said. He was kind.

"Maybe seeing a guy that you might actually like eating breakfast alone and then fleeing in fear." I tilted my head to the side, offering my version as a possibility.

"Maybe." He held out his hand for me. It was better than any private jet I'd ever been offered a seat on. "Come eat."

I slipped my hand in his and walked back to the café with him as if I'd known him for years. He was saving me from myself.

"What could go wrong?" he said.

You're going to be a star, Isla Monroe . . . Nothing will go wrong, I promise.

I sighed and sat in the seat across from him. The last breakfast I ate with a man was in New York with Cruz Allen, but compared to Dalton, Cruz wasn't a man.

What table we sat at didn't matter. We were just Mae and Dalton, having some pancakes together. No one—well, maybe Rita, but no one else—cared about the two of us. At least not here.

After the waitress took our order, Dalton sat back in his chair and rested his hands in his lap. He was much better at peacefulness than I was. I thought it was from maturity until he smirked, which made me sit up straight, preparing myself for whatever conversation would amuse him.

"Let's start with the easy stuff," he said to put me at ease. "Where are you from?"

I took a sip of my tea. "Got anything simpler?" He should know I wasn't an easy hill to climb. I never was, but in my current situation, he'd be lucky if I told him my favorite color.

"What's your favorite color?"

I raised my eyebrows at him. "Right now, black."

"Boyfriend?" he continued on having cracked me open a bit.

"Recently broke up."

"Was it difficult?"

"For me? No. Everyone else seems to be having trouble coming to terms with it."

"It gets easier as you age."

There was something so boyish about him compared to me. He was naughty, and I was guarded. I preferred him to myself. "Thank you, Yoda."

He laughed quietly. Dalton never seemed to need to be loud or in the spotlight. "You're difficult."

"You speak to me with the tone of someone twenty years older and infinitely wiser."

He leaned into the table and said, "I'm certain one of those is true."

"How old are you?" His body was that of a twenty-seven, twenty-eight-year-old. Hard and matured. His eyes told the stories of a few more years. Dalton's road had been a long one. Maybe thirty-three.

"Old enough to know better," he said and stared out the window I'd first seen him through.

"Still young enough not to care . . . I hope."

His eyes found me again. His attention bore down on me. The table between us disappeared. I imagined him throwing me on the floor and ripping my clothes off. Heat filled every inch of me, and I let him take me with his eyes. I inhaled and lost myself there. His lips parted to address my invitation at the same time his phone buzzed from his shirt pocket.

He reached for it and glanced at the screen. "I have to take this," he stumbled over the words as he stood. "It's about the job."

The job. Dalton walked out onto the sidewalk while I thought through all the calls that were occurring about my job. Victor must have been freaking out. He would have called my cell phone, and it would have rung in the apartment that I was sure was filled with people searching for evidence of where I'd gone. He'd call my brother, my sister-in-law, and everyone else he could find, but none of them knew where I was. I'd live the rest of my life completely alone to be without him.

He probably even went to my apartment himself, which would have seemed weird to those who surrounded him, but he wouldn't care. If they so much as looked at him strangely, he'd end their careers, and that would be just the beginning of the ways he'd torture them. Victor would search my bedroom—in the apartment I'd picked out against his wishes—for the remnants of my past life that I'd cherished. He'd rummage through my closet and see the first dress he'd taken off me prominently displayed in the middle. He'd find every memento and wonder if I'd been kidnapped, because I'd never leave those precious belongings behind. Then he'd trace me to the airport and realize . . . he had no idea who he was dealing with. I almost wished I could have been there to see his face when they'd told him I'd flown away.

He was as bad as Ian. Both of them thought they owned me. That I owed them a piece of me. I'd given myself to Victor. A stupid child, I was. Now he would know what it was like to lose someone.

I'd lost myself to this life he called fame.

I called it hell.

Dalton returned to the table without a care in the world. He had no Victor in his past. Nothing at all he carried with him that haunted him, it seemed. He smiled at me when our breakfast was delivered. The warm butter and syrup mixed together. The aroma took me back to the happiest days of my childhood the way it always did. "Life is what you make of it," Mama would tell us. She'd still have her sunglasses on to cover the bruises from the night before, but she'd smile and laugh while we ate. She'd never let my father define her life until eventually she'd found the strength to leave him. When we were safe and alone, she'd told me to forgive him, but I was only fifteen and I still wanted to kill him.

I left her behind in my mind and sank into the comfort of Dalton sitting across from me.

"Today is your day off?" he asked.

I nodded and took another bite.

"Don't take this the wrong way, but I've never seen a girl eat like you."

"What could be the wrong interpretation of that?"

"You're just so . . ."

I swallowed the remnants of the warm cinnamon.

"It's like you're making love to that plate of hotcakes."

"Food is to be enjoyed, and the last few years, I'd forgotten that. I'm just getting reacquainted with everything good in this life."

Dalton had ordered an egg white omelet with roasted vegetables. It smelled delicious, but it was a Kia compared to the Lexus stacked on my plate. I cut off a piece soaked in butter and syrup and held it on my fork across the table. "Here. Try this." I waited for him to argue, but he only regarded me as if he might eat me next before he opened his mouth. I fed him the pancakes.

"Hmm," he said, never taking his eyes off me, even after I'd nearly forgotten we weren't alone.

"See?" I tried to say, but my voice failed me, and the words were barely a raspy whisper.

"I do," he said. "Spend the day with me."

"Eating?" I asked and cut another piece of pancake. I fed him the next bite. "Or did you have something else in mind?"

Time didn't move as he chewed. His jaw accentuated the angles of his face that were softened by the tiny grin he wore while he thought. "Maybe we could go to the Rose Garden," he finally said. "You seemed intrigued by it."

I couldn't tell if he was teasing me. "I find it incredible. The forethought to save something beautiful from extinction due to war. Don't you think? Of all the tragedies in the world at that time, someone was worried about the roses."

Dalton studied me until I worried he thought I was crazy. He may have been right. I'd never argue against the assessment. "Do you like roses?" he asked.

"They're a bit cliché, I think." I placed my fork and knife on the edge of my plate. "They only seem to arrive when a person's been wronged or as a testament to a flawed love."

"That's dark."

"I know. Has it been your experience to give roses without an agenda?"

He laughed but just for a second before he stared at me while he thought. "I've never given anyone roses."

I leaned down, seeking the truth. "Never?"

"Never. Do you think that's why I'm alone?"

"I've been trying very hard *not* to imagine why you're alone. If you're some kind of freak, I don't want to know."

"Why?"

"Because that would mean I can't trust my own instincts, and they're all I have left."

Dalton paid for breakfast and walked me home. "I'll pick you up in a half hour," he said setting our plans without any further conversation.

I thought of the new book I'd grabbed in the grocery store, the fact that I should clean my apartment, and the loneliness associated with a typical Sunday afternoon. "Okay," I said and stared up at the sky, wondering if Mama would like Dalton or if she was up there screaming at me to run.

He crossed the street without another word. I needed more en-couragement. Some type of resume outlining his accomplishments in the field of being a human being and a long list of skills associated with safety and privacy. I'm sure that was what every woman my age was searching for on Internet dating sites. Someone who shunned the spotlight and was a decent person. Was it so much to ask for?

I spent more time selecting an outfit to wear to the Rose Garden than I had for the last Academy Awards. It had been my and Cruz's first public appearance together, and a dozen people had worked around the clock, perfecting my look before the event. That was the first time I'd felt lucky to sing. Movie stars had it the absolute worst when it came to fame, and it was never more evident than on the night of the Academy Awards. They were dressed up like tiny dolls and allowed only to speak to name the designer. They moved down a red carpet and smiled without thinking and were placed in their seats for the show. Little girls all over the world dreamed of being them.

Today, I'd attempt to wear something other than black. Was this a date? Something else I'd missed out on. Victor had seen me behind locked doors, and every boyfriend after that had used dates as a stage rather than an experience. Dalton was actually going to take me somewhere to see something together, and for that, I'd wear a dress.

I ran my hand over every hanger in my closet. The selection was limited. I wished I'd bought more clothes at the mall in Nashville. The dress I'd left New York City in hung off to the side. I pulled it out and thought of the only two times I'd ever worn it. The day I'd bought it in Australia because I'd had three hours to explore, and the flowy, thin fabric of the dress had felt like freedom in my hands in the boutique, and the day I'd escaped New York in it. That day it'd been covered with a denim jacket and I'd had a scarf wrapped around my head. For the Rose Garden, I'd wear it alone.

"Wow." Dalton appraised me as I locked the deadbolts on my

door. "You're beautiful."

"Thanks." This was definitely a date. Things were about to get more complicated.

I breezed by him and climbed into the passenger seat of his car. He glanced over at me before starting the engine and noticeably did not look my way the rest of the twenty-minute ride to Washington Park.

"Gorgeous day," I said and slipped on my sunglasses. They comforted me like a child's blanket. They'd been my hiding place for years.

"Yes," Dalton agreed but offered no input in return. I took to watching the clouds floating by in the sky.

We parked, read all the visitor's information, and picked up a pamphlet like the other normal tourists around us. We were decidedly nothing special except for the fact that we probably appeared like we belonged together, but no one could know that, not even us.

We meandered through the four and a half acres of roses. We had nothing but time. The pathways were surrounded by lush greens, trees, and in every direction, roses. Dalton read some of the information from the self-guided tour map, but I didn't care about any of the details, just the scents and the colors and the contrast to the blue sky above us.

I wandered down an aisle of roses and realized Dalton wasn't with me. I looked from one end to the other, but I couldn't see anyone but strangers lost in their own discovery. He was nowhere to be found. My chest tightened as I spun around in the direction we'd come.

"Looking for me?"

I exhaled. "Yes."

"I'm sorry. I was reading the sign and . . . you were gone."

"It's my fault."

"I'm not going to leave you here." He leaned in closer until his warmth floated across my arms. "Stranded in the Rose Garden."

"That would be tragic." The word fell from my lips, evoking the feeling of a light joke and not my reality.

Dalton held my hand as we explored the grounds. He led us through several distinct spaces until he stopped. I waited for him to say something about the space, but he only pointed out into the distance.

Mt. Hood stood majestic and snow-topped in the distance. The sight took my breath away. I followed it to the edge of the path we were standing on.

"It's gorgeous," I said when Dalton caught up to me.

"I tend to like the coast better than the mountains," he said. He was staring at me. I couldn't imagine how he could look away from Mt. Hood for more than thirty seconds. "But it is beautiful."

"You should go to the Big Island of Hawaii. You can have both there, and a volcano. It's my favorite place in the world."

"Have you been many places?"

I lifted my gaze, seeking the answer somewhere in the sky. "Too many." Dalton stayed still, listening. "With too little time to explore anything."

"Except for the Big Island?"

"It won't let you ignore it. It's full of ancient lure and spirits. The rain forest, the ocean, and the mountains all meet and bring the rest of the world with it."

Dalton raised his eyebrows at me. "You make it sound magical."

"If you go to the Big Island, the little voice inside you will finally find the words to tell you what you need to hear."

"Oh my. Not sure I want to hear it." There was sadness in his words I hadn't heard before. I wanted to know more, but I was too afraid he'd reciprocate with questions of his own. "When were you there?" he asked.

"A few months ago." I let my head hang, and the tense memories released into the summer air. "But it feels like a lifetime ago."

"The way you talk about it, it was," he said and pulled me to him. I closed my eyes and let the hickory scent invade me. It was strength and power and protection filling my insides while Dalton held me against his chest. I had some sense that I should move. This pause would become awkward, but it was the first time, in a long time, I'd found solace in another human being. I wanted to rest. Dalton turned, draped his arms over my shoulders, and together we admired Mt. Hood in all its majesty.

"Moments like this remind me of what's real in the world."

Dalton walked around and faced me. He was quiet. I adjusted to the warm air and the sense of isolation without his arms still around my shoulders. "This is real, Mae. This moment. Even if everything else is not." It was the first time Dalton was intense. It moved me a little closer to him.

Dalton leaned down until his dark eyes mirrored my own. He leaned his forehead on mine, trying to solidify the thought in my head by physically willing it in there.

My lips parted, wanting him to kiss me. I inhaled the hickory and closed my eyes. The silky fabric of my dress pressed against me with the wind everywhere I wished Dalton's hands would touch. A deep ache in my groin came back to life after years of distaste.

I wanted him more than I wanted to be alone.

Dalton moved away and the summer air rushed across the front of me, leaving me chilled in the humid breeze. "Let's keep moving," he said and took my hand. His was rough, but even though he held me tight in his grasp, I could sense that Dalton was gentle. It shook me more than the honesty in his eyes when he'd promised this was real.

He lingered at my doorstep when he dropped me off. We could spend the evening in bed together, but he was determined to leave. The three feet between us and his defensive stance were evidence enough that Dalton was most definitely not laying a hand on me, but it didn't keep him from swallowing me with his eyes. The way he stared at me was an accelerant to the burning inside I felt with him near. His not touching me was making me more insane than if he'd thrown me against the side of the house and taken me there. Although, I would have loved to have tested the comparison.

Dalton went home to sleep, and I rolled over and over in my bed. At one point, I sat up and considered walking across the street and knocking on his door. If it weren't for his claims of being complicated, I would have done it, too. When sleep finally took me, I dreamed of him. His hands were on me. His dick was in me. Dalton was everywhere around me except next to me, which was apparently where I needed him to be.

I woke and peeked out the curtains. Standing in his upstairs window without a shirt on was Dalton, and he was looking at me. His shoulders practically took up the width of the window. My eyes followed his body to the sill and back up again. We stood frozen in each other's stare until he lifted his cup of coffee to me. I couldn't tell if he saw me smile or not. I didn't care. I wanted to spend the day with him again, but I had to go back to work, and Dalton was probably getting tired of *not* having sex with me. Surely, there was some other fun thing he could avoid doing.

I put him out of my mind the rest of the morning. I couldn't sit around and pine over the out-of-work carpenter across the street. I locked the three deadbolts on my door and let the screen door close after it. On the bottom step of my stoop was a vase filled with every color rose I could think of before yesterday. A card rested in between the stems.

These come with no agenda, no apology, and no strings attached. They're evidence of nothing except how thankful I am for yesterday, and that you're beautiful.

I looked across the street at his house, but there were no signs of life.

CHAPTER 15

Dalton

PAUL WAS RIGHT. I HAD no idea how to talk to a woman. Every witty anecdote I used to get them into bed, I'd lost years ago, and I hadn't regained my game since. It took me six times to come up with what to write on the card for Mae. Not only because I was an idiot but also because she was unlike any other woman I'd ever met and she was only twenty-seven. My lack of words should have been a sign not to give her the flowers. It was playing with fire, but I wanted her to receive something from another human being who wanted nothing from her except to see her happy. So, I left the roses on her stoop and disappeared so I wouldn't have to deal with the result of my actions. That was what my job allowed me to do. Act without considering the consequences.

I didn't go back to my house until I was sure she was at work. Because at six four, I should be hiding from the terrified little creature across the street. I could probably whistle and startle her.

I ran through the rain onto my front porch and found my key in my pocket.

"Dalton."

"Ah!" I snapped, ready to kill.

Mae held up her hands in surrender. She stayed very still until my heartbeat almost returned to normal. "I'm sorry," she said. "I didn't mean to startle you."

What about enchant, inspire, and intrigue? What about those things? "You didn't," I rushed out, but neither of us believed it. "What are you doing here? Don't you have to work?"

"I brought you dinner," she said and leaned back onto the porch to grab a pizza box.

I let that sink in as I stared at the box. She was bringing me dinner—really, anything was noteworthy—to my house. The one she'd pretty much sworn to never enter. "You brought dinner here?"

"Yes," she said sweetly, knowing exactly the pieces of the gesture that I was stuck on.

"Do we have to eat it on the front lawn?"

She took a deep breath and glanced behind her. "We could if you'd like, but I thought maybe we could eat in your house." She had jeans on that were too long for her. The tips of her toes barely stuck out beyond the hem.

"Nice shirt," I said pointing to her Jack 'n' The Weed Stalk tee with a burning joint on the front.

"Thanks. Rita just got them in. Cute, right?" She walked past me and stopped a few feet inside my living room. Mae was inside my house. She must have given up the thought that I was going to kill her.

"Here," I said and took the pizza from her hands. I placed it on the coffee table. "What can I get you to drink? I have beer and . . . water."

"Well. I have to go back to work, so I'll just take water."

"I think in your line of work, a buzz is acceptable."

"That's why you're a carpenter, and I'm the pot saleswoman."

"Of course."

I brought plates, paper towels, and two glasses of water over to the coffee table. Mae had sat on the floor next to it. I did the same. I hadn't been planning on eating until after she'd taken her break and was safely tucked away in the shop, but here she was with dinner.

"Thank you for the roses," she said.

I stopped placing slices on our plates and studied Mae. She wasn't smiling. The words seemed to injure her as they left her lips. I couldn't decipher what horrors were running through her mind, but the roses were intended to make her happy.

"Did I overstep your boundaries?"

She shook her head. "No. You've been incredibly respectful. Suspiciously so."

She was right. I should have been trying to get in her pants since I'd first laid eyes on her to be believable.

"I'm sorry," I said for lack of any other response coming to my mind.

"Dalton, I've turned over a new leaf recently, and I've vowed to trust my instincts more."

"Good plan." I settled back against the couch and took a bite of my slice. "Is that the little voice you heard in Hawaii?"

Mae studied me. "Do you always listen to your own instincts?"

"I try." I put my plate down. Mae hadn't touched her own. "What do yours tell you about me?"

"You've got everything twisted inside my head."

"Maybe you were twisted before you met me."

Her concentration broke into a smile. "I like you, and I think you like me, too, but there are moments when you leave." I wasn't completely following her. "And I wish you'd stay." Oh. "At first, I thought maybe you were gay or infectious."

"Lovely."

"But now I think you've got something going on that's keeping you from moving forward."

"Mae—"

"It's okay. I've had years of getting exactly what I wanted and I realize none of it was worth having. Maybe if I can't have you, you're worth it." Her hair swept across her forehead. The light brown strands brightened the green of her eyes that were piercing me.

I moved closer to her, because it was the wrong thing to do and

I was tired of being right. "I know I've made this terribly confusing." The need to touch her was hurting me. I ran my sight over her arms and shoulder. Her lips and her soft, deceptive eyes. The muscles in my leg twitched from wanting to carry her to my bed. "I can be your friend."

Someone pounded on the front door. Mae leapt to her feet. She stood facing the door with her hands up, ready to fight. I was frozen in the wake of her fear.

"It's okay. Just someone at the door," I said, but Mae stayed in the exact same position. When was the last time someone knocked on her door? I looked out the curtain and rolled my eyes. "It's Rita's nephew."

Mae exhaled and let her arms fall to her sides.

"Is Mae here?" Ricky asked. "Aunt Rita's freaking out. There's a leak in the shop, and there's water everywhere."

Mae's hand rested on my back, and just that small touch made me want to slam the door in Ricky's face and throw her against the wall. "I'm here," she said and moved in front of me. "I'll be right over."

Ricky maintained his clueless demeanor and ran back to the shop in the rain.

"I'll see you around, friend," she said and followed Ricky out of my house. Her hand brushed down my arm when she went by, leaving a chill in its wake.

CHAPTER 16

Dalton

THE RAIN WOULDN'T STOP. EVEN by Northwest standards, we were drowning in it. The day had flown by with little I could do to see Mae. At least without sending a barrage of mixed signals that even I wouldn't have been able to decipher in my own head. She hadn't given me her number. I was going to have to resort to going over there, which I knew she wouldn't like. She didn't want anyone in that prison she'd created.

"Mae! Get more of the boxes," Rita bellowed out the side window of the house.

Mae was in the back shed with a flashlight, rummaging through a chaotic mix of everything that Rita owned that wasn't neatly displayed in the shop.

"Hurry," Rita yelled.

Mae ran to the back porch with large plastic boxes. She handed them to Rita and said she was going back for the lids.

I ran out the back door and helped her.

"Hi," she said, making me feel as if I were the person she wanted to see more than anyone else in the world. I inhaled the possibility that it was true and exhaled the satisfaction of it. I took in how cute she looked with her wet hair matted to the sides of her face and her damp shirt sticking to her body.

"Hey. I've been thinking about you."

"I know." She shook her head. "I mean, me, too."

"Mae," Rita screamed.

"One bad leak has become several," Mae said to explain the urgency of Rita's calls.

Mae and I helped Rita load all the merchandise into waterproof bags and boxes to be stored in the back room until roofers could get out and fix the leaks that were somehow producing only small drips from the second floor ceiling but causing the entire first floor to sprout fountains at different intervals throughout the day.

"Go. Get out of here. Both of you. There's nothing more we can do." It might have been the siding, but I wasn't about to stick around with construction suggestions when she was sending Mae and I away for a few days.

We silently stared at each other until a pleasant, satisfied expression settled on Mae's face. I took her hand, and we darted across the street to Bob's front porch. There we stood until he finally answered the door.

"The shop's closing," Mae said.

Bob labored through the door and stood with us. "What?" he asked as horrified with the realization as Mae might have been at the thought of opening her curtains.

"There's a leak. Rita has to close until the roofers can get out. How's your stash?"

"I'll be all right," he said and smiled at Mae. Before her, I wondered how long it'd been since someone had taken care of Bob.

She reached into her bag and pulled out a Ziploc with four joints in it. "These are for you. To tide you over until Rita reopens."

Gratitude overflowed from Bob's eyes as he stared at the joints. His gaze stayed fixed on the bag while he said, "I knew you were sent from heaven." He took the joints, held them up for a goodbye, and disappeared into his house.

"Any other drug deals you need to complete today?"

"That's it," she said, proud of herself. "Deliveries are all done."

"Rita said it's going to be a few days."

"The roofers laughed at her when she called." Mae stared out at the rain. "Apparently, hers is not the only roof leaking this week." It pounded on the roof above us and the trees lining our street.

"Go away with me," I said, even though I knew it was a bad idea.

"Just skip town with my friend," she said and moved closer to me. She leaned against me until I could smell the honey scent of her shampoo over the rain.

"Yes."

"I've changed my mind, Dalton." She laid her open palms on my stomach and watched as she stretched out her fingers over my torso. "I don't want to be your friend."

"I can be friends enough for both of us. You make the plan. Wherever you want to go."

Mae moved back until I could see her, but the distance never helped with reading the look in her eyes.

"The Big Island perhaps?" I suggested.

She broke into a smile. "Someday, maybe."

"Come away with me," I said again as I reached out for her hand.

She left hers by her side. "You plan one day, and I'll plan the next." Mae offered.

"What if you hate what I plan?" Because in my head it was something like her and me in a cabin in the woods, somewhere Addario and Wright couldn't find us. It included me telling her the truth about why I was here, and her doing the same.

"Well, I've lived here for weeks, and I've seen nothing, so I'm guessing whatever you come up with will be spectacular."

"What if we both plan the same thing?"

"Such a stickler for the details, you are," she teased. "You plan something to the east, and I'll plan something to the west."

"You'll need a sleeping bag," I said.

The significance of that staple moved from her mind to her

raised eyebrows. "We're sleeping over?"

I nodded. "Like friends do," I said, taunting her. "I'll pick you up in the morning at eight."

"What about me makes you think I like to get up early?"

I left her smiling on the porch and ran across the street.

I barely slept that night.

CHAPTER 17

Dalton

WHEN I WOKE, WRIGHT WAS sitting in a chair at the foot of my bed. "What the fuck is going on with you?" It was more of a statement that a question.

I sat up and opened my eyes wide to properly assess the situation. I listened for signs of other life in my apartment.

"I'm alone," he said.

"What are you doing here?"

"Trying to salvage your career before you throw it all away and take my business's reputation with it."

"I just need more—"

"Do not say time, or I will rip your tongue out and shove it up your ass."

I sighed. I wouldn't say anything else.

"I saw the report."

"So, you know we're in New Mexico?"

He leaned his elbows on his knees and threaded his fingers together. "I've known you for over a decade. You're the finest operative I have, but for the first time, I can't trust your actions. You're leaving me with no choice."

That I understood. "I'll take her and go dark."

"You're going to kidnap her now?" He was indignant. Rightfully so.

"She's in trouble."

"Well, then she should hire us to protect her, but I'll tell you . . ." Wright's glare pierced through my calm demeanor. "I wouldn't put you on the job. You're too close."

"I'm fine."

"You're done. Brief Paul and pack up." He stood and handed me a folder. "Here's your next assignment."

I scanned the papers. "Jordan?" The destination lodged in my throat. Jordan was too far. Across the street was becoming too great a distance. I couldn't leave her.

"It's what you begged me for before her." Wright stood. "I'll leave out her exact location when I send through the final report to Addario." He walked out of my bedroom and through the front door onto the street.

I listened as he started his car and drove away, all the while knowing what I had to do.

The rain slowed long enough for me to load the car and pick her up across the street. I helped her put everything into the back seat and watched as she locked the three deadbolts she'd installed on the door. With the turn of each key, my heart sank a little deeper for her.

I could protect her.

"Ready," she said and buckled her seatbelt.

I was protecting her. Even if Wright assumed I'd be on my way to Jordan before the day was done. He wouldn't think I'd defy his orders to leave her there, but that wasn't going to happen. I'd committed myself to her the first time I'd lied back in Denver. Not even Wright was going to separate us.

I drove while Mae sang along to the radio. I wanted to ask her to sing solo, but she loved switching the channels and moving from country to metal to pop.

When an Isla Monroe song came on, she shut the radio off and said, "That's enough music."

"What now?"

"How much longer will we be in the car?"

"About an hour more. We're going to Mt. Hood."

"Oh, I was hoping." She peered out the side window. "I've been afraid to go."

"Why?" I asked.

"It just seems like a great place to kill someone and where no one would ever find the body."

I nodded. "I think they have that on the brochures."

"Maybe it's not raining up there."

"I love the rain." At least I didn't mind it with Mae.

"What else do you love?" she asked.

"I don't know . . ." I really wasn't sure anymore what I felt about anything.

"What's your full name?"

"Pass."

"Oh, there are passes in this interview. You know, if you don't answer the question, they make something up."

She laughed until I asked, "Who's they?"

She sighed and tossed another question. "Who do you spend Christmas day with?"

"My parents if I'm not working somewhere far away."

Mae nodded. She was satisfied I finally answered a question.

"Do you believe in God?"

"Not in the same way that you do."

She tilted her head but never took her eyes off me. "How could you possibly know in what way I believe in God?"

Her hymns in the Denver cathedral had changed my own views on God. He lived in her, but I couldn't tell her that. "By the way you describe the Big Island. Your connection is more than physical." I recovered with. "Am I wrong?"

She seemed to accept my explanation. "How do you believe?"

"I'm hoping there's a merciful God." I'd certainly sinned enough for any man. I was going to need some mercy when this life ended.

"What's your favorite vegetable?" she asked. I silently exhaled. "Broccoli."

"Oh, man." She threw her head back in disgust. "Take me back. Deal breaker."

"What's your favorite vegetable?"

"The red pepper, of course."

"My turn," I said. She shifted in her seat so she was facing me. "Did you always know you wanted to work in a pot shop?"

"No," she said and laughed. "I wanted to sing and be famous . . . and wear designer clothes and fly private jets all over the world." She spoke of the little girl's fantasy that it was.

"Not anymore? It's in the past?"

"Now I just want peace."

I thought she'd found it in the middle of the forest surrounding Mt. Hood. We'd stopped for lunch, and she ate like a linebacker. I didn't comment on it out of an ancient need to be a gentleman, but when she asked for the fries off my plate, I couldn't help myself.

"We'll have another meal, you know."

"I know."

I started to wonder if she was pregnant and that was why she'd fled. "Would you like a beer? Something to celebrate our disappearance?"

The smile drained from her face. She didn't like the word. I had a few others I thought she would make her equally uncomfortable.

"I'm good," she said. I regretted opening my mouth in the first place. "On second thought, let's drink up. We're on vacation."

She signaled to the waiter, and we both ordered Rogue Dead Guy Ales. We sat and watched the rain until the afternoon was in full swing.

"If we don't leave soon, I'll be drunk." She tilted her head toward me. "And I'll take advantage of you."

I laughed, unable to stop myself. Her tiny finger pointed at me with her warning. So, we left and drove until the asphalt became a muddy dirt road, which ended in a wall of rain-drenched forest. Then we hiked through the woods in the pouring rain. I'd only mentioned it, but Mae jumped at the chance.

"I used to spend days outside in the rain," she said. "What's not to love about it?"

"Wet socks, sticky heavy denim, and soaked underwear," I offered, but if she could do it, I certainly could.

She waved off my comments and led the way into the woods. The rain beat off the leaves around us insulating us from the outside world with the sound. It was a dark, green cave we trudged through, barely able to discern a path. When the rain drove harder, we stopped under a tree with branches reaching six feet across, forming a leaky canopy.

"Do you want to go back?"

"No." She shook her head. "You?"

"No."

"When is your birthday, Dalton?"

Her question threw me. "It's November eighteenth. Why?"

"Mine's today." She twirled around with her hands in the air and her face pointed toward the rain.

I wanted to say, "No, it's not," but how would I know? I wasn't supposed to have a thick file in my apartment that included such facts as February second was her birthday.

"Why didn't you say something?" I asked her.

Mae stopped spinning. She tilted her head and regarded me as if I should have already known. There was something so familiar and comfortable about her. "I haven't told anyone in years." She shivered from a chill and crossed her arms at her chest.

"Come here," I said. She folded into my arms. I leaned over above her to shield her from the rain. This tiny woman that I feared might fly away as she twirled in the forest, warmed me with her touch. Her head against my chest blocked the frigid raindrops on my neck and filled me with nothing but memories of what it was like to need someone. "Happy birthday, Ida Mae." She wrapped her arms around my back and held me tight against her.

"Let's go a little farther before we turn back," she said.

I couldn't say no to her. Not today. I was beginning to think not any day.

I took her tiny hand in mine, and we hiked over the hill until we came to a clearing that looked out onto Timothy Lake. Its surface jumped with the rain boring down on it. Mae shielded her eyes with her hand to watch it.

"Are you cold?" I asked.

"No. I'm grateful." She leaned against me. "And that's amazing. Thank you, Dalton."

"You're welcome."

The rain slowed. It let us hear the drops that landed around us instead of just the loud roar of a deluge. Mae kept her eyes fixed on the lake.

"It's going to stop," she said. "We're going to see the moment the rain stops."

We stared out at the lake. The surface calmed, but it was several minutes before individual raindrops distinguished themselves as they hit the water one by one.

She moved a few feet closer to the lake and announced, "It's done." Lake Timothy was completely serene. Drops fell from leaves surrounding us, but none touched the lake from the sky. "The storm's over," she said with a smile.

Dark clouds circled around Mt. Hood and moved with the wind toward us. "For now," I said. Mae's expression dampened as she stared at the lake. "Let's go to the cabin before it gets worse."

"We're going to get your car soaking wet."

"I brought some towels. The place we're staying in is a bit primitive."

"It's an actual place? I was expecting a tent."

"Well then, you're going to be very pleasantly surprised." The same way I was almost every time she opened her mouth.

I threw her a towel to sit on. She used it to wipe off her face first. We drove to the cabin with water dripping off us everywhere. She looked even younger soaking wet, or maybe she made me *feel* younger when she was sitting next me to me drenched.

I opened the door and let her walk in first. "Welcome to Clackamas Ranger Cabin."

She took off her shoes and wet socks by the door and peeked into the room. "Wow." She leaned her hand on the doorjamb and took it all in. "It's very Revolutionary War."

"Not quite, but I knew you'd like it." Water dripped from our clothes and onto the wooden floor. "Change here and take a hot shower." I handed her backpack to her. "I'm going to wait outside." *Stand guard.*

"You don't have to do that. I trust you."

"How come?"

"You haven't killed me yet," she said and unzipped her anorak. She lifted it over her head and dropped it on the floor at her feet. Her tee stuck to her skin and outlined every inch of her body. My breaths were shallow as I watched her.

"I'll be right out back. Scream if you need me," I forced out.

Her gaze followed me out the door. I willed each of my legs to walk away from her. I was going to shower, make us dinner, and tell her everything.

I organized all our gear in the trunk of my car until the rain started again. Then I just leaned on the quarter panel and waited. She was right. The rain felt good, especially since I wasn't trudging across a Mexican jungle with forty pounds of gear on my back.

"Dalton, it's all yours," she yelled from the doorway she leaned out with only a towel wrapped around her.

She was willful . . . and beautiful. I should tell her before dinner.

CHAPTER 18

Dalton

I DIDN'T TELL HER. SHE walked around the cabin singing and smiling, and the words never left my mouth. There were moments I caught myself daydreaming that time stood still or that I really was a carpenter. Ignoring my better judgment was becoming a part of being with Mae. I showered and sautéed onions and peppers. We were just two friends on a camping trip to Mt. Hood. I added diced tomatoes and the cooked pasta I'd brought with me in the cooler.

"Wow, Dalton. I'm impressed." She touched my bicep as she peered around me at the stovetop. "You didn't seem like a guy who knew how to cook."

"Because I'm alone?" I asked, and her hand fell from my arm.

"No. It's because you're handy. I should have figured, though. Cooking's not so different than carpentry, is it?"

"I haven't always been a carpenter," I said. My heart raced in my chest from the statement.

Mae stayed perfectly still next to me. She didn't say a word until I turned to her and looked her in the eye. "I wasn't always a pot saleswoman," she said and reached for the bottle of wine. She opened it and poured wine into two mugs she'd found. "Never trust a man without a past."

The way she moved about the kitchen shut down the

conversation. She didn't want any more details. She avoided the truth to hide her lies, but I wanted to know everything about her. Even the things not related to how I got here.

We ate together while the rain continued to pour outside our cabin. Mae's playfulness returned. She was pure light in our dimly lit cabin. I almost forgot everything *I* was running from.

"We can play I Never."

"Sure." I laughed at the ancient drinking game. "Because what's a high school party without I Never?"

She eyed the empty wine bottle, stood, and grabbed two beers from the fridge. "At least the refrigerator still works."

"Who needs light?" I switched on the lantern and placed it in the center of the table between us. I sat in the seat across from her and ran through all the things I wanted to know about her in my head. I settled on something easy and in line with the game. "I never ever stole something."

She sipped her beer. Of course she had. I held back my laughter and asked, "What?"

"Oh, that's not how this game works." She took a deep breath and sat quietly. "I never, ever had a threesome," she said and left her beer on the table. I did the same.

"Interesting," I said.

"That's just a little bit about me."

"That's quite a bit." I sipped. It was suddenly rather warm in the cabin. "I never, ever had sex in a car."

She drank immediately and waited expectantly for me to do the same, but my beer stayed on the table. "Now that's a little bit about you," she said.

I tapped my fingers nervously.

"I never, ever killed someone," she said.

I stayed perfectly still. I hated this game almost as much as I hated all the lies between us. Mae looked from me to our drinks on the table and back at me again. At the same time, we both took a sip of our beers.

"We're going to come back to that one," I said and took another sip.

"Sleep with one eye open." She tipped her head to me.

This game had already gone too far. I needed to return it to its ninth grade roots. "I never ever told someone I loved them." I sipped my beer. My chest tightened at the sight of Mae's bottle still on the table between her fingertips. I leaned down until I caught her line of sight. "You've never loved someone?"

"That wasn't the question." Her voice was flat and full of darkness.

"It's my question."

The playfulness drained from her eyes. "I learned at a very young age how wrong people can be about love." She sat back in my chair to distance herself from the rest of the answers I'd take from her. "Who did you love?"

"My wife," I said. "But she hated my job, so she left."

"She hated construction?"

"This was years ago. I didn't work construction then."

"I'm sorry," she said.

The lantern flickered off. It was ten. The generator wouldn't come back on again until tomorrow night.

"We should go to bed. Lot of driving tomorrow. We're heading west, right?"

Mae nodded and carried our mugs to the sink. "Good night, Dalton," she said before leaving me downstairs alone. I carried my sleeping bag into the bedroom off the living room. The mattress was covered only by a quilt which I left in place and unrolled my sleeping bag on top of it. The rain hit the windows, and sounds of Mae moving around above me felt distant. She was too far away.

The room was black. The rain and clouds that still hid the moon amplified the darkness. I was hot and cold at the same time. The damp air swept across my bare chest, but the rest of me that was tucked under the sleeping bag was hot. I unzipped the side and slipped my foot out.

Mae had been eerily quiet when she chose her room. None of them had curtains, which I knew was a requirement for her. She ignored the beds and the décor and stepped right to the windows to assess the point of entry's weaknesses.

I'd almost told her the truth right then. She should know nothing was ever going to hurt her as long as she was with me, and if she told me exactly who she was afraid of, I'd kill them for her.

The door opened a foot. More darkness creeped in with the sweet smell of citrus and honey.

"Are you awake?" she whispered.

"Yes." I sat up in bed. Not that she could see me. I could only make out the outline of her movements.

She dragged her sleeping bag behind her and carried her pillow into my room and stood next to my bed. "Can I ask to sleep with you without you thinking it's a desperate ploy to have sex with you?"

"No." More importantly, I wasn't sure I could stop myself if she gave me an opening. I needed to tell her the truth or stay away from her. Paul was right. I was fucking this up beyond compare. "But come here." I laid my sleeping bag out beneath us. She climbed on the bed and covered us with hers. "I'll behave."

She rolled onto her side and snuggled her head onto my shoulder. I inhaled the hints of honey from her hair and warmed immediately. She was a fire lying next to me, and even though she was constantly on high alert, I felt safe next to her. She reminded me of a time before the isolation when anything was possible. I kissed the top of her head.

"Thank you," she said and tightened her arm across my chest.

She lay there until her arm rested heavy on me and her breaths were long and even. Mae was quiet and serene. She stole the hardened thoughts of my past and replaced them with her warmth in my bed.

She clenched up and squeezed my arm in terror.

"Mae," I whispered.

"No. No. No, no, no, Ian," she said and loosened her grip on me.

I ran through my mind every name I'd ever heard associated with her, searching for an Ian until the letters tucked in the pages of her Bible finally came to me. I rubbed her back until she was solidly back to sleep and fell away myself. I could watch her with me. Here in this bed with me, she was safe.

Mae was still clutching my chest when the sunlight draped across us. It felt like a month since the sun had shown. I would tell her today. On the way home in the car, so she couldn't hit me or run away. At least she couldn't run away. She stirred beside me, and I wanted to pull her on top of me and rip off the nightshirt she was wearing.

"Good morning," she said. Her eyes flitted open. She closed them when they failed to adjust to the light.

"How'd you sleep?"

"Better than I have in a year." She sat up and leaned on her hand beside me. "How about you? Did your arm fall asleep?"

"If it did, I didn't notice. I slept well, too."

"I don't want to go back."

"Back to reality?"

She paused and stared at me. It was the perfect moment to blurt it out. "Back to Portland, which I suppose is reality."

"Let's spend the day on the lake. Now that the sun's out, I think the whole world is going to be different."

She closed her eyes and fell back next to me again. "That would be amazing."

Isla, my love,

We were interrupted. I apologize for that. The next time I touch you, it will be just us. No one will be able to find us. I promise.

I felt your heartbeat as I said your name. I know how much you want me. When this is over, we'll be together. We'll go somewhere quiet that's just ours. Somewhere the rest of the world won't matter. They won't call your name anymore.

Trust me the way I trust you. I'll never believe a word they say because you are Isla Monroe, and I know how much I mean to you, but Cruz Allen has to go.

I know you think he's just a friend, but he obviously sees your relationship differently. He's taking advantage of your kindness. You are polite, and he is confused. If he won't listen to me, he's going to suffer.

You are mine.

Love,

Ian

CHAPTER 19

Mae

"I DON'T WANT TO GO back." I knew I'd said it in bed and I probably sounded like a child, but it was how I felt. I certainly wasn't carefree, but here in the primitive cabin in the middle of the woods with Dalton, I was more relaxed than I'd been in months. He noticed things. He listened. Dalton was aware so I could rest. I'd never been with a man I felt more at peace with.

He stood in the doorway to the kitchen and studied me. It drove me crazy how I could never tell what he was thinking. He was older. Not impetuous or impatient. He seemed wiser in every conversation we had, but there was something lost about Dalton. I wasn't even sure he knew what was missing.

"What is it that you're trying so hard to avoid?" he asked.

It was my turn to be silent.

"Because you seem to love our street and your job and your neighbors." He had a wry smile.

"Yes. Bob is wonderful."

"So, tell me, Mae, what is it that you're so desperate to stay away from?"

"Desperate seems strong. I merely said I'd love not to go back." I scanned our modest surroundings. We were a million miles from real life. "Is that so hard to believe?"

Dalton sighed as if he were waiting for me to give him something I hadn't delivered. If it was information he was interested in, he'd be waiting forever. That was the one thing I was no longer sharing. Not with him and not with the rest of the world. I owed them nothing. Not even a song.

"Something about your arrival in Portland seems extreme." He spoke slowly, testing the waters with his thoughts.

"One could say the same for you." I moved about the kitchen, filling two teacups with water from the kettle. "You seemed to have dropped right out of the sky and landed next door to the weed stalk."

He nodded, lost in thought, and said, "Yes. Divine intervention, some might say."

"Would you be one of those people?"

"The more time I spend with you, the more I believe the people we meet aren't random."

"That's sweet, I think." Dalton was so deep compared to the men I was used to conversing with. I had to dive further down than I'd been in years to comprehend his thoughts.

Mama believed everyone we met in this life was for a reason. Right up until she'd bought me the ticket to New York City and gave me to Victor Addario, she believed. After that, she was terrified. Neither of us had any idea what stardom was like. We'd only witnessed it in the pages of the magazines or on the television in the back room of my grandmother's house after we'd moved in. To us, celebrities had it all, and to Mama, Victor Addario was the only way to become one.

"He's a good man," Mama had said after he'd flown down to meet with us. Victor had brought Mama flowers. He'd given me flowers when he'd come to the first apartment he'd rented for me in the city. They were gardenias, and ever since, the scent still reminds me of how he'd held my elbows together behind my back while he'd bent me over the arm of the couch and stuck his dick in me.

I stared at Mt. Hood in the distance and remembered how small

I'd felt when he'd walked into our kitchen in North Carolina. I'd only been in high school two years. I shook my head. Mama always had terrible taste in men.

My brother had told her, "Mama, you bring one more beast into this house, and I'm going to disown you. Can't you meet someone at church?" She'd laughed at the time, but she never brought home another man. It was as if God himself had spoken.

I wondered what she'd think of Dalton. If she'd liked him, I probably should be afraid.

"Let's stay," I said. Dalton didn't move. Just kept watching me while his brow furrowed in consternation. "Just one more night." I waved to the outdoors behind him. "The sun is out, and the moon will come. It'll be totally different from last night."

He stayed perfectly still. Dalton was always solid. "That's what I'm afraid of."

"Big, strong guy like yourself shouldn't be afraid of little old me."

"I've seen you drop a guy flat on his back in the alley next to my house."

"Me and pepper spray."

"Something tells me you didn't need the spray." His eyes traipsed over my body, lingering at my chest and sinking to my waist. I wouldn't force him into something he didn't want. Although, there were times I caught him watching me, or studying me, that I thought he could have me just from the need in his stare. "I'm too old for you."

"I know," I said and smiled at him. He couldn't have been ten years older. He had no idea how many lifetimes I'd lived before him. "Pop-Pop."

"That's creepy."

"How old are you?"

"Thirty-four," he said it like an apology. His age meant nothing to me.

I sighed. "Over the years, I've become very good at reading

people, but you . . ." I shook my head. "I can't figure you out."

"Maybe you shouldn't try." He crossed his arms, protecting himself from the energy between us.

"Maybe *you* should invest some time in that area."

"Spoken like a young woman."

"Dismissed like an aging man." My eyes raked over his solid chest and his trim waist. His pajama pants were hanging low, and the band of his underwear was peeking out. "If we stay, we'll make love. I'll roll over on top of you in bed tonight, and you won't stop me."

The muscles in his chest and upper arms tightened ever so slightly as he inhaled. "Mae—"

"I know you want me." I wasn't allowing him to retreat. If I could face this, Dalton could. "I can tell by the way you looked at me at the lake yesterday and how you held me in bed last night." I moved closer to him, and his jaw clenched. I stopped two feet in front of him. Heat poured off him, or me. I couldn't tell anymore which of us was setting this attraction off, but I wanted to touch him and to feel his hands on me. I tore my sight from his body and made eye contact. "And because you brought me here in the first place."

"I thought you'd like it." His voice was rough.

I pressed myself against the front of him and stood on my tiptoes to whisper, "I love it," in his ear.

He lifted me off my feet and carried me to the counter. He set me down, took my face in his hands, and forced his lips onto mine.

I reached up, and he batted my arms away, holding them tight to my sides. Dalton was done with me being in charge. He tightened his grip on my arms and pressed his lips on me until the back of my head was pressed against the cabinets. I froze from the familiar power. *It's Dalton.* He reached up and gently held my face in his hands, igniting my body. Every inch responded to his hands on me. I tightened my legs around the back of him. My thighs pulled him closer still. He was turning me into an animal. I wanted him—his body—and nothing else mattered.

He let go of my right arm and yanked my shirt down until my bare breast was exposed. He cupped my breast and kissed me again. Sweet heat burned through my insides. I closed my eyes and enjoyed the fire. He lifted my shirt over my head and threw it behind him without taking his eyes off my chest. Dalton's fingers found my nipples as his lips dragged down the side of my neck. I gasped for air and sucked in the delicious hickory scent that followed him.

He took my nipple in his mouth and moved his touch up my inner thigh. A wet heat that been held captive too long crept up inside me and followed his hands up my legs. Dalton clawed at my skin until I needed him inside me to quiet the fire that was building. He let go . . . of everything, and stepped back. His gaze stayed fixed on the floor until he turned around and walked out of the room.

"Dalton," I said and followed him.

He didn't stop until he threw his bag on his bed and began filling it with the clothes hanging over the chair.

My body still wanted him. The air touching my skin sent a violent reminder to every place he'd touched. "Dalton," I said again. This time my voice was firm. I wouldn't be denied.

He stopped packing. With his back still to me, he said, "I can't do this."

I closed my eyes and fought back tears. His rejection was welling up at the back of my throat. I wouldn't cry. Not today. Maybe never again.

"Dalton." I was gentle. I couldn't goad him into making love to me. I shouldn't have to. "Have you ever let yourself lose control of a situation?" I placed my hand on his back between his shoulders and let my mind wander there. My other hand I rested on the back of his arm. He had to touch me again. "Just taken what you want without regard to the consequences."

"I'm too old for that."

"We all are, and it always ends horrifically, but I don't think that's what's going on here." I slipped my hands around his waist and touched his stomach. "I think you've put a great deal of thought into this, and you're scared."

"Mae—"

I reached down and rubbed his dick through his pajama pants. "You don't have to do a thing." When I cupped his balls, his breath caught. I came around in front of him where I could fully grasp the tortured look in his eyes. "Especially not think."

I lowered his pants and bent to my knees. I took his dick in my mouth and moaned as I pressed it farther toward my throat.

Dalton's hand found the back of my head, and he guided me against him. His fingers threaded in my hair. I could feel him relax as I wrapped my hand around his thigh. I kept going, sucking him harder and keeping pace with his hand until he pulled my head back by my hair.

I licked my lips and stared up at him. He wasn't tormented anymore. He was in charge.

Dalton laid me on the bed. There I stayed in his stare as he took off my underwear. He stepped back and let his eyes move over every inch of me, as if I might disappear and he was memorizing my features.

I waited for his command with the muscles of my thighs quivering from the need for him to touch me.

He knelt, lifted my leg onto his shoulder, and softly blew on me until he licked my clit and electricity soared through my veins. He pressed his hand on my stomach to calm me and asked, "Okay?"

Breathing was an issue. As was speaking.

He finally looked up at me as I nodded. He leaned down and pressed my leg open farther as he ran his tongue over me. Dalton was slow and methodical, and my body responded by rushing a wet heat to exactly where his tongue touched.

"Don't move," he said. Again, I could only nod.

He took my clit between his teeth and sucked until I wanted to cry out, but before I could, he released it and licked it until I almost came. His tongue flitted against me with his hands pulling me closer to his mouth by my hips. I wanted to curl into a ball around him. To force his mouth into me and release the needs he'd built since the kitchen.

"Hold still," he demanded.

"I can't."

Dalton stood and kissed me. He stared at me until I thought I could fly. "You can do anything." He slipped a finger inside me and moaned at the wet welcome he'd created. His tongue returned to my clit, and I anchored myself up with both hands on the top of his head. My leg shook beneath me until my whole body followed its quake. I came with Dalton's mouth still on me.

Dalton stared at me exposed beneath him. "I don't have a condom." His eyes followed the lines of my body to the place where he stood above me.

"I do," I said with a rueful smile.

"Of course you do."

I rolled over, slid off the bed in front of him, and climbed the stairs to my room. I found the pocket in my bag that held the condom I'd purchased at the grocery store the day before. It was a wish then. Now it was a must.

Dalton turned around with his dick in his hand. He was stroking it. The expression on his face was a tortured pain mixed with the desire I felt in his stare. I rolled the condom on him and laid back down.

He touched my neck with both hands, and an old instinct to run crept in. He was gentle as his fingertips traced my collarbone and my breasts. I closed my eyes and exhaled. With his touch, the sweet tightening returned.

"You're beautiful, Mae," he said and rammed his dick into me. It quieted the pounding between my legs for a second before I needed him again.

I pulled him to me with my legs, the look in my eyes, and my hands reaching out for him. Dalton held my hands above my head and leaned over me. The weight of his chest was forgotten when he pulled out slowly and thrust again.

"Oh . . ." He slowed and regarded me. "Don't stop." I shook my head. "Please, don't ever stop."

He didn't, not even when every muscle in my body surged toward him and I collapse around him, coming in a way I never had before. I rode the wave of erotic energy that followed each thrust and gasped for air until he said, "I'm going to come."

I let my sight linger on his body as his head fell back toward the ceiling and his chest rose from his breaths. He was beautiful braced above me, and I'd taken him for my own.

He was my first mistake.

CHAPTER 20

Dalton

I WAITED FOR MAE TO say something. She always had something to add to the conversation. She'd fix this.

She lay there staring at me with the sweetest expression. I wasn't sure if it was the same girl who'd just forced my dick into her mouth. "Come here," she said and held her arms out to me. "I have the chills."

Goose bumps covered her skin. I curled up next to her and draped my leg over both of hers to share my heat. I was still on fire. My dick was hardening again, and if she didn't say something to get us out of this cabin, I was going to fuck her all day long. I no longer cared about the ramifications of my actions. The only thing I cared about was Mae.

"Thank you," she said. "I know that was asking you to give something up . . . or away, and I want you to know I appreciate it." She laughed a little at the tail end of her statement and amused me, too.

"You're welcome." *Don't think, Dalton.* "Maybe we should go."

Mae rolled on top of me. She let each leg fall to my sides and sat up, facing me. Her breasts were round, swollen to perfection, and the color of her lips matched the areola I wanted to touch with my tongue again. There was so much of her I wanted to explore.

"Maybe we should stay in bed all day," she said with a naughty glint in her eye.

"You won't be able to walk." I squeezed her thighs between my fingers. Her flesh heated beneath my touch.

"Walking's overrated," she said and kissed me.

I let myself drown in her again, and then I fell asleep next to her. She was the warmest moment of my life and she was terrorized by her own existence. I was a liar, but I wasn't letting her go.

When she woke, I convinced her to put clothes on so we could go to the lake. Everything was soaking wet except the kayak I rented for the day.

Mae climbed into the front while I pushed us off the shore. "Do you know how to swim?" I asked.

"Yes, but something tells me you'd save me if I were drowning."

"Only if you tell me who you've killed."

She spun around in her seat and lifted her legs over the opening until she reclined back and faced me. I rowed us out into the middle of the lake.

"My mother was in a horrible car accident when I was eighteen. She spent ten days on life support. She laid there until they told me to decide to take her off."

"That's tragic," I said and wondered why none of this was in her file and what the hell else wasn't in there.

"I have an older brother, whom I love, but he's never been a doer. That was always me. Mama used to say when she died, I'd have to bury her because he would never get around to it."

"She sounds charming."

Mae dropped her head back and stared at the cloudless sky. "She was." She tilted her face to the sun. "How about your mother, Dalton?"

I laughed. She was determined to drag me along her stroll down memory lane. "How about her?" I asked.

"Is she still living?"

"Yes."

"She must be very proud of her carpenter son." She raised her eyebrows at me as if my profession was some secret we held between us. "Do you have any brothers or sisters?"

"Just a brother. He lives near my parents in Buffalo."

"Nieces or nephews?"

"Two nieces."

"Oh, how lucky you are, Uncle Dalton . . . but they probably call you something else. Perhaps your first name." She peered back at me with one eye still shut. "What do they call their uncle?"

"They call me their favorite," I said and paddled us farther away from the shore.

"Hm. Smart girls." She reminded me of a Greek goddess lying in the bow of my boat. "Do you think you'll have children of your own someday?" she asked without turning away from the sun.

I rested the paddle across my thighs. "Probably not."

She swiveled around in her seat. "Why?"

"My job makes it difficult to have a family."

"Carpentry . . ." Mae stared at me until I thought she knew the truth. "Don't rule it out, Dalton. You're going to make an excellent daddy."

Her comments warmed me and left me considering things I hadn't in years. With Mae, life was more than just my work, it was real in a way it'd maybe never been, which was crazy, because our entire relationship was built on lies. "Thanks."

Mt. Hood towered over us in the distance. Drops of water fell from my resting paddles into the water, and a single fish jumped above the surface.

Mae shifted and rested her legs on the front of the boat. She was more at ease than I'd seen her in the weeks I'd known her. This was the first hint of true relaxation. Her hand slipped over the side, and her fingertips grazed the surface of the water. "Out here, it's hard to believe there are crazy people in the world."

"There are dangerous people everywhere," I said and watched

her abandon the sky and face me again.

"I know. Even right here in this kayak."

I paddled again. "How so?" I tried to seem nonchalant. She was just teasing. She couldn't know more about me than I knew about her. There were no details anywhere to find.

"There's the danger that jumps out of the dark . . ." She cupped water in her hand and let it trickle back into the lake. "And the one you can't see clearly, even in the light."

"Which one am I?"

"The one that I want," she said and her steely concentration convinced me she could have whatever she desired regardless of the cost.

"I need to tell you something."

She smiled a little, but it wasn't kind. Her expression was one of vindication. "I know," she said. "It's complicated." She sat up in her seat and began paddling us farther from the shore. "Please do me the tremendous favor of not telling me a thing."

"You can't just avoid life forever," I said, and Mae stayed still. "You can't outrun the past." She lowered her head. I feared I was pushing her too far. "I can help."

"Will you hammer my problems away?" The cold returned to her eyes.

"Don't be an asshole."

She nodded and ran her fingers over the water again. "Are you usually attracted to blondes or brunettes, Dalton?"

If I didn't know her past, the question would have been ridiculous, but she was still searching for reconciliation between her many lives. "I don't think things are quite so clear cut." I stared at her golden brown hair that the sun had highlighted around her face. "I'm drawn to light brown with hints of honey and caramel and sunlight," I said.

"You're too good to me."

"I didn't bring you up here to have sex with you." I needed her to believe me.

"Well then, your plans are failing miserably." Her wit never took a rest.

"I just wanted you to know. It wasn't my intention. I didn't lure you here." There was still some honor left in me. Even if I was void of all professionalism and lying to the woman in front of me. I was still a good man, and that was who she deserved.

"Please. I'm a little old to be lured. It's not like you had candy bars on your dashboard. I did come up here to have sex with you." She bounced her eyebrows at me. "I was oddly attracted to you the day you bought the bird bowl, but I *wanted* you when I saw you running in the rain."

"Oddly attracted?"

"You are the first man in . . ." She shook her head and raised her gaze toward the sky. "Too long that I really wanted to put my hands on." The muscles in my groin tightened. "To let my fingers rest against your chest and drag down your arms." She closed her eyes and shook her head. "Your body is exceptional." Mae took a deep breath. "Everything about you is exceptional."

My dick perked up as a tingling crossed the back of my neck. I picked up my paddle and rowed us back toward shore.

"Where are we going?"

"Someplace quiet."

"We're on the side of the mountain. Every place is quiet."

"Someplace that won't tip over when I climb on top of you."

"Oh."

CHAPTER 21

Dalton

WE HAD THE GENERATOR UNTIL ten at night, but we didn't need it. I could have spent the rest of my life with Mae completely in the dark. I was hoping it'd be that way.

She'd finally risen from our bed and found a long dress to put on. It was soft and black and flowed behind her when she walked as if she was an angel of death. I laughed at the reference.

"What's so funny?" she asked as she poured two mugs of wine and handed one to me. Her arm was bruised where I'd lifted her and held her down. I ran my thumb over it until her body shook with a chill from my touch.

"I'm sorry."

"I'm not. You didn't hurt me."

"I'd never hurt you." At least, that wasn't my intention.

"I don't think you could," she said.

"Believe that, Mae. Trust your instincts."

She ran her thumb down the side of my face. I closed my eyes and concentrated on her touch. "My last boyfriend did so much cocaine he could rarely get it up to have sex."

I stared back at her. It was the first piece of the life she'd left behind that she'd shared. Her expression wasn't cold. She was giving this to me.

"He sounds awesome."

"You'd be amazed at how many people thought just that," she said. I recalled all the information I'd read on Cruz Allen. Hollywood's darling son who courted the pop princess until they'd gotten engaged.

"Was it serious?"

Mae almost spit out her wine as she laughed. She shook her head. "Sorry. The group of people I used to hang out with loved drama." Her eyes flitted to the ceiling. "Like, couldn't get enough of it. Anyway, it wasn't serious. I would say we were more friends. We shared a very similar life that was hard to understand unless you'd lived it. So, there was that."

"What kind of life?" I asked, hoping she'd end all the lies. Mae was brave enough to get us out of this. She was bold. I just needed her to realize it and let me in.

"The crazy kind," she said and took a long sip of her wine. She wasn't tearing down any more walls in this cabin.

"What happened to him?"

Her laugh was dry, sinister. "Depends on who you ask."

"I'm asking you." I pulled her down into my lap and kissed her.

"We broke up." She threaded her hands through my hair with the familiarity of a lover who'd touched me a thousand times before. "It seemed to me that we'd never really been together, but he was surprised by the ending."

"Oh." I tried to concentrate while she pressed her body tight against mine. "How'd he take it?"

"I'm sure fine." She wrapped her arms around my neck and kissed me on the temple. "Thank you for agreeing to stay another night."

"I'm beginning to think I don't have a choice when it comes to you."

"I'm from North Carolina," she said and kissed me again.

I held her in front of me, not letting her look away and

acknowledged the significance of her offering. "I love North Carolina," I said instead of "I love you," which flew into my head.

She leaned back and rocked her pelvis against me. I ran my fingers down her exposed neck and inhaled the honey scent. My body responded to her immediately. There was a deep ache that echoed through me and was only silenced when my hands were on her, my dick in her.

"You're the first thing I've chosen in a long time," she said, still facing the ceiling.

"Mae . . ."

She exhaled loudly with frustration. "Let's just enjoy a few days together before you ruin it."

The suggestion made me stop. Ruining this was what I was trying to avoid.

"Wouldn't that be nice? Just keep all your logical thoughts and reasons to yourself for, say . . . forty-eight more hours." She shifted her weight and stroked my dick. "Can we do that?"

She kept moving back and forth on top of me until the throbbing silenced the truth. I hung my head back and closed my eyes.

"Yes," I finally managed to get out.

Mae led me to our bedroom and climbed on top of me. She didn't let me think the rest of the night, not even hours later with her lying quietly next to me as if she were meant to be there. I rolled on my side and laid my arm across her. I knew I'd never sleep again without touching her.

When I woke, the bed was empty. I could hear voices in the kitchen. When I fully regained consciousness, I realized she was listening to the radio. Mae sang low to the songs, trying not to wake me. I slipped on my pajama pants and walked out to find her toasting a bagel in the ancient toaster.

"Good morning," she said. Her hair was sticking out on the side and pushed behind her ear. She wore a long T-shirt that barely covered her bare ass. If I could, I'd have kept her right there, just like that, forever.

"Yes," was all I said and walked over to her. I held her against my chest until the toaster popped and her bagel raised just above the top. She reached over without looking and pressed the handle down again.

"In Hollywood news, Cruz Allen and Dorothy Ryan hit the red carpet last night for the opening of their new movie, *Spaced Out*. We asked Cruz about his fiancée, Isla Monroe's, time in rehab."

Mae stiffened in my arms but didn't say a word. She tilted her head toward the radio. My heart beat against the wall of my chest.

"Cruz, how's Isla? When is she coming home?"

"She's great. Isla's such a beautiful soul. She's getting the rest she needs, and I expect her back very soon."

"Have you gone to see her?"

"I have."

"Did you talk about the wedding?"

Cruz laughed. "I can't give away any details. I can say this. I can't wait to marry her. Isla is truly the love of my life. It'll be exactly how she wants it to be, and nothing is going to stand in our way."

"Thanks, Cruz. Back to you in the studio, Natalie."

I leaned back and waited for Mae's reaction. I couldn't stand Hollywood before I knew how completely fucked up and full of shit it was. After seeing Mae's life for a few weeks, Wright couldn't pay me to live or work there.

Mae pried her bagel from the toaster and buttered it using a plastic knife. She turned to me, rested the knife on her plate, and asked, "How did you propose to your wife?"

Her question threw me. I didn't want to talk about my ex-wife with anyone, but especially not Mae. "We were in a cabin by Mt. Hood, and one morning I got down on one knee and asked her to marry me," I said and slowly lowered to one knee.

Her expression morphed from shock to pissed off before she threw the dishtowel in my face. "You're terrible," she said and took a bite of her bagel.

"I'm not the one dredging up horrible memories."

"I wanted to know."

"Just because you want to know something in life, it doesn't mean you should just ask. What if I was still nursing the wounds of my failed marriage?"

She touched the side of my face with her palm. Kneeling down, I felt closer to her height. "I can tell by the way you touch me that you're over it." She leaned down until she was staring me in the eye. "And I can tell by the way you look at me, you're happier now."

"How do I look at you?" I was afraid of her answer.

"Like you're in love with me." She kissed my forehead. I was a secret operative trained in covert tactical operations and this pop singer could see right through me. She was terrifying. "Be careful with that, though. I'm all smoke and mirrors."

"And pepper spray."

"That, too."

CHAPTER 22

Dalton

WE TRAVELED WEST TO PORTLAND, but Mae didn't want to stop in the city. I thought she was afraid the pot shop had been fixed and our road trip would be cut short. We drove almost two more hours and checked into the hotel she'd chosen. Our view was of the beach, but it was almost dark. If we left the balcony door open, we could hear the surf, but Mae closed it and the curtain before we'd even dropped our bags on the bed.

"Do you want to take a walk on the beach?" I asked her.

She was shocked when she turned around. "In the dark?"

"Why not?" I opened the curtain an inch. The moonlight shone enough to make out Haystack Rock in the water. "I'll protect you." I wanted to shout that at her. To wrap her in my arms and fall on the bed with her. To not let her up until she believed every word I said.

"Promise?" The doubt in her eyes physically hurt me.

"Always." I held out my hand. Mae took it without hesitation.

We walked out of the back of the hotel to the soft sand. We left our flip-flops by the fence post and didn't care if they were there when we got back or not. All I needed was Mae. Several similar stragglers were on the beach with their dogs or holding hands as they strolled along the shore. Mae walked straight to the water and let it wash over her feet. She reached out for me. I took her hand

and stood next to her in the Pacific Ocean.

"The sand feels different than North Carolina," she said.

"I've never been to the beach in North Carolina."

"Oh, how terrible for you. Where did you grow up, Dalton?"

"Buffalo."

"Wow. No wonder you're drawn to the beach. You've had enough snow for a lifetime."

"Yes. I have." In the faint light of the crescent moon, I could see her studying me. She was deciding how many questions to ask. Mae rarely just reacted.

"Where did you go from Buffalo?"

I took a deep breath and exhaled my fear that she'd leave me. "West Point," I said, and her hand slipped out of mine.

She turned until she was facing me. I didn't move. I couldn't have if I tried. I was trapped in realization that the truth was about to level us. If I touched her, just reached out and pulled her to me, I could survive this silence, but her being separate from me while she thought was causing my blood to race through my veins. This is the reaction my body had before I entered a building to take out a target. Right now, I was the target.

"Did you graduate . . . from West Point?" She was putting together pieces of information that would lead her to a career that didn't include carpentry.

"I did."

"Well, thank you for your service," she said a bit playfully.

I stepped behind her, wrapped my arms around her shoulders, and watched the clouds cover the moon. I let the conversation slip away on the night's air. The thought of losing her stole my courage. I wouldn't force any of this on her until she asked to hear it.

"Maybe you don't have to go to Hawaii," she said.

"What?"

"Just today, right here in Oregon, we've been to the mountains and the coast."

"But I'll miss out on all the magical voices." I leaned to the side to see her.

Her attention was focused on Haystack Rock. She closed her eyes and let the strong wind whipping down the beach blow her hair back. "Maybe you can hear it here, too."

"You were right." The words were fighting free. She was the bravest, kindest, most intriguing woman I'd ever known. I didn't just admire her. "I love you," I said. Every inch of my body stood at attention. The air touched my skin in a new way. The sound of the birds flying over our heads were distinct from every other voice around us. I waited for Mae.

She reached out, steadying herself with a hand on an invisible chair and opened her eyes. Seconds felt like hours until she said, "There's so much you don't know." Her words were level and defined. She lowered her head in shame, but none of it mattered.

I was afraid she might cry. I took her hand and kissed her fingers. Mae's gaze followed her hand to my lips. "I know everything I need to."

She reached up and threaded her fingers in my hair. She pulled me down and kissed me. I lifted her off the ground and held her against me until there was no doubt we needed to go back to the room.

We made love. I wanted her to never hide again. She deserved so much more from life than what she was letting herself have. I could give it to her. If she would just tell me exactly what she was afraid of. She'd always be safe with me. I knew as I watched her asleep beside me that no one was ever going to hurt her unless they killed me first.

We laid in bed while the light drape over us. Mae faced the sliding glass door. "No blackout curtains?" She rolled over and smiled. "No need to let the day in," she said to cover the fact that she didn't want any people in.

"Room service," came through the door with a harsh knock.

Mae's head shot around toward the door.

I placed my hand gently on her am.

"I'll get it," she said and exhaled.

"Check through the hole first."

She stopped moving and stared at me as if I'd told her to light someone on fire.

"What?"

"Nothing."

"Why did you look at me like that?"

"I'm not used to someone taking care of me." Her words were light like her footsteps on her way to the door.

She returned to our bed with a basket of muffins, a carafe of juice, and the morning paper. Mae poured us each glasses of the bright orange liquid while I laid the paper out flat on the bed next to me. She placed the glass on my nightstand and read the headline at the same time as I did.

"Cruz Allen Dies from Drug-Induced Fall."

Mae took a tiny step back from me and the paper.

"Mae," I said. My voice was gentle. I knew she'd been engaged to him right before she'd left, but I never knew if he was part of what she was running from. "You okay?"

She absently nodded. Her gaze was fixed on the newspaper. She leaned over me and picked it up. "Cruz Allen died," she said, but she wasn't talking to me. She was lost inside her head. "Do you mind if I turn on the news?"

"Go ahead." My heart sank in my chest. She could have been lying when she said she didn't love him.

She flipped through the channels until she settled on one of several that were reporting on Allen's death. She sat on the end of the bed and watched the video of police entering and exiting his house in Los Angeles.

The reporter said, "It's a sad day in Hollywood as one of their favorite sons passes on. Cruz Allen was pronounced dead at his Los

Angeles home. The cause of death has not been released by the Broward County coroner's office yet, but sources tell NNK news that Allen fell down a flight of stairs, and evidence of significant cocaine and heroin use were found in his house."

The video changed to silent footage of Cruz Allen before he died.

"Celebrity family members and friends have flooded the Internet with tributes and love for Allen. We caught up with music mogul Victor Addario, who worked with Allen on several film projects."

Addario stood outside of his office, appearing smug. Everything about the man made me want him to submit before I killed him. The newscaster disappeared. The screen filled with Victor Addario. "This is a sad day," he began, and I rolled my eyes. Mae was fixated by his image on the screen. "Our thoughts and prayers are with the Allen family in this horrific time." He stared down as if he had any idea how to actually pray. "What can I say? It's tragic."

"Mr. Addario, will Isla Monroe leave rehab to attend the services?"

Addario stared directly into the camera and said, "We're currently speaking to Ms. Monroe. We hope she's getting the rest she needs and that she'll be home in time to pay her respects. Of course, she knows we all . . . love her."

Mae leaned back, separating herself from the television. She pressed off on the remote and wrapped her arms tight around her chest.

I kneeled in front of her. "Are you okay?" I asked. There was an empty silence in her eyes that I couldn't decipher. I wanted to know every thought in her mind. The truth of why I came to Portland was fighting its way free.

She sat completely still. "I feel like this is all a dream that I'm going to wake up from." I kissed her on the lips and the forehead and on the cheek right by her ear. "And when I do, the reality is going to be a nightmare."

"Stay right here with me." I kissed her again and forced her back onto the bed. If this was a dream, I hoped neither of us ever woke up.

Isla, my love,

They're all liars. I need to see you, to talk to you and make sure you understand. I need you to hear the truth from you, not all these reporters who have no idea who you really are. You can't trust them. Only me, and I don't trust them, either. They tell me you're in love with another man. That you could possibly have feelings for Cruz Allen is the biggest joke of it all. If he talks about you the way he did his last girlfriend, I'm going to kill him. I don't say that to scare you, but you should know that I'll do anything for us to be together.

You don't have to worry about that, though. Leave the concerns for me. Just take care of yourself and know that I'll never believe a word they say about you. You're an angel. Sent from God up above to my mind every night that I dream about the two of us finally together. The rest of these people think they own some piece of you, but there's nothing left for them.

You belong to me.

Love,

Ian

CHAPTER 23

Mae

WE LINGERED WELL PAST DINNER on the beach. The people surrounding us packed up and left, leaving us with only each other to observe. Dalton hadn't been lying; he loved the coast. He was in the water, lying in the sun, and happy the entire day. He pulled me into his ecstasy with him, and like Mt. Hood, I wanted to stay forever.

I read the cheesy novel he'd picked up for me in the hotel lobby between short naps as the sun lavished us. It'd been years—possibly a lifetime—since I'd felt this relaxed and safe and loved.

The sun glistened off the calm, vast ocean in front of us. The water was a stone gray and electrified when it bounced in the light. On the other side of the world, there was a woman in an overcrowded raft terrified of her future. She didn't have the money, the family, the choices I had.

"What are you thinking about?" Dalton asked and pulled me from the waters off the coast of Greece.

"Just that I'm here. With you. And there's some woman, who did nothing in her life to deserve her current situation, trying to escape oppression somewhere. I'm sitting on a beach, lounging in the sand, and she's fighting for survival. Our days are so different, and I don't know why." He stared at me until the words and thoughts crept back into my mind. "Sorry." I shook my head. "I'm sure you don't want to hear all of this."

Dalton rolled onto his side and stared me down before finally saying, "Of course I do." He shook his head in wonder. "Don't ever apologize for thinking about the world or caring for the people in it."

He was too much to ask for. Something—someone—completely different from the world I was trying to escape from. Dalton was part of my freedom. "Thank you, Mufasa."

"You're welcome, my little cub."

I wanted to call my brother and tell him I'd found a new home and it was wherever Dalton was, but there was still so much to deal with before my life could begin again. Victor was waiting for his contract to be signed. He would never tolerate my leaving the business, my leaving him.

Dalton took sand in his hand and released it down the center of my back. He did it again and again until there was a pile that he ran his fingers through and dusted off me.

"I'm not your sand castle."

"You are my toy." The words revived some diseased lump in my throat I'd buried since the last time Victor had said them to me. "What? I'm just kidding."

I tried to recover. It was Dalton. No one else. He shouldn't be punished for the sins of my past. "I know." I shook my head and tried to be *normal*. Dalton wasn't some depraved sociopath who needed to own me. "It's fine."

"What's fine? What did I even say?" The way he scrutinized me made me feel like I was damaged and he was doing the initial assessment to figure out why I didn't operate properly. This was why he shouldn't be in love with me. I'd been ruined years before he'd ever ridden into Portland.

"What are you thinking?" he asked. More like demanded.

"Nothing."

"Please don't do that, Mae. I can handle anything but you not telling me something."

"You're setting yourself up for disappointment."

"And you're trying to protect yourself from getting hurt. Neither of which is going to happen. Now, tell me what you're thinking."

"I was thinking how lucky I am to have met you."

He paused and let those words sink in. "Do you want to head back?"

"God, no, but we have to, I think," I said.

Dalton ran his fingers down the center of my back. "We can wait until the sun goes down and make love on the beach."

"And when we're arrested, do you think they'll put us in the same cell? Maybe we can make love there, too."

"Oh, I'd be a lucky prisoner. My friend, Paul, would be so jealous."

"Is he your roommate from college?"

"One of them. Not the one I bought the bowl for."

"What does Paul do for a living?"

Dalton thought for a moment and said, "He's in a little-known branch of the military."

"I didn't realize there was such a thing."

His pause was so slight that another person would have missed it, but I'd be scrutinizing every breath he took since he'd said he loved me. I was waiting for him to take it back. "Let's get out of here."

Dalton drove while I sang along with the radio. We traveled twenty miles away from the coast and stopped for gas at a quiet station that felt in the middle of nowhere compared to the congestion of the waterfront towns.

"I'm going to get a snack," I said and left Dalton pumping gas.

The crackling sound of tires pressing against loose gravel caught my attention because there were no moving cars near me. I stopped walking and listened for the sound in the darkness, but it stopped.

"You okay?" Dalton asked from the car.

I nodded and smiled over my shoulder at him. "Just listening."

I grabbed a bottle of water and perused the snacks for something

Dalton might like and that would sustain us on our depressing drive back to Portland. I wanted to stay on the road with him and never settle in one place. He was the first man I'd ever felt safe with. Neither my father, who'd hit my mother when he'd been drunk, nor Victor Addario, who'd possessed me more than protected me, had ever made me feel intact the way Dalton did.

Salty, crunchy, healthy . . . The convenience store had a nice mix of chips, but nothing that was exactly what I wanted. I almost gave up, but finally my attention fell on the bright yellow bag of peanut M&M's. I raised my eyebrows at the perfect snack for the moment.

"Yum," I said as I lifted them off the shelf and held them in front of me.

The images clicked together and faded. They moved forward and retreated, but I chased them in my mind until I finally came up with one word: Denver. From there, I pieced together where I'd seen Dalton before. He'd been in the gift shop of the Four Seasons Hotel in Denver. I forced air down my throat and into my lungs. I dropped the candy to the counter and fled out the back entrance of the store.

I ran right into Dick and bounced off him into Alex's arms. Alex held me tight to his chest as I screamed and kicked at my disgusting former security detail.

"Stop it," Alex calmly said and held his hand over my mouth and my legs to the ground.

Dick's neck, his eyes, his groin—all the places I was going to strike when I got a limb free—ran through my mind.

"How's the vacation going, Isla?" Dick's tone was sinister and his brow was sweating.

Alex slowly removed his hand from my mouth.

"Still eating donuts, I see." Dick slapped me across the face with the back of his hand. The pain seared from my cheek to the back of both eyes and exploded there. "You're a dead man," I spewed and pushed against Alex's arms around me. "Victor will kill you for touching me."

Dick leaned in until his breath hurt the side of my face he'd just slapped. "Who says he'll know? Maybe you and I will find a quiet place somewhere, and I'll stick my fat dick in your foul little mouth."

"Come on now," Alex said.

Dick looked from my lips to my eyes. His face twisted in a monstrous way that rendered him unhuman in my heart.

"You should have listened to the lady." All three of us shut up at the sound of Dalton's voice behind us.

Dick raised his eyebrows and tilted his head. He almost smiled. His expression was a warning of the deranged ugliness of the next few hours of my life. "What did you say?" He twisted to face Dalton.

"Remember me? I'm the guy Addario hired to do your job." I leaned back at the mention of Victor's name from Dalton's lips. The two wouldn't connect in my mind. Dick's face was turning a deep shade of red. His eyes were bulging with anger. "And I *said*, 'you should have listened to the lady.'" Dalton never glanced my way. He focused solely on Dick without an ounce of exertion.

Dick huffed.

"You're a dead man." Dalton lunged forward at Dick, landing a blow to the center of his chest that launched him onto the ground unconscious at my feet. "And you're next," he said and pointed at Alex.

"Dalton, no," I pleaded as Alex pushed me away. "He's good. He'd nev—" I tried to get the words out, but Dalton snapped Alex's neck, and he fell to the ground next to Dick.

Dalton's chest heaved next to me. I covered my mouth with my hands to keep from screaming.

"I'm not going to hurt you," Dalton said in a gentle voice. One impossible to connect to what I'd just witnessed.

"Are they dead?"

"If not, they will be."

"I . . . I . . ." I couldn't put a complete thought together in my mind.

"Mae," he said, but I couldn't take my eyes off the bodies between us. "Mae, look at me." He held my arms and shook me a little. His voice was slow and calm when he said, "We have to move fast. Go get in the car and meet me twenty miles east of here on the side of the road. Keep the doors locked. I'll be a little while and I'll be on foot when I get to you."

"How . . ." Questions tried to form in my mind. What about the car? And *them*? I glanced behind him.

Dalton ran his hands up and down my arms. "Just go. I'll be there soon. Don't be scared, Mae."

I shook my head. What would be scary?

"Go now. I'll be there soon."

I stepped back and tried to take in Dalton . . . and Dick . . . and Alex on the ground beside us. "Alex wouldn't have hurt me," I said, but I was telling myself more than Dalton. I needed to know I could still tell if a person was good or not.

"He knew too much."

I digested each of his words and tried to understand. I turned away from Dalton and walked to the car. The guy working behind the counter in the convenience store was eyeballing me from the window. I waved to him with the same lightness as a woman who'd just peed in the woods behind the station. He nodded and went back to stocking waters in the refrigerator.

I drove away from the pump the same way I would have if everything were okay. If I hadn't just seen my new boyfriend murder two men sent for me from hell. When I cleared the area near the gas station, I floored it. I was heading south, not east. I was getting the hell out of here and leaving Dalton and Victor and everyone else behind.

He was a part of this. He'd been following me since Denver. *I'm the guy Addario hired to do your job.* I slammed my hand against the steering wheel. Since New York. I was an idiot. He was a liar and a manipulator. He was being paid by someone or he was sick, and I was tired of trying to figure out exactly what was wrong with me in order to escape them.

The green fur that covered the forest surrounding me was hidden by the night. Past the enchanting wet moss, there was only darkness. Gone were the skyscrapers of trees Dalton and I had stopped and taken pictures against on our way to the coast. They were replaced by shadows and dead men and secrets.

I exhaled and lightened my foot on the accelerator. I stopped the car in the Wheeler marina and rested my head on the steering wheel. I listened for that little voice I'd ignored for so long. It'd been silenced by corruption and greed and my own abandonment.

Things didn't add up. If he was on Victor's payroll, why kill Dick and Alex? Why hadn't Victor already found me to torture me back to him? Victor always got what he wanted, certainly when he was paying for it. Dalton was the only man I'd ever met who could possibly stand up to him. He was definitely the only one who would ever see the need to. Most people followed men like Victor around hoping to catch the scraps of their success and fame. Dalton was completely uninterested. You can't fake that.

I stared out the car window, closed my eyes, and listened to the emptiness around me.

He was different. The armrest I held his hand upon. The radio we listened to. The seats we'd spent hours in traveling across the state of Oregon were all safe. He'd never hurt me. Not until I heard him say he worked for Victor.

I didn't want to escape Dalton.

He held my hand and didn't push for what the others took from me. Dalton waited, without a word, for me to tell him what I needed from him. With him was the safest place I'd ever known, including tonight.

Without a word of the truth to rely on, I knew in my heart he was good. He wasn't like the others. He couldn't be, because I loved him.

No matter how far away I drove or how much I believed about him, I loved him. I couldn't get him out of my head, and the words my sister-in-law had said rang loudly. She'd been right. I'd never been in love before. I'd never even felt safe with a man . . . before Dalton.

I waited for some memory to dispute the facts, but the only thing I believed was that he loved me, too. I turned the car around and headed back toward the gas station, where I picked up the Route 26 toward Portland. About fifteen miles down the road, I pulled up alongside Dalton walking by himself.

I rolled down the window and said, "It's not safe to be walking out here alone."

"I thought you'd gone."

"I did." His eyes were filled with exhaustion and pain. "But for once, I came back."

"I'll drive. You've been through enough."

I stepped out of the car and met Dalton in the beam of the headlights. Dalton's sight fixed on the side of my face Dick had slapped. His jaw clenched. "He should have suffered more," he said and released the darkness within him between us.

I pulled his hand down. It was dirty and rough, and I squeezed it between mine.

Dalton drove us toward home. He constantly checked the rearview mirror for cars and inspected each one that drove anywhere near us. I didn't let go of his hand until we reached a Hampton Inn off the highway.

"Did you check into the hotel on the coast as Danielle Morris?" he asked.

"How did you know?"

He lowered his head, not able to face me. "I'll tell you everything, but first we need a room." He pulled out his wallet and an ID and credit card from the last pocket hidden behind the card slots. The name said John Ward.

"Nice to meet you, John." My words were flat. We were too far gone for teasing.

"It's the only identification that no one knows of. You should wait here."

"No. I'm with you."

He nodded. "You are. Let's go check in."

I grabbed my overnight bag from the back seat. Dalton took it off my shoulder, and we walked into the Hampton Inn like any other couple exhausted from our long drive, but we were only beginning to know our torture.

CHAPTER 24

Dalton

MAE SEEMED TINY IN THE elevator. Her tanned legs sticking out from her gray hoodie alluded to our drive east from a weekend on the coast. The sunglasses she wore, even though it was dark, covered the fact that we'd stopped vacationing hours ago. The images of that animal slapping her fought to the surface of my anger. I'd never killed someone before out of anger. Duty? Yes. Anger? No. We were trained never to let emotions into a mission. Now, I could only stare at her and fight through every emotion I'd avoided the last few years.

She must hate me, or worse, she was probably frightened of me. She didn't talk on the ride. I couldn't tell what she was thinking. I feared I was going to lose her.

She walked next to me without touching me as we counted off the rooms to number three forty-seven. It was at the end of the hall that I stared back down to confirm no one was watching us. I opened the door, and she walked in. An ominous silence followed in her wake with me drowning behind it.

I could smell those pigs on my clothes. Their sweat on my hands. I needed to clean up before I went anywhere near her. "Do you mind if I shower?"

She closed the curtains over the windows and turned to me.

"No."

"Will you be here when I get out?"

"Yes. We need to talk."

Yes. We did. I left her and took off my clothes in the bathroom. The thick odor of smoke filled the room as I tossed them in a pile on the floor. Any evidence of me in their car would be unrecognizable. Burnt to oblivion like the vehicle's interior and the charred remains of the men who dared to touch her. I ran the water until it was almost unbearably hot and stepped into the nondescript shower. The water washed away the stench of the last few hours and loosened the muscles in my back. I stood with my head hanging low and my back to the stream. I couldn't lose her. I had no choice.

"Dalton." I hadn't heard the door open. She'd stolen my senses.

Mae pulled back the curtain a few inches and stepped into the shower with me. Her arms were bruised where he'd held her while she was hit. Her cheek was cracked and bruised, and the blood vessel in her eye had shattered, covering her beautiful green eye with blood. I wanted to reach out to her, but I was afraid to touch her. Petrified by the notion that I could possibly hurt her more.

She lowered her head and looked at the wet floor between us. Her breasts rose when she sighed. I knew she was about to leave forever. I didn't blame her. I wasn't angry. The only thing I felt was lost.

She stepped closer to me and jerked her head back when the water hit her face. I moved to the left and shielded her from the stream. Mae took the soap and ran it across my chest and over my shoulders. Her eyes followed the movements of her hands. Everywhere she touched, my hardened body turned to warmth. The heat rushed through me to every corner of my being because she was next to me.

"Turn around," she said.

Mae washed my back all the way to my ankles. She kneeled down and washed my feet.

When she stood, I faced her. "Are you okay?" she asked. I nodded, still unable to find the words to beg her not to leave. "Because I need you."

With the soap still in her hand, I forced her to the back wall of the shower and kissed her. I drowned out every sin I'd ever committed with the taste of her lips and the touch of her tongue. She was my heaven.

I didn't let her speak. I wanted the air from her lungs, the heat from inside her. I wanted to take it all so there was nothing left I didn't have of her. The thought of losing her had left me crazed. Someone touched her. She'd been slapped. I would kill every single person who ever dared to lay a hand on her again. Because somehow, she'd become the only thing that mattered in the world to me.

Her grip on my dick brought me back to her naked in front of me. I let my head fall back and the water run over my face. She was right here. Not going anywhere without me.

"What would have happened if I hadn't found you?" I knew she thought I was talking about tonight, but I was asking about all of it. If I hadn't been assigned to watch her. If she'd somehow gotten out of New York without Paul knowing. If I hadn't put the GPS on her car. Where would I be right now . . . without her?

"You did find me," she said and rested her other hand flat on my heart. She was talking about all of it, too.

She held me close and stroked my dick between us. She tilted her head until her heavy breaths reached my ear and set me on fire. I lifted her against the wall and took exactly what I needed from her.

I pulled out and came on the shower floor beneath her as Mae clung to me. The water hit my back, the steam broke and let the air chill us, but I couldn't release her from between the wall and my body. It was the only place I knew she was protected . . . that she was mine.

"I feel this overwhelming need to possess you."

"You can," she said and ran her hands through my wet hair. I placed her back on her feet and she faced me. "Only when we're making love. You can have all of me then." She stood on her tiptoes and kissed my cheek as if we were sane. "I'm going to get dressed."

Mae moved about the room without saying a word. I watched her. Exactly how I'd been paid to. She was distracted. I could see her clever mind twisting and turning through the events of the last few weeks.

"Who are you?" she finally asked and climbed into bed. I was propped up on pillows against the headboard, and she sat facing me.

"I'm Dalton." I ran my hand up her arm. "This is real, I promise."

"Victor Addario hired you?" The truth was hurting the inside me. It should have been exercised like a demon days ago.

I nodded.

"I'm an idiot."

"No you're not. You're brilliant. I can't believe you've made it this far."

"Where have I made it to? The Hampton Inn alongside a highway in Oregon."

"Mae—"

"What do you know about me? Why did he hire you?"

"I know everything Addario told us, and I was hired to keep an eye on you through your contract negotiations."

She let her head hang low as she shook it. "I was a fool."

"I can help you." My chest shuddered with the truth. These were the words I'd wanted to say to her since I'd first spoken to her in the pot shop. "I can help you go wherever you want, and no one will ever be able to hurt you again."

"You underestimate *this*." She almost smiled, but it wasn't from joy. "What did you tell them? How much does he know?"

"I was taken off the job the day we left for Mt. Hood. I assume my superior provided him with all the information I'd gathered so far, including the identity you'd been using for all your financials. Who is Danielle Morris?"

"She's my sister-in-law's cousin, but we all spent the summers together when we were little. She gave me her entire wallet. Just like that. That's what it's like in North Carolina. The whole damn state has your back." She wallowed in her memories of her hometown. When she spoke of it, I heard nothing but love.

"Why didn't you stay there? Why Oregon?"

"I told you why. North Carolina wasn't far enough away, and the first place he'd look for me was my hometown. Everyone always goes home."

I started slow. "I understand leaving." I needed her to trust me, even though I'd been hired by Addario. "I wouldn't want to live that life either, but this is more than quitting a job and trying to start a new life. You're running . . . terrorized by something . . . or someone."

She shook her head and stared at the bed between us.

"Tell me, Mae." She was lost in her mind and left me trying to figure this out. "I just killed two people. I think I deserve to know why."

Mae stared at my chest while she thought. I didn't want her to choose her words. She didn't have to be careful with me. "Victor is twisted but manageable if he gets his way in the end. He relishes the chase but hates to lose." I stayed very still, willing her to continue. "He sent them to find me because he didn't like losing, but he would have killed the man you saw slap me, too. To Victor, Dick laying a hand on me would have been disrespectful to *him*, and that, in any form, would never be tolerated."

"Dick?"

"That's what I called him. It's not very nice." She wrung her hands. "We've always had a difficult relationship. Mainly because I caught him watching me change or touching my clothes. He's gross." She dropped her hands to her lap. "I'm not sorry he's dead."

I realized how tense I was when every muscle relaxed at her words. She wasn't angry or scared of me. She was still Mae.

"Victor is dangerous in his own way," she said.

"I've had a bad feeling about Addario since I met him."

"That's a good instinct. I wish Mama and I had it years ago."

I pulled her into my arms. If I'd known Mae a decade ago, both of our lives would have been so different. "So, Addario hired me because he thought you might leave?"

"He didn't think that. No one would think that I'd give up my career, but he was playing with fire, and something had to give." She thought for a second and then her expression softened before she said, "Victor is at least predictable." She ran her fingers up my arm. I felt like to distract me. "He gave me the world, and just like with all extravagant gifts, there were strings attached."

"Mae . . ." I wasn't sure what to say. She stopped talking, but her mind was wandering somewhere else. "If you want Addario to stay away from you, I'll make sure you never see him again." There was more to this than she was telling me, and I wanted to scream at her about it. My blood was boiling beneath the surface of my skin. Someone was hurting her, scaring her into isolation, and she refused to tell me.

Mae's fingers stopped at my wrist. She flipped my palm over and caressed the lines in my skin. "Victor didn't mention Ian?"

"No." Only she had ever said the name Ian while she slept, and I knew she'd kept the letters from him in her Bible. I shook my head.

"Up until I left the city, Victor was the least of my problems." Her gaze didn't falter. She only stared right through me as if she'd been waiting for this time to come and these were the lines she'd been practicing to say. "I was being stalked by a man named Ian." She let go, and my hand dropped to the bed. Frustration mounted in my chest. I could have protected her all these months. If Addario had hired me in the first place, she wouldn't be on the run now. "I told Victor he was getting closer. Bolder. He frightened me. Victor promised he'd protect me. He swore he'd never let Ian near me, but I was being hunted."

"What's his last name?"

Her head shook slightly, but instead of facing me, she stared at the wall beside us. "All we know is Ian." She refocused on me. "He's left me letters. Some he'd written while he sat right next to me in restaurants and bars, but I don't know what he looks like. I've never seen him."

"You must have. You just didn't realize it. Think back. Who scares you? Who haunts you in your dreams? What do *they* look like?"

Her tiny laugh was full of horror. I was an infant in the story of Isla Monroe. "He's taller than me, but who isn't?"

Good point. "Is he as tall as me?"

"No," she said and surveyed my body. "At least, I don't think so. I've never actually seen him." She sat and thought for a minute. It reminded me of all the times she chose not to tell me the truth about her past. "I think he killed Cruz."

My head snapped up.

"He threatened to in one of his letters."

"Do you have the letters with you now?"

"No. I left them in Portland."

"We have to go back there."

She ran her finger over the sheet between us. She was completely lost in her own mind. "I know," she finally said.

CHAPTER 25

Dalton

I CIRCLED AROUND THE BACK of Mae's house, checking every window from the ground and peering into Bob's house. He was sitting in his chair watching television with a puff of smoke above his head. "Are you sure you're going to be okay?" The world had shifted around me. Sometime over the past few months, I'd gone from watching her to needing her.

"No one knows where I live, do they?" Something was different about Mae, too. She wasn't young and afraid anymore. She was calm and resigned . . . the quiet from it was torturing me.

"Not your exact location. Just whose credit card you've been using, so don't use it anymore."

"I'm going to mail it back to her," Mae said and unlocked the deadbolts on the side door of her house. I inspected the knob, the doorjamb, and the staircase leading to her apartment. "Do you want to come in?"

The significance of her offer made my heart swell in my chest. I wanted to be invited in in every way, but first I had to meet with Wright, who was sitting on the front porch of my house. He sat on the chair, rocking as if he weren't capable of killing someone at any minute. He'd smiled when we pulled up. "I have to go see someone. I'll be over in a few minutes if that's okay." I stepped back, not wanting her to kiss me.

The movement registered in Mae's mind. I watched her put the pieces together. She tipped her head to Wright over my shoulder. "Is he involved with your work?"

"Yes. He's my boss." I touched her stomach where Wright couldn't see. "And he's not very pleased with my performance recently, so this could be a loud, but short conversation."

"Will you be fired?" she asked and stared me right in the eyes.

"It doesn't matter." I let my hand fall back to my sides. "I'll be over soon."

I stood back as she walked into the house and waited for her to lock the door. She was safe, and now I had to go deal with Wright.

He stood when I crossed the street. "She's lovely," he said without an ounce of admiration in his voice. Wright was married, but he never spoke of his own wife. I'd met her several times and had no doubt he loved her, but to him, business was separate from love. To me, too, until Mae had decided to drive across the country.

"Thanks. Want to come in?"

"Of course." He followed me inside. I switched on the lights. I'd only been gone a few days, but the house felt totally foreign without Mae somewhere nearby. I missed the honey citrus scent of her and the way her hair fell to the side when she tilted her head.

"I'm sorry," I said to Wright. He deserved more, but that was all I could muster at the moment. I had nothing to offer him that didn't include Mae.

"I know." He put his hands in his pocket and walked near the windows. "I underestimated your involvement with this woman. I should have trusted your instincts. I owed you more."

"I'm pretty sure I'm the one with the debt to repay."

He almost smiled. I found myself backing up to sit down. "What now?" he asked, but I had no answers.

"She's still in danger. I can't leave her."

"Is it something the firm can help her with?"

"I'm not sure. When we're done here, I'm going over—"

A shot rang out through the night air. Wright and I both froze and listened before I flew out of my living room and leaped over the railing of my front porch.

Mae's door was locked. Her curtains were still drawn. The muscles in my chest were strangling my heart.

"Mae," I screamed toward the second floor of the house. "Mae!"

I punched my hand through the glass of the door and unlocked the deadbolts. Blood ran down my arm as I took the stairs two at a time to get to her.

"Mae," I yelled once more and opened the door to her apartment, ignoring any recognition of the danger beyond it or the lifetime of training I'd had to deal with it. Baseballs congregated on the floor by the door, and it registered that the door had been unlocked. I stared at the balls for a millisecond. Someone had entered before me. He'd been in here when she'd come home.

Mae was standing in the living room with a gun in her hand. She glanced back at me when I walked in. "He said he's with you," Mae said and waved the gun toward her bedroom.

I walked over to her and touched her shoulders and her arms. I needed to confirm she was still here. She flipped over my arm and examined the gash from the door's glass downstairs. Her eyes, wide with terror, reminded me of the shot.

I turned away from her and saw Paul writhing on the floor, clutching his shin that was oozing blood. "What the fuck?" I said.

"She shot me!"

"He was in my bedroom," she said pointing the gun at Paul again.

I took the gun from her hand and watched Paul rock back and forth on the floor.

"He said he's here to see you," Mae repeated.

"First, I get hit in the balls with a baseball, then this crazy bitch shoots me."

She walked over to him like she was going to kick his teeth in.

"You were in my house."

"I'm calling Wright." I didn't have my phone, though. I'd run over here without a thought for what I might need besides Mae.

"Call an ambulance," Mae said, but we didn't go to regular hospitals and we didn't involve the police. It just made more work for us.

"Can I get a towel or something?" Paul asked from the floor. His blood-covered hand was losing the battle against his entry wound. He tried to sit up, but toppled over with his face twisted in pain.

Mae rolled her eyes and grabbed a towel from the hook on the bathroom door.

"I mean, seriously. Can a guy get a second to explain himself before you fucking shoot him?" Paul said as the kitchen door swung open, and Mae tensed at the sound.

I raised my hands to calm her. It was Wright with his weapon drawn.

"Do you see what I mean? This is not normal. She's a loose cannon."

"Shut up, Paul, before I let her shoot you again."

"Right. This is my fault."

Wright entered the room. Everyone morphed into a silent mound. He scrutinized the situation. "What the fuck?"

I half smiled and said, "She shot him."

Wright's eyebrows rose as he took in Mae's petite appearance. "I don't believe we've met. I'm Joseph Wright."

"Mae." She almost smiled. "Pleased to meet you."

"I must say, foreign nations, heads of corporations, and oil-rich sheiks have never caused as much havoc in my business as you have."

"It was never my intention."

"Of course. I'm not blaming you." His stare fixed squarely on me. Wright walked into the living room and made a phone call. His words were too low to hear, but I knew he was arranging for Paul to be transported for medical care somewhere.

I put Mae's gun down on the nightstand. "Where did you get this?"

"It came with the car I bought in North Carolina."

"Where did you keep it?"

She thought before she answered. A chill ran down the back of my neck from her stare. "Why?" Her spine straightened. "Because when you were in here, you never found it?"

"It was before . . ."

"I didn't keep it anywhere. I carried it with me every day in case I needed it."

"Even when we went to Mt. Hood?" The idea that I could hurt her was inconceivable.

"Everywhere."

"I was just looking around, and then she came in. I was trapped in her carnival cave," Paul said from the floor.

"I knew someone'd been in here. I was paralyzed in the kitchen . . . until I heard German music playing from a phone."

I laughed. Almost uncontrollably. "I told you that woman would be the death of you."

"Yeah, well, I'm telling you now." He tipped his head to Mae. "This one's not too stable, either." He grumbled under his breath some more until two paramedics showed up with a gurney. They lifted Paul onto it and rolled him out and down the stairs. He'd have the bullet removed within the hour and be back at work tomorrow. Mae, Wright, and I were left with nothing but questions for each other.

"Can I see the letters?" I asked Mae, who was staring at the door I'd just closed behind Paul.

She handed me her Bible from off the kitchen counter. The folded papers stuck out every so often between the pages. She removed them one by one until five letters sat on the table in front of me. She laid them out, making sure the order was correct.

"They started out not too disturbing. In fact, had they come through my label, I would have never even seen them, but he always hand-delivered them." She picked up the first one and cringed as she read parts of it. "This one he left for me in Baltimore." She handed it to me.

I re-read it with a sick feeling growing inside me. "This bar he mentions . . ."

"I went to a local bar after the show. I was supposed to be meeting a few of the dancers there, but I was the first one to arrive. You wouldn't have even recognized me. I was all bundled up. It was last fall and a cold night on the harbor. I sat at the bar and ordered a drink." She shook her head, defeated. "I don't remember anyone around me. I'm always trying so hard to not be seen, I never noticed anyone else."

"This one mentions Christmas . . ." I held up another one.

She nodded and took the paper from my hand. She sat and read it silently. "My last show of the year was at the United Center in Chicago. I stayed at the Waldorf that night. There was a tree in the courtyard. I stopped and took a minute to admire it . . ." She choked up a little. "It was beautiful. I missed Mama, but I don't remember anyone near me who I didn't know."

Wright walked back into the room.

"Can I keep this?" I asked her, and she nodded.

I handed it to Wright. "Any way we can have the lab do a rush on this? She's being stalked."

He ignored the paper in his hands and regarded Mae. Wright was gentle with her in a way I'd never seen him before. "I'm sorry."

Every day that Mae had peeked out her window to see if her stalker was watching flew through my mind.

"Me, too," she said.

Wright read the letter while I picked up the others and read them. Sick fuck Ian was. "This one says you two were interrupted."

"Yes." She rubbed the back of her neck. She was tensing again at the memories we were forcing her to share. "He was in my dressing room in Australia. There was a rain delay during my concert. I went there to wait out the storm." She was lost inside her mind. "I was pouring myself a glass of water." She stared at the letter in Wright's hands. "He said, 'Isla,' from behind me and then put his hands around my neck." She exhaled. "Alex walked in. He ran out." Mae shivered when she spoke. "Alex said he didn't get a good look at him from behind. The letters were all we've had to go on." The fear in her eyes made me want to pick her up and carry her away right now.

"How long have you had these?" Wright asked.

"That one since last October. I get a new one every five or six weeks. They were beginning to terrify me." Mae took the dishtowel hanging from the oven handle and wrapped it around my forearm. She stared into my eyes until I thought she was apologizing for something that wasn't her fault.

"Did Addario know about this?" he asked her.

"Of course."

"Why would he leave that out of the file?" Wright was thinking aloud more than asking.

"He also gave us the wrong birth date for her," I said.

"That was me. There was a mistake on my original birth certificate, and Mama never fixed it. She said I'd get my license sooner and that summer birthdays were no fun for kids." Mae half laughed at the memories. "I guess she never minded living a lie. I never gave Victor the right one."

Wright studied her without questioning.

"I couldn't let him have everything. He took every piece of me and created Isla Monroe. I kept my real birthdate for myself."

Two men came in with cleaning supplies and began removing Paul's blood from the floor. Mae moved out of the way. She stood in the living room and stared out the window. The curtains were opened wide.

"I need to meet with you," Wright said to me. "About Tel Aviv, if you have a few hours."

"Go," she said from the other room. She never turned away from the window. Her hands were balled into tight fists at her sides. "I'll be fine here."

I wasn't sure I was going to be unless I was near her. I walked toward her, but she met me in the middle of the room and kissed me.

"I'm okay. What could go wrong?"

I kissed her again. "Nothing. I'm sure." I needed a few moments to think about everything that had happened. I wanted to sort out all the information and figure out where Mae and I should go next.

"Leave the gun," she said. I realized how far ahead of me she was when it came to this. She'd been thinking through these details since she'd left New York.

A chill ran down my back. It was going to take a lot for Mae to ever feel safe again.

CHAPTER 26

Dalton

MAE SPENT THE AFTERNOON AT the pot shop. She'd said help-ing Rita set the store back up kept her from thinking. I walked her home to her apartment at ten. Everything appeared to be back in order, except Mae. She walked around touching knobs and moldings as if she was putting together a puzzle in her mind.

"Are you sure you're okay? You've been through a lot," I said, and she only smiled in return. "We could go to a hotel. Maybe something downtown, or go back to the coast. There's nothing keeping us here."

"No. I love this street."

I felt her moving away from me. She barely looked me in the eyes. She was lost in her head. I was worried she was wandering through thoughts of leaving me. Going over the events of the night before without talking about them.

"I don't want to lose you," I said. Mae stared at the door, the window, and the wall next to us. Anywhere but near the words that were tearing apart the two of us. "I meant what I said at Cannon Beach, and I know that you love me, too."

She stopped moving, stood in front of me, and let her hands fall to her sides. "How long were you following me?" There was a twinge of anger in her voice. The evidence of betrayal that I'd hoped she wouldn't latch onto. "What did you see?"

I leaned against the doorjamb between the kitchen and living room. "I saw . . ." I was part of the group of people who were hurting her. I fought past the guilt of betraying her and all the other idealistic notions about my work. I would only focus on Mae because she was all that mattered. "I saw you shopping in Tennessee and how kind you were to everyone you met in the mall." She stayed completely still and watched me. "I listened in Denver to your God-given gift and the way you shared it with the congregation. I learned you had something to confess."

She lowered her head and stared at the floor between us.

"It was there I realized you're human. Not just Isla Monroe, a spoiled, rich girl I was forced to follow." I moved closer, and she tilted her head to the side. "I saw you take care of Bob with dignity and respect, and I watched this entire street fall in love with a young angel they called Mae."

I closed the distance between us and held her face in my hands until she finally made eye contact with me. "But mainly, I just watched the most fearless woman I've ever laid eyes on take back control of her life." I kissed the side of her face. "And she inspired me to do the same."

She reached up and pulled my hands down. "I never lied to you," she said. Disgust was laced in every word.

"Did you always tell me the truth?"

"I didn't lie."

"I had no choice. I didn't even want this assignment, and I certainly wasn't planning on falling in love with you."

She walked in a circle around the apartment. Stopping at the front windows to peek out and then focusing her attention on the kitchen behind me. The pitching machine stood still facing the door, and the curtains kept out the light. She might have loved this street, but her apartment was a cell she'd been encased in for the past couple of months.

I followed her into the bedroom. I wasn't sure what to do, what she wanted me to do, but she was making me nervous. She paused and ran her fingers across her barren nightstand. Mae tapped her fingers on the wood and surveyed the floor around the furniture.

"Stay with me," she said. She almost whispered it. "Stay in my bed." The invitation had some greater significance to Mae than me. She brightened at the invitation. "In the sheets I picked out and put on it. In the apartment I rented in the city that I chose." She was almost playful again. "Be part of that, with me."

She tilted her head to the side in a way that would guarantee I'd do anything she asked. Her power over me should have bothered me, but it made me feel alive. Loving someone was exhilarating, even if that someone shot people in their bedrooms and attracted killers at night.

"I'd love to," I said and followed her to her bed.

We didn't make love. She curled up in my arms the same way she had the first night at the cabin. I slept with the same peace I had that night. Mae fell asleep. She took one last deep breath and then sank onto me with even exhales. I stopped playing with her hair for fear I'd disturb her.

"Where is it?" she mumbled. She rolled back and forth, saying, "Tell me."

"Mae, wake up. You're having a bad dream." I shook her shoulders.

She thrashed in my arms. "Where is it?" she said and rolled on top of me.

"Mae. You were asleep." I held her tight.

She moved to the side of the bed and switched on the light. She didn't say a word as her gaze searched all around the room before she stared at her nightstand. I thought she was confirming we were safe, but when she turned off the light again, she whispered, "Bastard," before lying back down.

Isla, my love,

I'm writing this while sitting at the counter in your kitchen. Your home is exactly how I imagined it would be. Beautiful. Your view of the park is what I would have chosen for you if I'd been included in the search. There are no pictures of us, no sign of our love. I was disappointed until I found where you kept my letters. God will bless us, in the same way he'll forgive me.

You've been home almost a week. I came here to talk to you about Cruz Allen. The reporters say you are engaged, but that's impossible. You love me. This must be more of Cruz's lies. He hasn't been here in a few days. Once I move in, he'll never be back.

Summer is coming and now that your tour is over, I think it's time that we're together. I'm putting the final pieces of my plan together. You'll be the first to know when it's complete. You've waited too long for this, too. Thank you for your patience, Isla. You are a gift.

Your doorman, of course, tried to keep me away, but nothing—no one—ever will. I've promised you we'll be together for all eternity, and we will be. We have Victor Addario to thank for it. He finally helped me get into your apartment. All I had to tell him was that I needed to be close to you. I told him how I've watched you for months and how I protect you. Mr. Addario said he'd heard about me and knew exactly who I was. He understands what you mean to me and how you're nothing without me. I always hated the way he stood so close to you and put his hand on your back, but now I'm appreciative. He must love you, too. As a father, of course.

I left you a surprise in the bedroom. I hope you like it.

With the love of a warrior,

Ian

CHAPTER 27

Isla

"I NEED TO SEE YOU," I said into the phone and tried to keep my lunch down.

"Isla, you have no idea how long I've been waiting for this call." Victor's breaths heaved into the phone. "I'm in Oregon. Tell me where you are."

I peered out the window again. The man was still there. Standing next to a car two houses down from Dalton's. He kept one eye on Jack 'n' The Weed Stalk and the other on my house at all times. I was trapped. Exactly how he liked me.

The average build, blond, curly haired man that I'd seen so many times before, but never really noticed because he was always among the others. It's not that I recognized him. The familiar feeling of being hunted sank down to my knees. The way he stared up at my window without reacting to the wind or the sun or the cars driving by him. He was fixated, and now I knew what he looked like. How long would he let me stay in here? How many states would he follow me to? Without speaking to him, I knew his name was Ian.

"Why are you in Oregon?" I asked Victor. "Thirsty for some craft beer?"

"I came to get you, of course. Surely you're ready to come home."

"Why didn't you just send the goons you always had follow me around?"

There was nothing but silence on the other end of the line. He'd sent them, but they'd disappeared. The same way I had a few months ago. Victor Addario had to be tiring of this game we were playing. He liked the chase, but only when he won in the end.

"I wanted to see you myself. I need to talk, Isla." The name, spoken from his lips, churned the contents of my stomach again. "I miss you."

Victor'd let Ian into my life in New York City. Now, he was going to have to deal with him. "I miss you, too, Victor. I've been staying at a cabin on Mt. Hood. Would you be able to come up here? It's a bit out of the way, but we'll have some privacy. You know how I've needed that lately."

"Yes," he said, but the enthusiasm drained from his voice. "Whatever you need, Isla. It's yours. I just want you to come home."

"And sign your contract."

"No. I don't care anymore if you sign it. I'll leave my wife. We can go away somewhere together. Whatever will make you happy is what I'll do. I just want you to come back. Isla, I need you." The thought of being happy anywhere near Victor was absurd.

"Meet me at the Clackamas Lake Historic Ranger Station at eight."

"Is that near the Kimpton Hotel?"

I laughed a little and hoped he'd heard me. Tonight, I would be making the decisions. "It's a lifetime away. I'll see you tonight, Victor."

The meager furniture in my apartment had been pushed to the side for Paul's gurney. The paint tub no longer rested beneath the window. I pulled back the curtains and hooked them on the ancient holders to the sides. It was time to let the light in. I'd have to leave my fortress to ever truly be free.

I searched the street below me and found nothing out of the

ordinary except Wright moving around in Dalton's apartment with him. Mama's words rang through my head: "A man can't set you free—only you can." Dalton was going to be impossible to eliminate from my plans, but he couldn't be a part of them. Someday, I'd give him the truth I owed him, but that was not today.

I texted him: *I'm going to the grocery store. There's no food here.*

Dalton texted back within seconds: *Wait and I'll go with you.*

It's just groceries, was all I responded.

If I made it sound mundane enough, maybe I'd convince him that it was. Dalton thought I was fragile, shaken by Dick's death, but I'd dreamed about it the first time Dick had lingered too long at my costume fitting. He hadn't deserved to live. Alex was different, but I couldn't think about him until after tonight. Then I'd mourn Alex and hopefully some others.

I found the heart necklace Ian'd left on my pillow the day Victor had let him into my apartment. The moment Victor'd fed me to the wolves. I fastened it around my neck. It was the last time I'd be collared by fame. I left the house without scanning the block around me and every inch in and around my car. Tonight would be different. Starting with the menu. I took 12th Avenue south to Whole Foods. No expense would be spared for our last meal together. I drove slowly through the neighborhoods separating mine from Burnside Street and made a list in my head along the way.

Fresh pasta, sauce, perhaps some shrimp. Victor loved shrimp. Wine, of course. He often drank it at lunch. When I was seventeen, I'd thought it was the most romantic thing about him.

I breezed through the grocery aisles without an ounce of fear. I knew it would come later, but I had to focus on the details. I owed Victor that much. He always perfectly executed his plans.

"Have a nice night," the man checking me out said.

"Thank you. I plan on it," I said and carried my two bags to my car.

Just as I'd hoped, he was standing there. Three cars down. Not leaning on anything. Not sitting in his car. I'd feared I was wrong when I saw him from my apartment window, but deep down, I knew. He was in Portland, and from the look in his eyes, he was a tortured soul. The lonely guy who could just stand and watch me for hours. I stood very still. This wasn't how he'd planned things in his mind. I didn't want to upset him.

His eyes were filled with wonder. I stared back at him and smiled. I let my emotions die inside me. Tonight was about thinking. I could feel something tomorrow. I left my car behind and walked over to him. He rocked back and forth preparing to run, but he held firm. I took the last step to stand directly in front of him. He swallowed hard.

"Ian?"

He didn't respond. His eyes were wild. His gaze jumped to every feature of my face and glanced over my shoulder as if he might be taken into custody right from the Whole Foods parking lot.

"Is your name Ian?"

He nodded. Still unable to speak.

I lifted the bags a little higher. "I was hoping we could have dinner."

His breathing splintered to almost a pant before he finally smiled back at me. I didn't hate Ian, but the terror was seeping back in. The thoughts of his hands around my neck tried to penetrate my plan, but I pushed them to the back of my mind, where they'd have to stay for the remainder of the night.

"Yes. I'm Ian."

"Would you mind driving? I thought we could go someplace special . . . for a new beginning."

Exaltation covered his face as his gaze fixed on the necklace around my neck. He exhaled deeply all the months of being held behind a barrier or not allowed in. Ian had finally been invited into my life. In his mind, he always had been, but today in the Whole Foods parking lot, he truly was.

Ian took the bags from me and placed them on the floor of the back seat. He opened the door of his Ford Edge for me and watched me buckle my seatbelt. Ian was still trying to put all the pieces together in his mind.

I steadied my nerves. He couldn't sense anything but my openness. "Ready?"

"Yes," he said and practically ran around to the driver's side of the car.

What did one talk about with their stalker? He already knew so much about me, and I didn't really want to hear anything about him. A text came through from Dalton. *Where are you? Getting worried. Hungry. Want to touch you.*

I turned my phone off completely and threw it in my bag.

"Is this your first time in Oregon?" I asked.

Ian nodded without saying a word.

"How did you find me, Ian?" I liked to use his name. It made this seem less like a suicide mission in my mind. Ian and I were in this together. He couldn't hurt me if I said his name. "How did you know I was in Oregon?"

"I followed Victor Addario's army. That's how I always found you. They're careless."

He must have known what happened at the gas station. "Did you see . . . Were you with me when . . ."

"When that animal slapped you? Yes." His grip tightened on the steering wheel. "I wanted to kill him myself, but your friend did." He stumbled slightly over the word "friend."

"He's a good man. Like you. Someday I hope you'll get to meet him."

"I've been watching him. I don't like the way he looks at you."

I took silent, deep breaths and pushed Dalton from my mind. "You're very intelligent, Ian."

"Thank you. My mother always says that I'm smart."

I didn't want to talk about his mother or anyone else who truly loved him. "What's your last name? You never told me in any of the letters you wrote to me."

"It's Grayson, Ian Mitchell Grayson." He held out his hand. It laid between us like a burning piece of wood. If I touched it, I'd be hurt, but it couldn't be ignored.

I rested my hand in his and willed my stomach to settle. I could still call Dalton. I could text him and tell him to meet us at the cabin, but there was only one way this could end. I couldn't ask Dalton to kill again. The events of this evening wouldn't be so easily erased. Victor Addario would never just disappear. He loved all eyes on him.

"Where are we going?" Ian asked as I gave him directions.

"Someplace quiet that is just ours. Somewhere the rest of the world won't matter." I was careful to quote him exactly. His face lit up at my words. His breaths were shallow. I'd succeeded. In what, I wasn't sure.

We rode the hour and a half to Mt. Hood and the cabin. We parked out front. Images of Dalton waiting in the rain for me to shower tore at my resignation.

"Isla," Ian said and threw me back into reality with him.

"Yes?"

He'd grabbed the groceries from the back of the car. "You ready to go in?"

"Of course."

Ian followed me into the cabin I'd rented. Memories of Dalton were everywhere. The kitchen counter, the chairs, and the bedrooms I hoped to go nowhere near. I wanted to be home with him before midnight, but I couldn't escape him here. Love's grasp was stronger than a cage.

"Do you like to cook, Ian?"

"You know I'm terrible." His words were rushed with insult.

My movements slowed. He'd clued me into how this whole thing worked in his mind, and I needed to incorporate it into the next few hours.

I shook my head and laughed it off. "Of course. It's been too long."

I emptied the bags. Ian came up behind me. He stood perfectly still with his hot breath reaching the tips of my earlobes. I closed my eyes halfway and steadied myself on my feet. A wave of nausea followed his breath through my body. I kept moving for fear of what he was going to do next. If he touched me, I'd have to shoot him, and it wasn't time for that part of the plan.

"I bought your favorite," I said and prayed silently for some help. "Pasta."

Ian moved my hair to the side and ran his fingertips on the back of my neck. "Perfect."

I stepped away too fast and silently chastised myself. Ian and I were in this together. At least that was the way I needed him to see it. I selected the largest pot and filled it with water. I might need the boiling cauldron before the night was over.

"I brought you something," he said.

"You did? You're always so thoughtful. I need to talk to you about that."

Ian took a step back. The childish excitement over his gift drained from his face.

"Nothing serious. I'm just afraid Victor Addario has tried to take advantage of your kindness." Ian's expression twisted into a suspicious glare. "He's not like you, Ian. His motives aren't pure. He's evil."

"Mr. Addario helped me get close to you."

I nodded and stirred the sauce. "I know that's how it seemed, but he was actually trying to keep us apart. Victor—Mr. Addario—told me horrible things about you. He said you were dangerous and told me to run . . . from you."

"What?" Ian's sight dragged around every corner of the room, but mine stayed fixed on him. Anger seared off him when he stared at me again.

I fought back my debilitating fear and answered, "Yes." I steadied myself in his hateful glare and continued. "He said that you're insane and that I need to be protected from you. He swore he was the only man who could keep me safe." Ian Grayson may have been insane, but Victor Addario was a monster.

"He wouldn't." Ian's head was shaking against the logic that was fighting through his mind.

"I didn't understand what was happening until you left me the letter in my apartment that mentioned he'd helped you get in." I reached up and touched the necklace around my neck. "The day you left me this heart. Thank you for it, too."

"What did you realize that day?"

I rested the spoon against the side of the pot. "That Victor was telling us two different things. He'd told me that morning that he loved me and that he'd kill you to have me all to himself."

"No."

"He's a coward, though. He couldn't kill anyone. He's not you." I felt dizzy. I didn't want to hear it, but I had to know the truth. "He's more like Cruz Allen."

Ian laughed. It was a thin, veiled guffaw at my ex's demise. "To think people actually thought you were going to marry him."

"You're telling me." I laughed a little, too. "I could barely stand him."

"That's what he said right before I threw him down the staircase."

A deep pit in my stomach rolled up and lodged in the center of my throat. I couldn't move. Tears were filling my eyes. I wasn't going to be able to hide them. "Thank you," I managed to say and wiped a tear with the back of my hand.

"Don't cry. I'd do anything for you. That's love."

"Yes. That's what Victor Addario doesn't understand. He thinks he can control us with lies, but nothing can defeat the type of love we share. He said he's coming here. To talk about us."

"He'll die, too."

There were no words left that needed to be said. I continued to prepare dinner while Ian sat at the table and watched me as if I was a show on television he could rewind and play over and over again. I glanced at him twice. The second time, he was twirling a fork, pushing the tines into the wooden table and staring at me with his mouth open just a little. I promised myself that I wouldn't look again.

At seven minutes to eight, Victor's headlights traced the back of the room. They shut off with the engine of his car.

I froze in the center of the kitchen.

"I'm going in the back room. I want to hear what he has to say."

I could only nod in response. The table was set. My hands shook while I poured wine in the mugs Dalton and I had drank out of.

I was going to see Dalton again. I inhaled deeply and exhaled the stiffening fear.

Victor's steps echoed through the silent cabin as he approached the door. I could scream and tell him to run. I could run myself, but this cabin was where I was going to reappear. Ian promised me that.

"My love," Victor said and opened the door.

"Victor. You found it."

"I was glad I wasn't driving the whole thing in the dark." He took in the simplicity of the cabin and smirked at me. "You've picked quite a spot." He was back in control. It suited him. "Definitely not near the Kimpton."

"It has a certain personality. Don't you think? A story of its own to tell."

Victor ran his hand along the table and eyed the adjoining room. "Are there bedrooms here?"

"Are you tired?" I asked and poured the sauce over the pasta. I carried the plate to the table and set it down next to his wine. "Sit. Please. I think we should talk and eat."

"There are many things we should do, but we can begin with dinner if you'd like."

"Yes."

As I passed him, he reached up and grabbed my hair, pulling me by it back to him. He held me in front of him. I would have fallen except for his fist in my hair. I stifled the cry in my throat.

"Tonight, I'm going to show you what it feels like to be owned by me," Victor whispered in my ear.

I knew his dick was hardening in his pants just from the thought of what he'd do to me. I moved against his steely grip and whispered to him, "I'm counting on it."

Victor let go of my hair and sat. His satisfied grin spoke of his lengthy journey to Oregon to claim me once again. He placed his paper napkin in his lap and rested his forearms on the table. I rode the wave of Victor's psyche. It was as familiar as my childhood.

"Your fans miss you, Isla," he said and settled into a kind stare.

I sat across from him. "Why? They seem to be keeping up quite well." The fake Instagram posts and fictional news stories should have been enough to satisfy their curiosities.

"If you're talking about that dickless psycho who keeps leaving you letters, you know he's of no consequence. He comes with the territory."

What's a starlet without a stalker? Victor had used him like a sex tape or a wardrobe malfunction. But Ian wasn't just for publicity. Victor pulled the strings on him, too, in hopes I'd come running back to him in fear for my life. Instead of sending Ian to the police, he gave him a key to my home. Victor deserved this night even more than I did.

"Ian?" I said and watched Ian step out from the doorway behind Victor. His eyes were fixated on the back of Victor's head.

"He's a dead man if he comes near you again," Victor said. He paused, probably a reaction to what I was sure was a stunned expression on my face. Victor was confused, and that annoyed him. "What the hell is wron—"

Ian sprung forward. The tool he'd been working on for the last hour came into view as he wrapped it around Victor's neck. It was fishing line tied to a broken broom stick. He turned the stick behind Victor's choking head. Ian almost lifted Victor out of his seat with the force of his movements. Victor was defenseless. I was frozen by the sight of him weak and helpless. He only struggled for a moment before his body went limp across from me at the dinner table.

Ian kept tightening it until I feared he might sever Victor's head completely. He was lost in his grotesque task, and I didn't know what to do.

Ian glanced up and released his hold on the broom. He lowered his eyes to the ground in front of him as if expecting me to scold him, but I felt nothing but gratitude . . . and fear. I'd come to Oregon to find peace and had left a string of bodies behind me. No one would believe I'd killed Victor. I couldn't possibly have had the strength to defeat him. Not some pretty little pop star.

The sight of his lifeless body was like hot molasses being poured over my body. It slowly sank in with the pain and history of a tortured lifetime. I fought against the sensation. I had to be the one in charge. It was *all* part of a plan. "Are you hungry?" I asked Ian. I needed to draw his attention away from Victor. He had to stay calm.

"I never got to show you what I brought for you," he said and stepped away from Victor.

I was grateful to be able to look away. "Oh. I'm sorry. What is it?" I asked and moved toward my purse in the living room. One shot. That was all I needed, but instead of Paul's leg, it needed to go into Ian's brain. The man who'd stalked me for months had shown up and killed my dear old friend, Victor, and so I had no choice but to shoot him in self-defense.

Ian ran over to his backpack and searched through the main compartment until he held up the snow globe from my nightstand. He shook it and handed it to me. His expression was full of misplaced pride. The little girl's arms followed her song to the heavens.

I turned my back on him and watched the snow drift down

around the little girl and stick on her hair and fingertips. She was my last gift from my mother, and he'd taken it. She was trapped in this little globe like me with no place to hide. She'd told me he'd been in my apartment. When she went missing the other day, I knew Ian had found me. He was a bastard for taking her.

Ian brushed my hair off the back of my neck and placed his hands on both sides. Energy coursed through me from the locations of his fingers to my own clenched around the snow globe.

"I love you," he said.

My hands shook. I tightened the muscles in my arms to steady myself.

"We're going to be together now, Isla."

"My name is not Isla," I screamed at him and bashed the snow globe against the side of his head. I swung again, but he blocked my arm, and the little girl flew across the room.

Ian punched me in the face harder than I'd ever been hit before. A black light shot through my head with a pain searing behind it. I fell to the floor next to the couch and reached for my purse. He stepped on my wrist until I thought the bones were broken.

"That's enough," he said. "Game time's over."

Blood dripped from above my eyes. It fell over my lashes and down my cheek.

"I win," he said.

CHAPTER 28

Dalton

"WE'RE GOING TO FIND HER," Wright said. I wanted to punch him. He was barely exceeding the speed limit. I should have driven. I knew the roads better. He'd never been here. It was now dark, and he was behind the wheel because based on the way he spoke gently to me, I was crazy.

"She went to the grocery store. What the fuck?" I yelled into the passenger window.

"She's okay."

"I shouldn't have let her out of my sight."

"What are you going to do? Follow her around the rest of your life?"

"Maybe. It's been a good run so far."

"It could be nothing. Just a misunderstanding," he said and turned onto Route 42. He didn't know Mae. He didn't realize how careful and calculating she was. "This is the last place we had a signal from Addario's cell phone."

Wright could tell himself all he wanted that she was fine, but I knew she was in trouble. "Her car was abandoned in a parking lot. Her phone was completely off." I felt sick at every word. I'd watched her for weeks. I knew the rhythms of Ida Mae Malone. The possibility of this not working out okay was eating away at the inside me.

Wright answered his own phone that hadn't even rung.

"Yes," he said. "Uh-huh. Yes. Okay. Thanks." He hung up. "They finished the parking lot security footage. She willingly got into a Ford Edge with a guy about her age. Average build. Blond." He glanced over at me, but I was picking through every mental file of people I'd seen her with. Rita's nephew. Bob. Neither of which fit the bill. The other regular customers at the pot shop. Photos I'd seen of her brother. No one came to mind. "They're running the plates now."

"Thanks." I stared out the window.

"Are you going to make it if she's choosing someone over you?"

I closed my eyes and said, "No." She wasn't choosing someone.

His phone rang again. When Wright hung up, he said, "Ian M. Grayson. Last known Bogota, New Jersey. Ring any bells?"

A chill ran across my chest and over my thighs. I swallowed before I could speak. "He's the guy who left the letters."

"Oh." Wright accelerated and passed the car in front of us. At least we were finally on the same page.

Ian's Ford Edge rental was parked next to Addario's rental about thirty feet from the cabin.

Wright surveyed the yard through the front windshield and to both sides of the car. "Well, there goes the element of surprise." I grabbed the door handle and yanked it before he pulled me back. "Whoa. Let's not be stupid."

My chest heaved. If anything happened to Mae, I was going to burn this place down. I waited for movement inside the cabin. It was still, like my heart.

"I'm going to go wide around the back. See if I can tell where they're at in there. If they're even in there."

"I'm going through the front door and killing everyone but Mae," I said, not so under my breath.

"Great," Wright said and opened his door while barely making a sound. I took the gun off my calf and walked to the cabin. The sinking feeling I'd had the entire ride up had become a throbbing in the back of my head. This job was impossible with the addition of emotions. I'd be sure to mention to Mae how she'd fucked this up for me when we were sitting on a beach somewhere sipping mai tais.

Through the window, I could see Addario seated at the table. He was oddly still until I saw the broken stick twisted in the makeshift garrote around his neck. The throbbing fell from my head to my chest. My mouth was dry.

I couldn't see Mae anywhere else in the room. I opened the door and walked through it. I would rip Ian's arms off his body before lighting him on fire if he killed her.

"Mae," I called. She didn't answer, but I could hear a male's voice from the bedroom.

I walked through the first place we'd made love and listened as my hand rested on the door.

"I'm sorry, Ian. Maybe I'll see you in heaven," Mae said.

"Isla," he pleaded.

I opened the door slowly with my weapon drawn. Ian was on his knees on the floor. Mae was standing in front of him with a gun pointed at his head. She was bleeding. The blood ran down the side of her face onto her torn dress. She had fingernail marks running the length of her forearm. She kneeled in front of him.

"My name is not Isla," she said and pulled the trigger.

Ian fell over when the bullet hit him in the head.

Mae closed her eyes and lowered the gun to her side. She was battered and bruised, but the sense of terrifying hatred I'd carried with me on the ride to the cabin was replaced by the peace that surrounded her.

I lifted her into my arms and kissed the top of her head while my hands wandered over her shoulders and her arms. I needed to feel her to believe that she was still with me.

"Wow," Wright said from behind me. His single word was a testament to the carnage surrounding us. Furniture was out of place or on its side. The lamp from the nightstand was on the other side of the room with the cord and plug still in the socket by the bed. Books had been thrown from their shelves and the mattress was half hanging off the bed. Ian and Mae's time together had been violent. Destructively so.

I didn't respond to Wright. I only wanted to hold on to Mae for as long as she'd let me. I pushed her hair off her face and grazed the battered side. She winced from my touch causing the anger to burn inside me again. "Are you okay?" I asked. "Are you hurt anywhere else?"

"My stomach hurts."

I lifted her shirt. A bruise the size of a boot print was already forming. "My God, what did he do to you?"

She looked up at me with a blank stare. "He set me free," she said. She leaned over and picked up a bronze disc with a little girl statue attached to it. She held it upright. The little girl was singing with her arms above her head. I'd seen it before.

"Why did you kill him then?"

"He knew too much." Her gaze drifted around the room and landed back on me. "I have to call the police. You two should go."

Wright's eyebrows shot up in complete fascination. He was usually the fixer. The man with the plan, and this little pop star was taking over. "We can help you with this."

"I know." She shook her head. "I don't need any help." Her voice wavered a little at the end. She was on shaky ground. "Once I'm done with the police, this will all be over."

For the first time since I'd first laid eyes on Mae, I thought she might cry. Something inside me broke off and fought to be with her. I pulled her tight against my chest and held her there until she reached for her phone.

"I've got to go to the end of the road and call 9–1-1."

"Mae," Wright said from behind us. He was staring at Ian's body slumped over on the floor. "Why did you kneel down in front of him?"

She studied Ian, too. A cold demeanor descended around her. "So the angle would be correct. If you shoot someone on their knees, is it really self-defense?"

Wright never took his eyes off the body.

"I'll call you when I can," she said to me.

"That won't be necessary. Wherever you are, I'll follow."

She wiped away the tears with the back of her hand. "Thank you." She pulled out another letter from Ian. "Take this with you?"

"When did you get this?"

"The day I left New York."

"Why didn't you show it to me?"

"Because sometimes you have to let the evil in to fully escape it."

CHAPTER 29

Dalton

I WATCHED FROM THE SHADOWS as Mae was taken from the house. Hours I waited in the forest surrounding the cabin. When she was finally transported to the hospital in the back of a police cruiser, Wright picked me up on the side of the road, and we followed her.

He made some phone calls. Anyone local who could help us find out what was going on inside the emergency room. Mae being alone in there was killing me. According to Wright's source, local detectives were confirming her claims that she'd arranged to meet Addario in an out-of-the-way spot to discuss her contract and increased security against her stalker named Grayson. Shortly after Addario arrived at the cabin, Ian Grayson showed up with a gun, beat her, and strangled Addario. She fought for her life before fatally shooting him inside the bedroom.

My head spun at the details. If I hadn't been following her for so long, I'd never believed what she was capable of, but Mae could do anything. The police would underestimate her. That was one of the things she'd counted on.

After hours of questioning, and the receipt of the initial ballistics report, Isla was released to my waiting car at the back entrance of the hospital. Wright drove the crawling car through the exit and the throngs of reporters six-deep and leaning over the car while I held up a blanket in front of Mae.

"This was what your life was like in New York?" Wright asked her when we cleared the crowd.

"It was like this all over the world." She leaned her head on my shoulder. "I couldn't escape it," she said, but she had. Her eyes finally shut when I wrapped my arm around her and we were on the highway headed back to her beloved street.

We didn't speak of that night again. Mae woke hungry. I walked down to the café to get her pancakes to go. Our neighborhood remained peaceful. Rita, her nephew, Bob, and anyone else who recognized her from the news never told a soul where she was hiding. The people of Portland minded their own business and they loved Mae.

"Why do you think professional athletes aren't hunted the way other celebrities are?" she asked as she unplugged the pitching machine almost a week later. We'd spent the day lounging around her apartment. The time flew by when I was with her, even if we were lying on her couch reading.

"I don't know." It killed her that she still couldn't make sense of her old life.

"I mean, they're making millions of dollars. They're celebrities working for other's entertainment, but I couldn't tell you who one of them is dating or where they went to dinner last night."

"They're part of a bigger brand."

"Huh?" She stood straight.

"Professional football players, even the ones who make millions, are all a small part of the overarching brand of the NFL. We only hear about their personal lives when it suits the NFL. When their child is born minutes after a game, when they donate toys to the children's hospital. The NFL controls that brand." She played with her hair and concentrated on my explanation. "If they're arrested, they stand to lose everything, because the brand might drop them. If a celebrity gets arrested, it's publicity." I took her hand and kissed it. "For a singer or actor, they are the entire brand."

"A hundred million people follow me on Instagram, more than most of the world's leaders combined, and they've never heard one word that I've actually thought. It's insane."

"It's showbiz." The constant state of confusion had been with her since she'd been released from the hospital. "I guess it's like anything else. I don't want to hear my plumber's thoughts on the world. Just fix my sink."

"You also don't buy magazines to see what your plumber wore last weekend or who he's dating. Can you force a person to share their life and then dictate what parts?"

"I hope so," I said. I wanted her to share this life with me. All of it. "You're right."

She scrutinized every wall of her apartment that housed too many memories of the violence she'd endured over the last week. "I'm not sure that I am." She exhaled loudly. "Life's a choice." She was sinking deeper.

"Come to my house tonight. We can make dinner and go to bed early," I said.

Her shoulders sank at my suggestion. "You make it sound so easy."

"It is." Her eyes rolled ever so slightly at my words before she caught herself. "It will be. I promise."

I held out my hand to her, and Mae sighed. She slid hers in mine. We walked across the street to my house, where nothing bad had ever happened to her.

She sank into the red corduroy couch and rested her head on the pillow beside her. She lounged as if she'd been there a hundred times before. "Did you decorate this place?" she asked me while I searched the cabinets for food.

"No." I peeked from behind the wall and saw her rummaging through the magazines on the coffee table. None of which had my name on them.

"It's nice. Where did you live before you followed me to Oregon?"

"I was in the Middle East for six months before I landed you."
I laughed and hoped she still found me funny.

"Can you actually fix anything?"

I opened a bag of tortilla chips and brought them into her. "Like a broken heart?"

She smiled at me. Finally. "No. Like a broken door. Mine is still covered in plywood from where you broke in."

"Oh. Like a real carpenter."

"Yes. A real one."

"I don't know about replacing glass. We generally break it and leave."

"Of course. Where will you go next?" Mae's voice was flat again, as if the answer meant nothing.

I shook my head. She seemed so small sitting on the couch in my rented house. "I don't know. I have no plans. I want to spend some time with you if that's okay."

"Sure," she said and added, "Mr. Dalton," but I wasn't sure of the significance.

"Are you going back to New York?" She hadn't spoken a word about her former life since Addario had died. Her silence wasn't good. Victims needed to talk about their experiences. That night in the cabin had been gruesome and was trapped in her head ever since. "Back to singing?"

"Back to my old life?" She was often melancholy these days. I wanted to snap her out of it, but she wouldn't let me far enough in. We hadn't made love since our drive home from Canon Beach. Since she'd discovered I was one of the monsters she'd been running from. I was losing her. "It wasn't a life," she said while she stared at the ceiling.

"Build one with me."

She stood and put her hands on her hips. Her lips pressed into a fine line while she searched around the room for the answer to some question she refused to ask me for help with. "I have to go."

"No you don't." I could feel her moving away from me, and I had to stop her. "Mae, this is a lot for me. I haven't had anyone in my life I wasn't willing to lose for a long time, but I promise this is real."

"I've built too many relationships on a lie. They always crumble. I don't want that for us." I stepped toward her. She moved back, but she had nothing to fear from me. "I don't want to watch us break."

"It's not going to be like that." I took another step toward her, and she held her ground. She was the bravest woman I'd ever met and she was five foot four inches tall. She could send me to my knees just with the look in her eyes. I couldn't let her out of my life. "I know I've done all the things you hate them for," I said, recognizing our less-than-perfect beginning.

"At least you were paid to do it."

"I was paid to follow Isla Monroe."

She exhaled a bitter laugh. "That's not my name."

I nodded. I knew her better than I thought it was possible to understand another human being. "I was hired to *follow* her. I fell in love with Ida Malone." I devoured her with my eyes. Every inch of her face, I committed to memory. I leaned down and pressed my lips to her cheek, willing her to love me the way I loved her. She tilted her head toward me as my lips dragged down the front of her neck until she tilted her head back and exposed herself to me.

I turned her back against the wall and lifted both hands above her head. I held them there and ripped open the front of her blouse. Buttons hit the walls and floor around us. Mae didn't flinch. Her tiny shorts clung to her body. I lifted her up until she wrapped her legs around my waist. I carried her to the bedroom and let myself forget what we were talking about.

I dropped her on the bed. She bounced onto her knees and reached for the button of my jeans. Mae's focus suddenly became razor sharp on my body. She unzipped my pants and lowered them until my dick fell out in front of her face. She considered me with her sweet eyes and said, "Thank you, Dalton."

"For what?"

"For finding me."

I leaned down and took her face in my hands. "You're welcome." I was the one who was thankful. She'd finally let me in. Now, I was refusing to leave, even if she pushed me away. I kissed her until we both fell back onto my bed. Mae rolled me over and climbed on top of me. The nights I'd dreamed of her here with me ran through my mind. She was finally mine, in my bed, and she knew every truth between us.

Mae pulled herself up until I could reach to take off her shorts.

"I don't have a condom," I said.

"You don't need one." I didn't know what she meant. "I want all of you." And I wanted her to take it. Her breath hit my ear and felt like a sob. Mae was giving in to me. She'd sworn she'd never concede again. Especially not to a man. My hands found her shoulders. I wouldn't take this from her. She'd come too far.

Without a word, Mae climbed on top of me. Her desperate stare told me she loved me and that she wanted to stay right here, in my bed in Portland, Oregon. She rode me while I watched her rise and fall above me. The sight of breasts, the touch of her skin, engaged every nerve in my body. They ignited beneath her. My groin rose to meet her each time she lowered herself around me. She was a second chance, sent to me, and I wasn't letting her go.

That was what the others had thought before me. Ian and Addario. Their names anywhere near my love for her enraged me. They didn't deserve her.

Mae slowed and stared at me from above. "What?" she asked. It wouldn't surprise me if she could read my mind.

"You've left me defenseless. I'm not used to wanting something the way I want you," I said and dragged my grip up her thighs.

She leaned down and kissed me until every thought in my head slipped away with the honey scent I loved about her. I rested my hands on her and closed my eyes, letting her set the pace. The air touched my neck like a thousand volts of energy. I sat up and took off my shirt to feel her on my skin.

Mae climbed off. I laid her beneath me and took from her what the whole world wanted. Except I loved her. They barely knew her.

She pulled my face down to hers. I swore she was going to tell me. She was going to speak the words she'd never told another man, but instead, Mae kissed me. When I came, she tightened her arms around my neck and whispered my name in my ear.

There, on top of her, I fell asleep, finally in the safety of her arms.

I woke to the absence of her. I closed my eyes again and fell into the memories of Mae. She belonged with me, but she'd left. The dreams I'd had the night before were only that . . . dreams. The nightmare was waking without her.

I already knew she was gone from my apartment and gone from hers. She'd take to the road and leave me behind, because I was a part of everything she'd worked so hard to forfeit. I was a member of the darkest time in her life, and no matter what I did to move forward, too much had happened in the past.

I picked up my phone off my nightstand and activated the GPS I'd installed on her car. The blue dot raced across I-84 on its way out of the city. She couldn't outrun me, but I'd let her go. I couldn't force her to love me the way I loved her. I wouldn't become another person in the world who took from Ida Mae what she wasn't willing to give.

Wrights name came up on the screen before the phone rang.

"We need you," he said when I answered. There was no need for me to say hello. His voice was stricken. Wright was never *not* in control.

I sat up in bed.

"Paul's been captured," he said.

"I'm on my way."

Six months later . . .

Dalton,

I'm sorry. Incredibly so. Bone-aching, head-throbbing, regretful that I left you in Oregon the way that I did. I just couldn't . . . I'm not even sure what part of it I was incapable of. I think maybe the happily ever after, because I've only heard of those in books and movies. Fairy tales never existed in my world. I couldn't reconcile the concept—and you—as a part of my life.

You must hate me. I lie awake at night and wonder if you do. I miss you so much that I talk to myself at breakfast and in the car and standing in the rain. I want you in my life, and if you give me another chance, I promise I'll never run again. If you're reading this letter, it's because Wright wouldn't help me find you. I know if you don't want to be found, you won't be, and that you'll live alone forever out of spite for what I've put you through, but if I could just see you once again, I'd tell you not to.

You are magnificent, and your life should be shared. Please call me. I need you, Dalton.

I'm sorry.

Love,

Ida Mae Malone

CHAPTER 30

Mae

I HAD NO IDEA WHERE to send the letter to Dalton. Men like him didn't leave forwarding addresses. Every corner I turned, I hoped to see him standing on the other side. I waited for him to call, to show up. I stopped listening to music in my car, because every hellish song reminded me of him.

He wasn't coming back for me. That was the only thing I knew in my heart. I lay on top of the floral comforter in my brother's guest room and stared at the ceiling. It was a perfect flat white. Not a crack to be seen. How utterly boring perfection was?

I had to return to New York.

"Hey." My brother's familiar voice broke through my study of nothing above me.

I rolled onto my side. "Hi."

He sat on the edge of my bed as if it were too strange for him to just flop down beside me. Our personal space had been invaded so many times in our childhood, he still respected it whenever we were together. "Are you sure you don't want to talk to someone?"

"I got my hair done the other day and talked to your wife for hours."

He smiled at me with the same collusive expression of our childhood. "She's a gifted therapist."

"What stylist isn't?"

He stared down at the flowers in the fabric between us. "I was thinking of someone trained to deal with the victims of violent crimes. People who've seen someone murdered before their eyes."

"Oh. Are you sure she hasn't worked with that before?"

"I'm serious, Mae. This is a lot. Even for us." He sounded like Dalton. The way my brother scrutinized me reminded me of him, but so did everything else in existence. Wanting him was the only pain I felt.

"Do you think in the midst of an ocean full of lies, and a race to be as far away from your past as you can run, that it's possible to find the one person you're meant to love?"

"No," he flatly said. I rolled over onto my back. I preferred the ceiling to the truth. "But I'm not you. You can do anything, including falling in love in a nightmare."

"There's quite a bit wrong with me, don't you think?"

"I've always thought you were completely fucked up." I laughed before he did. "A bit spoiled, too." He threw the extra pillow on top of my head. "What are you going to do about Isla Monroe?"

I took a deep breath and exhaled loudly. "I'm going to bury her with all the other secrets." The clouds broke outside the window. Sunlight flooded the room. "In Bogota, New Jersey."

"I don't know what that means, but you can go back to all of it. Without Addario, things can be different . . . better."

"Can they? When I first thought about leaving it all behind, it had little to do with Victor or Ian. I just wanted to be . . . normal. I wanted to be me. The industry will never allow that."

"You worked so hard to just walk away."

"I'll still sing. Just for a dozen people instead of millions. Mama told me to lift my voice to the Lord."

"She also said a shot of whiskey will stop a cough." I laughed at his retort without making a sound. "When we were four."

"She could have been a nurse."

"She could have been a lot of things, I guess."

"I'm just glad she was our Mama." We'd never talked about it, and God knew there were nights when we both would have traded her, but she loved us. More than she loved herself.

I'd been to Mama's grave at least once a week since I'd moved home. The groundskeepers were beginning to talk to me like I was their coworker. The other day, they were complaining about the heat and "our" boss. They were kind, and it wasn't like Mama was giving me any great advice from her grave. She'd had so little of it to share when she was alive.

There'd been a small article online. Only a few sentences in a paragraph about the funeral arrangements for Constance Grayson's son, listed only as I.M. Grayson. I didn't attend. I couldn't face her. Ian was sick, but I was the one who took his life. I'd carry that with me the rest of my life.

Bogota, New Jersey was due west of the George Washington Bridge, but the cemetery Ian was buried in was south of there in Union City. I asked the driver to park and wait outside of the green iron fence that surrounded the property.

Ian's grave had already matured to fit in with the others around it. Beside the date on the gravestone, you'd never know he'd died six months ago. I placed the bouquet of white roses on the ground near the stone. I was surrendering. The fight was over.

"I'm sorry this happened to you," I said. There was no one around to hear me. Ian had always been around. Only a few steps away even when I didn't know it. "I'm grateful. You may not know this, but your letters made me realize I didn't want that life anymore. It was a child's dream that turned into a nightmare."

I stepped back, and the February wind swept across my face. Across the center of Ian's gravestone was inscribed, *In Heaven, All are forgiven.* In my heart, too.

CHAPTER 31

Mae

"THANK YOU FOR MEETING ME. I know in the past, I've caused you a great deal of inconvenience," I said and took the seat Jason Wright offered me. Victor's former secretary had been nice enough to give me Wright's number.

His office was nothing like I'd imagined. It was warm and soft. Hardly indicative of the lethal services his business afforded its clients. Wright sank into the couch across the coffee table from me as if we were having a drink after dinner together. In the absurd times I'd been with him before, I'd never seen him anything but calm and in control.

"It's been a while." He held me in his stare. "Six months. I trust things are going well for you."

"They've been going very slowly, which is exactly what I needed." I threaded my fingers together and placed my hands in my lap. "Thank you, again, for your help. It was an impossible situation." I never spoke of Victor Addario anymore. That part of my life I'd put behind me. I never wanted to return to it.

"Not impossible, and you were quite capable of getting yourself out of it, but I'm glad we were there."

"Yes." I nodded. "I need your help one more time."

"I assumed. What can I do for you?"

"I need to find Dalton."

I didn't know what Dalton had told Wright about the ending of our relationship or even if he knew the extent of it. I hadn't spoken to him since I'd left. Jason Wright was the only person who'd know where he was.

"Dalton is capable of being invisible. He'd be impossible to find if . . ."

"If?"

"If he didn't want to be."

I sighed. It was silly of me to think Wright would assist me in locating him. I reached for my purse. The letter I'd written was with the few other items in it. I'd leave it in hopes that Wright would get it to him, and that Dalton would read it and respond. There was little hope, though. He'd told me that he loved me, and I'd run away in the morning light. I didn't deserve for him to read it.

"Dalton's been off work for several months now."

"He has?"

"Yes. We had a situation involving his colleague. Once they were home, Dalton requested not to be considered for future assignments."

In saving myself, I'd managed to ruin Dalton's life. He loved his work. "For how long?"

"Indefinitely."

My heart stopped. Where was he? He wasn't working. He wasn't with me. "Has he been in contact? Do you know where he is?"

"I haven't spoken to him." My heart sank. What if I never saw him again?

"But his friend, Paul, has. He's apparently in Hawaii."

My breath caught. "On the Big Island," I said more to myself than to Wright.

"How did you know?"

"I didn't," I said.

Wright walked over to his desk and handed me an envelope

from it. "Everything that can help you is in here."

I stared at the envelope.

He genuinely smiled at me. "I hope everything works out, Ms. Malone, and I hope you're able to convince him to return to work. We miss him."

I nodded, still entranced by the envelope. Dalton was on the Big Island. "Thank you. I can't thank you enough." I jumped into his arms and hugged him tight.

Wright awkwardly patted me on the back. "You can repay me by bringing him back."

"I'll see what I can do."

My heart strummed against the inside of my chest while I waited for the elevator. I knew I wanted him, but now that I knew how to find him, I couldn't slow my pace enough to get to him. I was running in circles inside my head.

When I was safely tucked on the plane back to North Carolina, I read the details of John Ward's vacation on the Big Island of Hawaii. He was renting a house in the rainforest. A three-bedroom near the volcano. He'd been there for over four months.

A lot of voices could be heard in that length of time.

"Sorry," the young girl in the seat next to me said. She shifted so her coat didn't hang over the armrest.

"No problem."

She pulled out a celebrity magazine and flipped through the first few pages. The familiar urge to hide returned, but I swallowed it down with the realization that that part of my life was completely over. Forever.

"You know all that stuff's a lie, right?" I leaned over and asked.

"Totally," she said. "I only read it for the hair colors."

I relaxed in my seat. There was hope for this new generation.

"Yours is great by the way. Nice caramel highlights."

"Thanks."

I barely stopped at my house to pack. It was like the day I'd left

New York City in the summer, except this time, I was running to someone instead of away from them. The information on Dalton didn't include a phone number, but I wouldn't have called him anyway. I needed to see him. I'd missed his birthday and Christmas and the New Year. He'd been alone for all of them.

I stopped shoving my underwear into my bag and stood as the thought cemented in my mind. What if he wasn't alone? What if Dalton was living in Hawaii with someone else? What if he was in love?

I sat on my bed and took a deep breath. It didn't matter. I was going to Hawaii and regardless of who I found there, I was going to tell Dalton I loved him, because he was the only man I'd ever truly loved, and for that reason alone, he should hear the words from my mouth.

"Where are you going?"

I jumped at Denise's question. "What are you doing home?"

"I came to pick up the donations for the auction at the school."

"Oh, right. They're boxed on the kitchen table." I'd signed every CD, T-shirt, and book about Isla Monroe I could get my hands on. Since she'd "moved away from New York and sought a quiet life out of the entertainment industry," her memorabilia had quadrupled in value. The local school district should make a fortune off the ridiculousness I'd engaged in for so many years.

"Now, back to my question." My sister-in-law would not be ignored. "What's going on?"

"Dalton's in Hawaii."

"His boss told you that?"

I nodded. "And I'm going to get him."

"And do what with him?"

"Love him."

Denise only stared at me with all the support I'd lost since my mother died. She and my brother were more than most people even knew to ask for. I was a lucky girl. "You're coming back, right?"

I laughed. What I had put them through these past twelve months. It was three lifetimes. "I'm not sure, but I'll be in touch, and you can call my phone. I'll always answer. I'm not hiding. I'm seeking."

"Good luck."

CHAPTER 32

Mae

FROM SAN FRANCISCO, I FLEW direct to Kona, rented a car, and drove to where Dalton was staying. It was a long day, but grueling travel was my specialty. I was just happy not to be driving the entire time.

Dalton's house was only two turns off the main highway, but a world away. I left the pavement and found a skinny road with trees and brush hanging over the shoulders and practically touching above me. The houses were difficult to discern from the road unless you were going slow enough to read the signs attached to a tree or hanging from a rock. Dalton's had a sign hanging from the gate, which was locked and blocked the driveway. I stopped in front of it and put my rental in park.

I climbed the fence and jumped down into Dalton's property. There were sounds all around me, but not one associated with human life. The squawks and grunts followed me as I walked farther into the forest. At the end of the path stood a house almost completely obscured by trees. There were lights strung along the porch and stairs leading to the door.

The ground crunched behind me, and I twirled around to see two wild pigs walking through the yard. They weren't interested in me, but I couldn't take my eyes off them. They grunted and snorted in a fun way and kept exploring the yard.

I left the pigs and walked up the stairs to the house. A hammock hung from the corner of the roof, and a hot tub was covered at the opposite end. It was cozy in Dalton's hideaway. I knocked, but no one answered. The truck in the driveway told a different story of its occupant.

I opened the door a crack and called out, "Dalton."

Sounds of movement from the hallway slipped through the house to me.

I stepped one foot in the door. "Dalton, it's Mae. I need to talk to you."

The sounds stopped. He was listening or in shock or already running through the forest behind the house.

"I love you," I said, and the weight of my life flew off my chest and up into the air. I would tell him every day if he let me. "Dalton, I love you."

"I love you, too," a squeaky, fake-girl voice said from the kitchen. It wasn't Dalton.

Paul hobbled in front of me on two crutches. Over his eye was a scar I didn't remember, and his wrist was in a brace.

"What are you doing here?"

He raised his eyebrows and lifted a pint of ice cream out of the purse hanging around his neck. He found a spoon in his bag and took a bite before saying, "I could ask you the same thing." I watched Paul eat two more bites of ice cream, and then he added, "Except now I know you're in love with him."

I had even less patience for Paul than I had the day I'd shot him in my bedroom. "Where is he?" Paul maneuvered himself—and his snack—to the couch. He sat with great effort. It was painful to watch. "And what happened to you?"

"Tough day at the office." He motioned to the other end of the couch he was sitting on.

I felt lost. The plan was to arrive, profess my love, and tear his clothes off. Instead. I was being offered a seat next to a battered Paul, and I wasn't even sure if he liked me. I sat. "Thank you," I said and let my gaze wander around the house.

The rooms weren't extravagant except for the sense that the house had been handmade by the owner with love. Knotty pine beams and wood counter tops were highlighted by soft colors on the walls. There were windows everywhere and not a treatment to be found. Who could see you through the trees?

"So, you love him?"

I refocused on Paul. "Yes, and I need to see him."

"Ah. The hunter becomes the hunted." He stopped laughing and looked me in the eyes. "I've known Dalton for a few lifetimes now. I've never seen him act the way he did with you."

"I'm guessing that's not a compliment."

"I'm not sure what it is," he said and repositioned his foot on a pillow atop the coffee table. "But I liked who he was with you."

"And who was that?"

"Someone with a reason to live."

I hid my reaction from Paul. I didn't want to share my shame in leaving Dalton without a goodbye with his best friend.

"But . . . then you left, and he was worse off than he'd been before he'd ever heard the name Isla Monroe."

"Is he here somewhere?" I couldn't have this conversation with Paul. I wouldn't squander my remorse on him. "I really need to talk to him."

"I get it." He was losing his patience, too. "I just want to make sure you've thought this through, because I'm tired, you know? I'm cooped up here with him. He's kind of . . . sad," he said with great disgust. "If I tell you where he is, I need to be sure you're not going to leave him in a worse place than I've gotten him back to."

"I'm not going to leave him again." I quieted the anger building inside me. I needed information from Paul, and hurting him wasn't going to help me. I sighed loudly, losing the fight against my emotions.

"He's at the beach. Punalu'u. It's the black sand beach south of here. He goes"—Paul rolled his eyes—"and listens, he says." He shook his head as if it were the most ridiculous thing he'd ever heard.

"Thanks," I said and stood to leave. "Do you need anything before I go?"

"I need love, too, but instead of being nursed back to health by a German angel, I've been stuck in the jungle with mopey."

"Can you shorten this speech?" I pointed toward the door. "I'm on my way somewhere."

"Of course. Far be it for me to hold you up with talk of my extensive injuries and loneliness."

"Thanks, Paul."

CHAPTER 33

Mae

WHAT IF I PASSED HIM on the way? What if he wasn't there? I couldn't go back to the house and wait with Paul. I might accidentally kill him on purpose. Based on his injuries, he'd had as rough a year as I'd had.

It was a straight line and forty-five minute drive from the house in the rain forest to the beach. I tried to decide what I'd do if he rejected me, but there was no way for me to imagine him speaking those words. The man had killed for me. How could he not still love me?

What if he was seeing someone? Maybe a Hawaiian woman or someone else he'd met on the job. Surely, I wasn't the only female he'd met over the last six months. The thoughts ran through my mind until my stomach was so twisted in knots it was hard to get out of the car in the parking lot.

I should have asked Paul what Dalton was driving or where he hung out or if he still loved me. I should have done a lot of things. Like, not leave without saying goodbye in Portland. But I'd been through so many endings, I'd just wanted to be away from every part of it, and even though I knew Dalton was different, he was absolutely a part of the death of Isla Monroe.

The sea spray hit my face when I stepped out of the car. It blew off the ocean as the waves hit the shore. People meandered near campsites and across the black sand of Punalu'u. Not one of them was Dalton, though.

Couples held hands. Children hopped across the rocks. No one was in a rush on the Big Island of Hawaii except for me. I was desperately searching for the one man I'd come to see. I scanned the faces around me until I was sure he was nowhere to be found. I sat on the black sand and became lost in the vast ocean before me.

I'd go back to the house and wait for him there. He'd have to come home at some point, and I'd tell him. I'd endure Paul to be with Dalton. The wind blew my hair across my face and my clothes against my body, but it felt more like a whisper than a shout. It caressed me. I sat and listened to the sounds of the earth. There was magic here, even if Dalton wasn't.

I laid back and closed my eyes to hide from the sun. I covered my face with my arm and remembered what it was like to lay next to Dalton at Cannon Beach. What his voice sounded like when he said my name. My real name.

"Ida Mae," I heard.

I almost burst into tears when I realized the words weren't in my head.

I opened my eyes. He was standing above me, blocking the sun from my eyes.

"What are you doing here?" His voice was stern. Dalton didn't like to be surprised.

I stood and brushed the sand off the back of me and shook it from my hair. I fixed the jeans and tank top I had on since San Francisco and straightened my posture in front of him.

"I love you," I said and waited for the long months to end.

He didn't break down with relief or pull me into his arms. Dalton's last six months hadn't been spent waiting for me to find him here. The emptiness was creeping in, but my need for him overpowered it. I would stand right here until he wanted me again. "There's so much you don't know."

"I don't care about any of it. Just you."

"Mae." He shook his head, denying us both, but the doubts he had didn't matter. This was our time.

I walked over and pressed my body against his. "Look at me," I said and stole his attention from the spot I'd just stood. Dalton's eyes were deeper paths than I'd remembered. He'd grown a beard. His hair was out in loose curls around his face. "I know I'm young. I've been through a lot. We started in the wrong place. You're fucked up, and I'm a little insane." He didn't smile, but his defensive stare softened just a tad. "But I love you more than anything else in the world. That has to mean something."

His hands rested at his sides.

"It does to me," I said and stood on my tiptoes to kiss him. "I miss you, Dalton." I kissed him again. The hickory mixed with coconut suntan lotion and the salt from the water. I didn't think he could appeal to me any more than he already did. I was wrong. "And I need you, and I miss you, and . . ." I slid my hands down his chest where I pressed them against his hard stomach and the memories of him ached throughout my body. He was as solid as I remembered. Every night since I left him, I'd imagined touching him again. Dalton reached up and covered them with his own. "I want you to come to church with me . . . and throw me down and knock me up." I laughed a little. "Not all at the same time." He ran his thumb across the top of my hand, and his heat invaded me. "And help me put up a proper Christmas tree and build a fire in our backyard and carry me to bed when I'm too drunk on New Year's Eve and—"

He kissed me, and the whole world stopped around us. The wind ceased, the birds silenced, and the sun paused to witness the moment when the man I loved, loved me back.

When he released me, tears filled my eyes. The stress of my journey to him welled up and poured over my lashes and down my cheeks. Dalton took my face in his palms and wiped away my tears as more followed in their paths. There was a time when I'd thought he was more than I deserved, but in his arms, I knew no one earned this. It was bestowed upon you in mercy and love.

"Say something," I managed to get out.

Dalton kissed my cheek where a tear had fallen. He stared into my eyes until I felt his thoughts in my own head. "If you're not here when I wake in the morning, I'm going to hunt you down and kill you."

I nodded and smiled through more crying. "Deal."

"I'm serious, Ida Mae Malone."

"Oh. Full-name serious. Got it."

"It'll be a painful death. I'll take out the last few months on you."

The mention of what I'd put him through dampened the humor. "I'm sorry."

"I am, too. I never wanted anything the way I wanted you. It was too much for you to deal with along with everything else."

"I just needed to separate you from . . . the rest. I couldn't start something in the wake of that ending. I could barely function."

"Did going home help?"

"How did you know?" I almost laughed. I'd wondered a thousand times if he knew where I was and was staying away on purpose.

"I still have a GPS unit on your car. Every time you drive, I get a notification on my phone."

"Even here you get the information?" I was in shock.

"Yes." He kissed my forehead and the tip of my nose. "And I must say, it was good to see you were still eating pancakes as often as possible."

I rested my head on his chest and tightened my arms round him.

"If you'd gotten a new car, I'd have had to come find you."

I sank into his words. He'd been thinking of me these last months, too.

"How did you know I was here?" he asked.

"I went to see Wright."

"He told you?"

I nodded and took a step back from him. "I think he likes me."

"Oh yeah?" Dalton laughed. It should be obvious that Wright didn't like anyone.

"Well, I think he likes you *with* me."

He held out his hand, and I jumped back into his arms. I couldn't stop crying. I squeezed him in my arms and tightened my legs around his waist. "Hey, hey," he said and rubbed my back. "I'm right here. I'm not letting go." He put me back on the ground and leaned down to see my face. "What has gotten into you? I've never seen you cry before."

"I've never been afraid of losing someone the way I am about you." I shook my head, disgusted with myself. "If this is what it's like to love someone, it's absolutely horrible." I was appalled at myself. "I'm a complete mess." I held my hands out to my side, displaying what was left of me for him.

Dalton burst out laughing. "You're a beautiful mess, Ida Mae. I love you." The darkness lifted. The damage inflicted by all the men before him healed in his touch and with his words. I could have floated away if he'd come with me. He pulled me close to him and led us back toward the parking lot.

"How come you've been traveling as John Ward? Were you trying to hide from me?"

"Maybe that's my real name," he said, and I stopped walking. "After spending a few months with you, perhaps I needed to find myself again, too."

"What?"

"Maybe . . ." He raised his eyebrows and leaned against me on the back of his car.

Dalton kissed me until I practically forgot my name. I lost myself in him and the possibility of us and voices of the island that told me I belonged right there.

"Did you hear any voices while you were here?"

"I tried, but I couldn't stop thinking about you long enough to hear anything. You've been haunting me."

"We'll talk about that later," I said and kissed him again.

His hand slid down my neck and brushed against my breast. "Yes. Later," he said in my ear before opening the passenger door for me.

Dalton and I drove my car back to his house with my hand on his thigh and my lips on his neck. I wanted to taste every inch of him. I realized how much of my long road to Hawaii had been spent imagining the feel of his body against mine. The wait, the distance, the lengthy conversation with Paul were maddening, but now he—this—was in my grasp.

"I've thought about you every night since I left," I whispered in his ear.

"You have?" he asked and fought to keep his attention on the deserted road in front of us.

"Yes."

As soon as he locked the gate to his house behind us, I climbed on top of him.

He'd barely put the gear in park when I said, "It's time to rectify the 'I've never, ever, had sex in a car before.'"

He ran his hands down the sides of my body, cupped my buttocks, and tightened me against the front of him. "What about the threesome?"

"Don't push it," I said and kissed his neck. "Unless you want to go get Paul."

"Oh, God no. I'm going to lose my hard-on."

I rubbed it through his bathing suit. "Seems unlikely."

The sun dipped low in the sky, and in the thick cover of trees, it was almost completely dark. Dalton grabbed a lever on the side of his seat, and we reclined back, giving us a few more inches to work with.

He threw my shirt and bra in the back seat and took my nipple in his mouth. He swirled it with the gentleness I'd come to know in him. Lovemaking didn't have to be violent. It could be this, with Dalton, every day of my life.

I opened the door and stepped out of the car to peel my jeans off. The air was wet. I lifted my face to the trees above me. Movement and life surrounded me. I inhaled the atmosphere of Hawaii and was grateful.

Dalton followed me and lifted me onto the hood of the car. He untied his bathing suit without ever losing eye contact. I could see through to his soul. Here, on the Big Island, it was impossible to believe I ever couldn't trust him. My love for him mixed with my need. My chest caved in to be near him as I reached out.

He spread my legs wide in front of him and plunged into me, answering every demand of my body. Energy coursed through me from Dalton to the center of my core. His moan drowned out the sounds of the forest around us. He pulled me closer by my thighs as he continued to remind me that his version of rough was welcomed, too.

"I love you," I said.

He thrust into me. "Say it again." He panted between words. "Tell me, Ida Mae."

I leaned up and looked him in the eyes. When he came, I told him, "I love you."

I surrendered to him in every way. He was the first man I'd ever told I loved, because he was the first one I truly did. He didn't have to take me to own me; I gladly gave myself to him. Heart and soul.

I held him until the night air dropped to the mountain temperatures it held every night. He helped me put my clothes back on, dressing me with gentle motions foreign to the way my clothes had been removed.

"I'm happy," I said when I sat in the car next to him.

He held out his hand. I rested mine in his while we drove the last twenty feet to his house. He walked around and opened the door for me as if it were our first date. In some ways, it was. From now on, our conversations would be different. There'd be no secrets or untold truths. John Ward and I would begin today.

"Glad to see you guys are back together," Paul said from the porch. He was leaning on his crutches with binoculars hanging around his neck. "I was just out here bird-watching, and you would not believe what I saw." He pointed toward the road with a shit-eating grin on his face. "Two people were having sex in our driveway."

My mouth fell open. "You watched us?" I was more than appalled.

"That's the point of having sex in public, isn't it?"

"I should have shot you twice," I said, making Dalton laugh behind me.

"You're going to love me," Paul said and hobbled back toward the door. "Not the same way you do him, because *that* was something."

Dalton lunged toward him, but Paul closed the door between them and locked it.

"Everybody just needs to calm down," he said and smiled through the door. "You two, in particular, should be relaxed."

Dalton pulled me into his arms and kissed me. He pressed my back against the door Paul was speaking through.

"Okay, now you guys are just taunting me."

Dalton's lips moved to my neck.

"You two are *disgusting*," Paul said and limped away from the door.

"Wait until we tell him we're getting married." My breath caught. Dalton straightened to face me. "Oh, yeah." He nodded with a huge grin covering his face. "You're mine."

ALSO BY ELIZA FREED

The Devil's Playground (Book One in the Faraway Series)

Former U.S. Attorney, Meredith Walsh, took some time off to raise her children. But the time took away everything she once trusted about herself. She's lost within the mundane confines of her children's schedules of lacrosse, soccer, Cub Scouts, and math facts. Desperate for a sliver of her former passion, and isolated in the small town her corporate husband relocated her to, she counsels herself on risking her family for the rush of a fling.

But Vincent Pratt, the local chief of police, weakens Meredith's abhorrence of affairs and her dedication to her family. With him, she finds a new version of herself, one capable of contributing in her new world, and thriving in her lonely home. In spite of the fact, she's not the kind of woman who has an affair.

Turn the page for an excerpt from Eliza Freed's *The Devil's Playground*.

There were times when I felt completely alone.
Even when he was standing right next to me.
He would tell me that's ridiculous.
He would convince me I never felt it.

ONE

I SCANNED THE BALLROOM OF the Downtown Club in Philadelphia. Brad was standing near the bar, laughing with his high school friends, the ones he rarely saw anymore. He towered over most of them. His six-foot-three body an anomaly among his childhood friends. His height matched his power. He could stare you down with his jet-black eyes, or melt you with them, and he always knew which way to proceed. Most people were at his mercy. I was at his side.

I barely smiled, but Brad caught it and winked at me. He kept watching me as he half listened to his friends talking. There was little Brad didn't notice.

"Meredith, I want to introduce you to my father," the bride said, pulling me away from Brad's stare. I stood even straighter. The introduction was the reason I'd been excited about the wedding. It was why I'd spent weeks finding a dress. And it was why I'd barely drank a sip of alcohol the entire day. The bride's father was Judge Warren of the U.S. Court of Appeals. He was an Army veteran and Harvard Law grad who'd made his way to Philadelphia and an appointment to the Third Circuit. One didn't fall into that position.

I followed the bride across the dance floor. My Norwegian cream skin, the same as my mother's, was perfectly highlighted in the light-green dress I'd saved three months to buy. I'd been told before that I was angelic. Looking, at least. My skin and light eyes—not quite green, not quite blue—had garnered comments from passersby even as a child.

"She's beautiful. Why she looks like an angel."

My mother would take me aside each time and tell me *they* say that to everyone. "You're no prettier than anyone else, which is fine, because beauty will get you nowhere."

Beautiful or not, I'd capitalized on others' views of my appearance since they'd first noticed me. I knew what colors looked best, what cuts of clothing to wear to accentuate my lean figure. I wasn't voluptuous or petite. I was statuesque. At least that was the word my mother's boyfriend chose when he'd inappropriately blocked the doorway to my bedroom to discuss my future plans.

I'd been high at the time, like the rest of my senior year. I'd skipped school as much as I could and had driven the three and a half hours east to the shore. I wasn't challenged by my coursework, not inspired by my teachers, and easily ranked in the top of my class. If it wouldn't have killed my father, I'd have dropped out and surfed every day.

I was sitting on the floor of my room, leaning against my bed, and he was standing at the foot of it. I hadn't noticed the thirty extra pounds he carried around his waist or the bald front of his head until that day. He was a drycleaner. My mother had brought him home for dinner after having a pair of pants tailored at his store.

He picked up my bra from the hamper and held it to his nose. He closed his eyes and tilted his head toward the ceiling as he inhaled deeply. He ran his fat fingertips over the lace at the edge of the cups and pressed the silk against his cheek. My stomach churned with disgust. No one—man or woman—had ever made me feel that afraid.

His grotesque leer had made me want to change something. Something bigger than anything I'd ever imagined while swimming in the ocean, or lying on the sand. I stopped getting high and started making a plan. It started with locking my bedroom door every night until I moved in with my father.

"Dad, this is my friend, Meredith." Judge Warren turned and paused at the sight of me. The candles' soft light highlighted the chiffon crossed at my chest and tied behind my neck. "She's an attorney with the Justice Department."

His eyes widened, and he took one step to my side, blatantly appraising me in front of his daughter. She smiled to put me at ease, but I wasn't uncomfortable, I was prepared.

Game on.

The judge and I spoke of his path to the bench. We went all the way back to his military service, and I memorized every word he said. Judge Warren was the human equivalent of a tufted leather chair in a warm, ornate library. He was broad and upright, commanding attention, but reserved. He was a powerful man, whose generous smile relaxed you immediately. And to me, he was fascinating.

I was intelligent and interested and, above all, innocent in my intentions. I would not sleep with this judge to get ahead. But I would learn from him in whatever limited time I was allotted.

When he asked for my business card, I presented him with the one I brought with me. It'd been placed in the side pocket of my purse, all by itself, waiting for the judge to request it. I promised to have lunch with him the following week. He wanted to discuss my future, the one he knew would be bright. The judge had found me "remarkable." My work here was done.

I walked back to our friends, still high from my introduction. Two pregnant wives anchored the table; their waters with lemon rested between their swollen fingers. One was due that month, the other the next. Both were uncomfortable, tired, and annoyed by the shots their husbands poured down their throats and chased with beers, and I couldn't bring myself to sit with them and listen to their complaining. My life was too short.

"Do you want to dance?"

My body relaxed at the sound of his voice. It would forever be recognizable. I turned to find Brad standing just inches behind me. His smile was collusive. He was saving me from this table of lost joy, and it reminded me of the first night we met. He had rescued me from a guy hitting on me in a bar. He'd walked up and asked me if I was ready to leave. And without even knowing his name, I'd left with him.

"Yes," I said, and he took my hand in his and led me to the dance floor. The orchestra slipped into a slow cadence, and Brad held me the way he had a thousand times before. I'd been dancing with him for six years. Through weddings and promotions and thirtieth birthday parties and drunken holidays together. We'd been to the mountains, the islands, and to Europe, and we hadn't found a reason to stop dancing. But this would be the last dance for a while. The babies were beginning to come; the parties were beginning to end.

Brad leaned in as he whispered in my ear, "Frank and Tom were just telling me how lucky I am you haven't begged me for a baby yet."

"Is that how it works? We women beg you for your DNA to make the perfect baby?"

"According to them." He laughed and pulled me closer. "You smell amazing." He wanted me again. He'd had me when we woke up that morning, and again in the shower before the ceremony.

Brad's needs were simple. He wanted me, and power, and money. Not always in that order. Brad didn't care about changing the world. He cared about running it. But somehow we worked. Our goals were completely different, but the road we traveled to reach them was perfectly balanced between us. I forgot what we were talking about and let Brad lead me.

"I saw you wrap His Honor around your finger. I almost felt bad for the man." The smile on my face hid my disappointment. Lately, I'd sensed tiny moments of jealousy from Brad. Not jealousy of other men, but of me. As if he feared I might eclipse him. It reminded me of my mother. "Do you want to have a baby?"

I leaned back to see if Brad was kidding. "You want to talk about babies now?"

"Yes. You're twenty-nine. I'm thirty-one." Brad kissed me again. His eyes lit up with the same excitement of the days we'd set our wedding date and settled on the condo in the city. Brad liked when things were decided.

"I have so much left to do."

"None of our friends died when they had their babies," Brad said, pointing out the obvious, of which I was still not convinced.

"I don't want to have a baby just because everyone else is having one."

"You won't. You've never given a fuck what everyone else is doing. It's part of your charm." Brad admired me with the strangest expression. He was right next to me, and yet felt so far away. As if suddenly he didn't know me at all. "You're beautiful," he said, but *they* say that to everyone.

The song ended and took the discussion of babies with it. Brad and I walked over to the windows overlooking Independence Mall. The Liberty Bell was lit up, proclaiming our independence on this hot summer night. Brad handed me a glass of champagne. He put his arm around me and stared out the window as well. I leaned into him, feeling him solid beside me and forgot the last few minutes. No, it was not time for babies. We were on the verge of something brilliant.

TWO

Nine years later.

"MOMMY, CAN BRIAN HAVE A snack?"

I'd started locking the bathroom door, but I was too nervous to lock it while I showered. What if one of them fell and hit their head and bled to death while I was shaving my legs? What if I couldn't hear their screams, or their banging on the door? No matter how old they got, I never felt sure they'd be okay.

"Brian who?" I told Liv never to open the door for anyone. No one was allowed in the house. *Do. Not. Open. The. Door. Do you understand me?* I said it every time I got into the shower.

"This Brian." Through the fogged shower glass I could see Liv and the four-year-old boy from across the street staring at me in the shower. Brian was not fazed by my nudity.

I opened the shower door and stuck my head out. "Brian, can you wait in the hall for a minute?"

He shrugged and walked out of the bathroom, probably wondering what was taking so long with the snack.

"I thought I told you not to open the door?" My teeth were clenched. She would be the death of me.

"I didn't. I unlocked it, and then *he* opened it."

"It's not funny, Liv!"

"He's hungry. And that's not funny, either. You fed that dog the other day. The one that was lost."

"Brian's not a lost dog. He has a kitchen across the street."

"Does that mean no snack?" She had the sweetest face, that of an angel. And even though I knew that she knew exactly what she was doing, it was impossible to be mad at her.

"I'll be down in a minute."

As I walked into the kitchen, James told Brian hot dogs were the gross part of pigs. "Like all the stuff you'd never want to eat on a pig." Brian insisted he didn't want to eat any part of a pig, and Liv told him he had to eat a pig to have bacon, and everybody loved bacon. It seemed every conversation was some equally mind-numbing variation on the gross parts of a pig. I tried not to listen. *How much can one woman take?*

"You know a hamburger is made from a cow," James said.

"Milk, too," Liv added.

"Nobody likes milk."

"Lots of people like milk. Mommy, don't lots of people like milk?"

I nodded my head and grabbed three bowls from the cabinet. I poured goldfish into the bowls and took a handful for myself. My hair still had soap in it. I was in my robe. I wanted to be standing under a hot shower, not feeding these tiny people fish.

"Without milk, there'd be no ice cream."

"That's not true."

"Yes, it is."

Brad walked through the door. His eyes were glassy. He had that goofy I'm-kind-of-drunk smile on his stupid face. "Hey, Brian! What are you doing over here?"

"He's scavenging for food," I said.

Brad's smile disappeared. He looked like he wanted to disappear. My nasty tone was ruining the afterglow of his golf outing. I couldn't even pretend as if I cared. At least not until I rinsed the soap from my hair.

I carried a glass of water to my plant dying in the foyer and watered it. It continued to die. It couldn't stand hearing about the gross parts of the pig either. "Why can't you live?" I asked the plant, and heard Liv walking around, searching for me.

"Mommy, can you make ice cream without milk?"

My eyes bulged at Brad as I walked back into the kitchen, and then I closed them tightly, attempting to shut all of them out of my mind.

"Man, you're an angry woman," he said without an ounce of sympathy.

"It's because I can't be clean. Even inmates are allowed a shower. Not me, though."

"Go shower now. I got this." He opened a beer and sat down at the island. "Do you want me to shower with you?" He winked.

God, I hate you.

I DID SHOWER. I SHOWERED for forty minutes. I was in no rush to be anywhere else. We were always late whenever we left the house, but that was because I never wanted to be where we were going. I had 77,000 miles on my car. Three hundred and ninety-eight were to places I wanted to be. But who was counting?

After the shower, I put the kids to bed. I sat on the couch and listened to Brad's day. Who he golfed with. What business was conducted. How it affected him. He didn't ask a word about my day. He'd stopped a long time ago. He'd stopped after the thousandth time he'd returned home to find me unhappy.

His arrival was usually timed perfectly after I'd cooked dinner, listened to the kids' riveting conversation while we ate, cleaned everything up, and completed elementary school homework. I packed their lunches and signed their assignment books. Tomorrow's outfits were picked out, and notes were written. Permission slips were signed and money was paid. And then Brad would walk through the door and wonder why I was miserable. *Don't you want to hear about my day? I cleaned two fish tanks and plunged the toilet.*

I wanted to *need* to take a short shower. I missed having some-place to be. Having something to talk about that was about my life and not Liv's and James'. I let my mind drift to when the next interesting thing in my life might occur. Five years . . . ten years . . .

Maybe I'll cut my hair.

JOSH & ANNA AND GABE & CLAIRE

No marriage is perfect.

Josh and Anna Montgomery are trying to have a baby. Well, Anna is. Josh is making the minimum contribution necessary, and it's ruining their relationship.

Gabe Hawkins is trying to survive the wild ride that is life with his wife, Claire. It's passionate everywhere but in their bedroom.

For these four friends, the difficulties of their marriages are camouflaged by hazy happy hours, extravagant vacations, picturesque weddings, and sleeping in. The possibilities of their youth are wilting in the light of their waning twenties, and on one fateful night, four friends become two. Survivors become lovers. Truths are told, and nothing seems like forever anymore.

Turn the page for an excerpt from Eliza Freed's *Josh & Anna and Gabe & Claire*.

"You need to be careful with perfect. It's brilliant at hiding its flaws."
~Jason Leer in REDEEM ME by Eliza Freed

STAGE I

INTOXICATION

ONE

Anna

HE THRUST INTO ME ONE last time before relaxing his muscles and resting his weight on my chest. He was breathless, panting softly against the crook of my neck as I ran my fingers through his hair and kissed the side of his face. I didn't have an orgasm, but neither of us cared. That wasn't what our sex life was about anymore. We were trying to have a baby. Desperately trying. We no longer wanted each other in the same way we once had. Before the irregular periods and the journals, logs, and temperatures. Before I asked my husband to jerk off in a cup so we could analyze his sperm.

Back when I didn't hate myself.

Now, our sex life was a new job that wasn't working out.

"I love you, Anna," he said. He always said it.

Josh had wanted a baby more than I did. He'd brought it up first, but once we'd started trying, I'd become consumed with the idea of a little one joining us. "Fixated"—that was Josh's word for my focus on conception. When he drank too much, he used the word "obsessed."

He rolled off me and walked to the bathroom. The dim light highlighted his ass, which hadn't changed since the day I'd met him in a dingy room of an off-campus house party. His eyes were a soft blue, and while he was a few inches taller than I was, his body was soft as well. He wasn't rock hard like the gym crew, but gentle in his stance. Something about his exterior had told me he was kind. When he'd made me laugh that first night, I'd told him I thought we were going to be married, and two years later, we were.

This morning I felt as if I'd been tricked all those years ago, and Josh seemed to feel nothing. Like a soccer star playing with tremendous skill but only half a heart because he thought he might not survive the big game loss, Josh had launched the idea of our family and then disconnected when we didn't score on our first try.

"I think we should have a baby," he'd said. I'd always assumed someday I'd get married and then have children, but I'd been happily not planning past the next few months of my life, and those plans had *not* included a baby.

At the time, I'd been a bridesmaid in my college roommate's wedding, and I'd already bought my plane ticket for the upcoming bachelorette party in Las Vegas. Babies weren't welcomed on girls' weekends. Josh had been quiet and irritable the entire week leading up to my departure. My new shoes and fresh highlights had done nothing to quell his abrasiveness.

"I guess you're not getting pregnant this month," he'd said, as if we were already trying. I hadn't even gone off the pill.

"Why does it have to be right now?"

Josh had never answered. Somehow over time, when there'd been a lull in the weddings, the birth control had been thrown away, and my focus had shifted from my own life to creating another. The first few weeks of trying had been the happiest of our marriage. It was inconceivable how we'd gone from him wanting me pregnant two years ago to me crying alone every month when my period came. The concept of a child wasn't as appealing to Josh if we had to work for it. With each month I didn't get pregnant, a baby became the only idea I'd let in my head.

Josh turned off the light and returned to our bed. He picked up his phone and read the screen while his sperm made itself at home inside me. I laid still. His carefree movements beside me annoyed me. He'd done the very least he had to for me to get pregnant and turned his attention to an article about the Eagles preseason. Everything he did, besides coming inside me, told me he didn't care if we had a baby or not. His face reacted to something in an article, making his lips pull up at the edges. I resented that look. Why did a piece of technology get it when I didn't?

I already knew I wasn't pregnant. I could sense the emptiness. The same feeling of being alone I had every day.

"Did Claire ever tell you what time we're supposed to meet them tomorrow?" Josh asked without looking up from his phone.

I stared at the popcorn ceiling above us and sifted through the endless things Claire had told me about tomorrow. What she was wearing. Why she absolutely had to get out of her house for the night. Gabe's dimmed enthusiasm. Her lack of care regarding Gabe's opinion. "Seven, I think."

"Why so late? It's Friday."

Partying with Gabe and Claire always started early and ended late, or rather, whenever we all passed out somewhere. Josh preferred couples to girls' trips. He'd be happy if we spent every weekend with them, even if Claire drove him mad.

"Gabe said he has a late meeting tomorrow."

Josh stayed perfectly still, clueing me in to the lie that had passed between a different husband and wife. If Gabe had a meeting, Josh would know about it. They ran a group of three hundred people together.

I rolled over and rested my head on my husband's shoulder. "But there is no meeting, is there?" I remained nonchalant.

"There must be something if Gabe said there is." It was the perfect answer. Non-collusive, non-committal, yet seemingly in agreement.

"I'm sure he'll tell us all about it." At this, my husband stiffened. I wrapped my arm across his stomach and closed my eyes. Josh was the least fun person to torture. Josh was a rule follower, but he struggled with his dual role of my husband and Gabe's friend whenever the four of us were together. I'd save my torture for Gabe. He didn't struggle with anything.

"Why don't I come home early and we'll go somewhere first. Just the two of us."

"Just like it will always be." The words escaped before I could catch them. The wave of regret they rode upon was always flowing below the surface. No matter how hard I tried, I couldn't stop the thoughts.

"Would that be so bad?"

I was sick of the question. I'd considered the reality a thousand times. When I was driving in my paid-off car, when I arrived each night at our lovely home, when we were laughing with Claire and Gabe over possibly nothing but the fact that we were all hilarious to each other, a little voice would always lament, *it is that bad*.

"I love you, Josh." He didn't want to hear the rest. Even if I spoke the words, they wouldn't penetrate through his own disgust at our situation. Josh acted as if it didn't matter, but a baby was the one thing he'd failed to plan. He couldn't provide a son or a daughter. One came when God decided.

He kissed the top of my head, and I fell asleep next to my husband.

TWO

Gabe

MY WIFE WAS DRUNK. NOT completely wasted, but drunk. I watched as she poured herself a glass of water, trying to detect whether this was the pull-my-dick-out-and-suck-it drunk, or the hateful-crazy-bitch drunk. I was a fan of the former. Terrified of the latter.

Claire sipped her water. Her large almond-shaped eyes softened the harsh edges of her latest haircut. The style accentuated the sharp collar bones that protruded like a shelf her head rested upon. She watched me over the rim of her glass and said, "I talked to Anna today."

Fuck.

I wasn't getting a blow job.

"Oh yeah?"

Anna was Claire's best friend. Closest friend was probably a better definition. They were together at least two weekends every month. Sometimes it was every weekend. They drank. They gossiped, and they left Josh and me alone to quietly enjoy our beverages. Anna balanced Claire. She stabilized her, but Claire couldn't get past some minute piece of jealousy when it came to Anna. When she drank, it came out in these ridiculous conversations.

"It's so funny . . ." Nothing would be humorous about this. "I still can't get over how different she is than I expected." Claire had met Anna four years ago. Anna was funny and gracious and always kind to Claire. Even when my wife's over-the-top ideas of what we should do or where we should go would have exhausted any other acquaintance. Under the umbrella of Anna's acceptance, Claire and her ideas didn't seem so ridiculous.

"Really?" I walked up the stairs to our bedroom, leaving my crazy wife to her insane thoughts.

She followed me. "Really."

Claire wasn't going to leave me alone. I'd neglect her to avoid the subject of Anna Montgomery, but to ignore the topic altogether would only enrage her. "What did you expect?" I asked.

"Well, having met Josh, I thought she'd be ultra-respectable."

I brushed my teeth. My reflection in the mirror was as confused as I was. I shook my head a little. "Anna's not respectable?" I needed to get my wife to sleep. Especially if there was no hope of a blow job.

"Of course she is. I guess I just expected her to be prim. Not so much fun." This was her bait, and I wouldn't let her catch me.

I'd spent hours with Anna. Every single one of them with my wife, too, and I'd never felt a thing from her but warmth. She wasn't as loud as Claire. Not as obvious. Her humor was dry and almost obscured by her petite figure and tailored politeness, but she could be as hilarious as the rest of us. "I haven't really thought about it. I had no expectations before I met her, and now I have no opinion."

Claire huffed past me, hiked up her dress, and sat on the toilet. She'd taken to the ugly intimacies of a relationship the same way I'd embraced her naked body the first time—without a thought. Within the first week of knowing her, Claire had flossed, peed, and snored in front of me. Ours was like a five-year-old marriage within days of its conception.

The toilet paper roll wobbled on the holder, and I continued to brush my teeth without looking at her. There was a time when I couldn't keep my eyes off her. Claire's openness had been intoxicating. Strangers, coworkers, and friends all fell under the spell of Claire's connection to this life. She shared pieces of herself without a thought. The longer we were together, the more I understood how small those pieces were.

Claire's loud laughs and monologues on the meaning of life were only to distract her audience so she could examine each person further. Her hair and attire were mere props to trick the eye. The people who fell under her spell never knew the real Claire. They only ever knew the parts she'd arranged. Most people we met were mesmerized by her, but I was unnerved. It was getting worse. A chill ran down my neck.

I replaced my toothbrush in its holder and walked out of the bathroom. If I could be asleep in the next three seconds, that'd be great.

"What are we doing tomorrow night?" she yelled from her perch.

I waited for her to finish in the bathroom and climb into bed with me. "Where were you tonight?" I asked, hoping to find a new topic. One which pleased my wife.

"My team went to happy hour. We finally finished the acquisition and deserved a good night out." It worked. She was satisfied with my attention.

"Congratulations." I kissed her cheek and rolled over in bed.

"What are we doing tomorrow?" she asked as if I'd answered and she'd already forgotten what I'd said.

"Meeting up with Josh and Anna. You made the plans." Claire's mind was a scary place.

"Oh, yes. That's right." She intertwined her legs with mine, and her cold toes rubbed against my shin. It was almost painful. Within minutes, her breathing deepened and fell into an ominous rhythm. When I knew she was asleep, I finally allowed myself to relax as well.

ELIZA FREED

ELIZA FREED GRADUATED FROM RUTGERS University and returned to her hometown in rural South Jersey. Her mother encouraged her to take some time and find herself. After three months of searching, she began to bounce checks, her neighbors began to talk, and her mother told her to find a job.

She settled into corporate America, learning systems and practices and the bureaucracy that slows them. Eliza quickly discovered her creativity and gift for story telling as a corporate trainer and spent years perfecting her presentation skills and studying diversity. It was during this time she became an avid observer of the characters she met and the heartaches they endured. Her years of study taught her that laughter, even the completely inappropriate kind, was the key to survival.

She currently lives in New Jersey with her family and a misbehaving beagle named Odin. As an avid swimmer, if Eliza is not with her family and friends, she'd rather be underwater. While she enjoys many genres, she is, and always has been, a sucker for a love story . . . the more screwed up the better.

To keep up with all of Eliza's new releases and giveaways, sign up for her newsletter on her website:

www.elizafreed.com